FIGHTING *for your* TOUCH

NIKKI ASH

Find the courage to fight.

To my mom,

who spent hours upon hours fostering my love for reading.

Prologue

CALEB

Seven Years Ago

"WHAT THE FUCK IS GOING ON?" MY DAD YELLS AT ME, RED faced, fists tight at his side like it's taking everything in him not to punch me in my face. He's not even questioning *her*. He's already made up his mind I'm to blame. Of course I'm to blame. There's no way his precious wife could be.

I'm standing face to face with him in my bedroom with my pants and boxers around my ankles. My dick is flaccid, but let's be honest, it usually is when I'm around *her*. Don't get me wrong, there's nothing wrong with my dick. I know it works properly since I've spent most of my teenage years fucking women I wish I could forget about. You don't know how many times I've jacked off hoping it wouldn't get back up again for them. If it can't get up what good am I to her, or any of them for that matter? Maybe if it stopped working she and all those other fucking women would leave me the hell alone. Unfortunately my dick doesn't work that way—it doesn't just shut off. After a while it goes hard again whether I want it to or not, and trust me, I definitely don't want it to.

Before attempting to answer his clearly rhetorical question, I reach down and pull my pants up so my dick is no longer hanging out. The conversation is already awkward as fuck as it is, no need to add to the awkwardness of my father coming home early from a business trip to find his slutty wife with her mouth wrapped around my cock. I shoot a glare at the woman who is the reason behind all this, hoping she'll for once do the right thing and admit the truth. I know it's not going to happen, but I can hope. I have learned two things about women, they're gold digging bitches and they can't be fucking trusted. Every time I think I can trust a woman she proves me wrong.

She raises her eyebrows in defiance at me and I know I'm on my own here. I wouldn't expect anything less from that cunt.

Closing my eyes, I take a deep breath in and then exhale slowly, attempting to calm myself before I try to persuade my dad of something I already know he isn't going to believe. My hands are shaking, and I have a horrible feeling this is going to end badly for me. It's just the way my life goes.

"Dad, please listen to me. It's not what it looks like. This is all *her*." There is so much more I want to say. So much more to this whole fucked up ordeal. But my dad is under enough stress as it is. I don't want to add to it. Sure, he has made mistakes. He's definitely not perfect, but he's been through a lot these past few years and I don't want to be the reason he goes through even more.

Tears of anger and frustration are clogging my tear ducts, and the lump in my throat is making it hard to breathe. The most frustrating thing is trying to prove to someone you aren't lying without having any proof, especially without being able to explain the entire story. Because of the secrets I've been forced to keep, my dad's caught me in too many lies to count that I couldn't explain. I don't blame him for not believing me now. Trust is hard to earn and easy to lose. Shit, if I were him, I wouldn't believe me.

Even if I was a complete saint, the evidence stacked up against me looks bad, and judging by the look on my dad's face, he doesn't believe a damn word I'm saying. I want to tell him the truth. I don't want to keep these secrets from him, but once the truth is out there, I can never take it back, and I don't know how *she* will react. What if she makes good on her threats? Then every nasty, fucked up thing I have endured from all these women will be for nothing. My dad has lost so much. He deserves more than to have his entire life destroyed.

"He's lying, Adam. He came on to me. I was scared," she says with crocodile tears streaming down her face. Her cheeks are stained black from the overdone mascara her fake-ass wears. The truth is, her cheeks aren't stained from crying, it's from her taking my cock so deep down her fucking throat it choked her to the point of tears. Just thinking about her mouth on my dick makes me want to throw up.

When he turns to me, she shoots me a glare making it clear to keep my mouth shut. If he only knew the truth about his precious wife, he would run the other way and never look back. The problem is, she's a smart, manipulative bitch and he has no idea the person she really is—not like I do.

He looks at me with longing in his eyes then looks back at her with what looks like disappointment, and for a second I think maybe he's going to believe me over her, that he can see through all her bullshit and lies. Out of the corner of my eye, I see Gloria tense up. She's thinking the same thing I am.

"I didn't want this," I blurt out as a last chance, praying he believes me. Praying he chooses me. Maybe he will kick her out and she'll be out of our lives for good. I'm not sure if she'll make good on her threats if he kicks her out, but we can deal with it all together. I'll do whatever it takes to help my dad, which is precisely how I got in this fucked up position to begin with.

My dad looks back at Gloria one more time and her face goes stoic. She gives nothing away at first, but then with a small lift of her one eyebrow, she silently tells him something causing him to visibly stiffen. They appear to be having a silent conversation of some sort. I wish I knew what the fuck they were saying.

Instantly my dad's demeanor changes from sad to pissed. He cocks his fist and punches the wall I'm standing in front of, his fist going through it.

Dry wall crumbles everywhere.

Gloria screeches like she's afraid.

Give me a fucking break. That woman eats up and spits out grown men on a daily basis.

He walks up to me until we're only inches apart, his face right in mine. I'm tall at six-foot-two. He isn't quite as tall as me, but he's still a big guy. He looks slightly up into my eyes and with an eerily calm voice says, "I don't know why you would do this, but I am not going to have you destroying this family with your lies. I'm going to give you one chance to change your story or you're out of here."

My shoulders sag in defeat and my head drops down shaking back and forth knowing this was coming but still shocked. I look back up into his eyes and see a glimpse of something...it's almost as if he's begging me to change my story, but I can't do that. I might not be able to tell him the entire truth, but I'm not going to take responsibility for choosing to fuck that money-hungry, lying, blackmailing cunt. He thinks I'm trying to destroy this family with my lies...If he only knew I'm actually trying to save this family...No, fuck that. I'm trying to save him. We don't have a family; they're all dead.

I swallow back the hurt and stand straight up. I lift my chin and, with the little bit of respect I have left for myself, say the only thing I can say. "I'm out of here."

Turning my back on him, I grab a backpack to pack my shit. I can feel his eyes on me, watching me, but I can't look at him. The only family I have left just chose that piece-of-shit woman over his own son. I hear the door close behind them and a few seconds later my phone dings indicating a text.

Nasty Bitch: Don't fuck with me.

I don't bother to reply. I completely understand her text. If I try to tell my dad the entire truth she will destroy everything he's worked for.

I open the drawer of my nightstand and grab the two pictures that are tucked away under my boxers. The first is of my older sister and me. It was taken the same day Colette went missing, a few days before she died. Running my fingers over her smiling face, I remember how happy she was that day. It was my twelfth birthday and our parents took us skiing. Colette loved to ski and she was damn good. She would drag me up and down those slopes for hours.

I choke up remembering how amazing the day was until we got home. Colette was four years older than me. The entire ride home she was texting with someone. I saw her smiling and asked if it was a guy. She lied to me. When we got home she asked to go to her friend's house. She lied to our parents. Three days later she was found in the woods with no clothes on, bruises covering her body. The autopsy said she was raped and then strangled to death. After investigating, the police said she was chatting with an older guy in an online chat room. She met up with him when she said she was going with her friends. The cops were able to locate him. He was tried for her murder and found guilty, sentenced to life in prison. But that doesn't change the fact that she lied, and because of her lies, she's dead.

The day my parents found out Colette died I lost a piece of them as well. They began arguing all the time blaming each other. Nothing tears a family apart quicker than the death of a child. My mom cried for months after, saying a parent should never have to bury her own child. My dad turned to work. He went from working the standard forty hours a week to barely ever coming home. Instead of being on my best behavior, I lashed out, getting into fights, skipping school, and causing trouble. That was until I found out about the next lie. This one told by my mother.

I bring the second picture to the front. It's of my mom and me a few weeks before she died from cancer. We are both smiling, but my smile isn't real. I was thirteen at the time—almost a year after Colette died, and we knew my mom only had a short time left. I was homeschooled those last couple months so I could spend my days with her. As much as she tried to keep me away, not wanting me to see her body quickly deteriorating, I refused to stay away. I didn't want to miss a moment with my mom, with the little time she had left. She knew she was sick for a long time but didn't tell me. Another lie...More lies.

Pointing fingers at my sister and mom won't change anything, but it still hurts knowing they both lied to me. I trusted them completely and yet they didn't trust me with the truth.

I try hard not to let those be the last memories I have of them. I try to remember the good times. The times my sister would let me tag along to the local ice cream shop or hang out with her and her friends at the mall or the movies. I try to remember all the times my mom would take me to breakfast, just the two of us, or when she and I would play cards until late at night talking about nothing, yet it felt like everything. My mom and my sister were good people, they were my entire world, and I get they aren't anything like my stepmom, but a lie is a lie, right? Lies destroy and hurt people, and I'm so sick of all the damn lies.

The pictures used to be on top of my nightstand for me to see, to try to remember all the good times over the bad, but Gloria made me put them away. I guess she didn't want to see my mom and sister's smiling faces while she was forcing herself on me.

I shove the pictures into my bag and finish packing some clothes, money I have stashed away, my toothbrush, deodorant, and an extra pair of shoes. I take one last look at my bedroom and head out knowing I'll never be back.

I throw my bag into the backseat of my car and head to Cooper's Fight Club. It's a UFC training facility I work out at as much as I can. I came across the place a few years ago while walking home from school. In exchange for cleaning the gym a few nights a week after it closes, the gym owner, Marc Cooper, agreed to let me workout here for free. I hear he's an asshole, but luckily he lives in Las Vegas and runs the gym there. The gym manager here, Diego, is really cool and lets me train after hours.

While my dream is to be a UFC fighter one day, I'm also going to college full-time. After I graduated from high school last year, I agreed to go to college because my mom left me a college fund when she passed away. She wanted to make sure no matter what happened I would have the money to go. I don't want to let her down so I'm majoring in business and finance. My dad is an investment banker so it made him happy to see me major in something similar. While I can't see myself ever using my degree to do anything like what he does, I'm determined to finish it.

I'm pounding away on the bag for God knows how long when Diego walks over to me.

"What's going on, kid? It looks like you're trying to kill the bag. You know it's an inanimate object, right?"

I can't help but laugh. He's such a smartass.

"Just a bad day. I'm apparently homeless as of a couple hours ago."

I'm not sure why I let that slip out. I usually keep to myself. Nobody knows the shit I've endured the last few years and it needs to stay that way, especially if I want to make sure my dad stays out of prison.

My phone vibrates, letting me know I have a text, so I check it quickly.

Nasty Bitch: You have an appointment at 8 p.m. Don't be late.

She can't be fucking serious right now. Does she really think I'm still going to be her fuck boy? Diego goes to say something and I put up one finger, signaling for him to give me a minute, and text her back.

Me: I'm done.

Her response is almost immediate.

Nasty Bitch: What are you going to do for money? Did you forget our deal?

Me: I would rather live on the streets broke. I'm done.

I'm hoping she won't turn my dad in if I walk away quietly. I'm not her only source of income, and if she turns him in, she'll lose her main source of income as well. She might be a poor excuse for a human, but she isn't stupid.

Nasty Bitch: You need to go to your appointment tonight. You know who it's with. I will let her know it's the last time.

I do know who it's with and it's a woman I don't want to piss off. She has the power to fuck my life up. The first time I met her at the hotel I didn't know who she was. How would I? I was a seventeen-year-old senior in high school. After I started college I learned she's the dean of admissions. When I barely made it through high school and needed to get into college I was shocked to learn I actually got in. Little did I know she pulled strings and got me accepted. As much as I would like to blow her world apart by outing her ass for fucking a teenager, it would also fuck up mine for a few reasons. One, it would out my stepmom and ultimately fuck up my dad's life. And two, it would destroy the last two years I've spent in a college I don't belong in. I only have two more to go to graduate, so I can honor my mom.

Me: Fine. Last time, though.

Nasty Bitch: That's what I thought, and remember you say a word to anybody about our arrangement I will destroy you and your father. You'll be visiting him in prison.

While I don't give a shit about her threats to me, I'll never say a word to anybody. I wouldn't do that to my dad. He's lost enough. His one mistake shouldn't cost him everything.

Putting my phone back in my pocket, I look up and see Diego still staring at me. I completely forgot he was there.

"Homeless?"

"Yeah, I had to move out of my dad's place."

He thinks for a minute. "Look, I got an available room at my place..."

Before he can continue I cut him off.

"How much is the rent? I have some money, but I need to find a job. My school is paid for, but I don't have a steady income anymore."

While I despise Gloria for what she's put me through the last four years, she did pay me. I think she justified her sick actions by paying me for my services. Like if I'm receiving money, it isn't statutory rape and blackmail. If I'm accepting money from her, I must be willing, right? Fucking wrong!

"Like I was saying, I have an extra room at my place and it's empty. It is actually an old mother-in-law suite. It's separate from my house, back behind the pool. I'll start paying you to clean the gym instead of you doing it for free, and that way you can afford food, and still keep training and go to school."

I would be a fool to say no to his offer. I definitely don't have a better one, and if I want to keep training and graduate in two years, getting a full-time minimum wage job is only going to get in the way.

"All right, I'm going to take you up on your offer. Thanks, man."

"No problem. Come by later and I'll get you settled in. It's completely furnished so you don't need anything."

I shake his hand. "I appreciate it."

I glance at the clock and see it's almost seven. I've got to shower and get ready for my last appointment. Suddenly it feels like I can breathe again. Knowing I'll never have to unwillingly fuck another woman makes me feel like a hundred pounds has been lifted off my chest.

I head to the locker room to change and run into Bentley and Cooper. I met them here at the gym. It's actually Cooper's dad who owns the gym, but I guess they don't really get along too well. Bentley and Cooper are both cool, though. They're both fighters and are training to be in the UFC like I am. They've invited me to chill several times but with everything I have going on, I've found it best to keep people at arm's length. They're always going out, chasing females, and the truth is, I want nothing to do with women. Over the last few years I have been forced to fuck every kind of woman, but a few things are always the same. They're users and cheaters, and they can't be trusted. They want a man for his money and cock. I can't even tell you how many married women I have fucked. And do they care that they've been fucking a teenager? Fuck no, they don't. I hate the female population and I'm definitely not interested in chasing one.

One day I'll be in the UFC. I'll be a fighter like I've dreamed of, and with my business and finance degree I'll be able to manage my own money. There is no way I am busting my ass to have some untrustworthy, cheating woman use me for my money and then fuck me over. Fuck that shit.

Now all I need to do is get through tonight and shit will be looking up from here on out. I say what's up to the guys, shower, and get dressed. Maybe after tonight I'll actually be able to chill with them.

Norma Silverstein, the dean of admissions, is of course a married woman. She is married to a professor at the business college so we meet at a local hotel for our appointments since her home is off limits. When I pull up, I send her a text to let her know I'm here. She texts back the room number and I head up.

I knock and she lets me in. She's dressed in nothing but the hotel robe and her hair is up in some messy bun shit women always wear. She smiles at me and holds the door open while I walk through to the main room to wait for her demands. I hear the door close behind me and then feel her hands come around me moving straight to my dick. What I want to do is take her hand and shove it away from me, tell her to never fucking touch me again, but I can't. So instead I stand there and let the woman put her hands on my body.

"You aren't hard." I can't see her since she's standing behind me, but I can hear the pout in her voice.

Of course I'm not hard. Do women seriously think guys walk around hard twenty-four seven? Do they think paying someone for their services is going to make that person instantly attracted to them? Well, I can tell you from experience, it doesn't. What's worse is these women know what kind of service my stepmom provides. They know she pimps out her barely old enough teenage stepson to service them at their demand, but do they care? No, they don't. They care about one thing, themselves. My job is to do as these women say. It doesn't matter if I don't want to or if I'm not in the mood. My job is to fake it.

The first time I had sex with Norma I was almost eighteen. I was about to graduate high school and my stepmom said if I had sex with Norma she could ensure I would be accepted to the University. Not that I had a damn choice anyway. I had already been having sex with other women for a little over a year. At least having sex with Norma would mean I would get into college. Unfortunately once wasn't enough and every time we're done she reminds me she's the only reason I'm in college. I would say I should have just gone to a local state college but would it have mattered? I still would be forced to sleep with Norma. Gloria gets what she wants or my dad will end up in prison. I don't want to see my father in prison...even if he technically deserves it.

Norma stays standing behind me and rubs my cock, hoping it will magically get hard. I close my eyes and will my dick to do something. I'm not sure if I should will it to get hard to get this shit over with or will it to stay soft so I won't have to fuck this cheating whore at all. Of course my dick has a mind of its own and after a few minutes of her rubbing on it, it gets hard. It's science, really...it doesn't matter how much I beg it to stay soft, it always ends up getting hard. It's as if it's been trained to get hard against its will, and I guess in a way it has been, by Gloria. Turning around, I decide to get this shit over with.

"What would you like tonight?" I robotically ask, because that's my job—to ask what they want and then give it to them. They all want pretty much the same thing—to get off. They want orgasms that are almost impossible to give and receive. They think because they have read some porn shit in a romance book that means it's really that easy.

"I want it rough tonight," she shyly responds. If I didn't know better I would think she's some sweet, innocent woman, but I do know better and she's neither of those. I don't know why she insists on acting shy every time she makes her demands. You're paying for sex while cheating on your husband. Do you really need to act shy? But because I don't need to piss this woman off, I go along with it.

I take her by her hand and bring her to the room, straight to the bed. I push her onto the mattress roughly and begin removing my clothes. She gets excited and strips herself of her robe. Stroking my cock to keep it hard, I climb on onto the bed and flip her over onto her stomach, pulling her ass up in the air.

"Spank me!" she screeches, so I do. Kneeling behind her, I smack her ass several times with one hand while I find her pussy through her opened thighs with my other. I push two fingers straight into her cunt and begin pumping them in and out of her, getting her wet. I add a third finger and attempt to find her G-spot. The sooner I give her what her husband apparently can't, the sooner I can get the fuck out of here.

I know I've found the spot that will make her go off when her thighs begin to close shut. I give her ass another hard smack just like she likes.

"Keep your fucking legs open." Within a few seconds of my fingers hitting the spot, she's coming. *One down.*

"Ohhh...that feels so good. I want you to fuck me in the ass now," Norma moans, coming down from her orgasm.

I grab a condom from the nightstand she left there for tonight and roll it onto my dick. I stroke it a few more times to make sure it's hard again. Then I drag her to the edge of the bed so she's leaning over the edge with her ass in the air.

Taking the wetness from my fingers, I stick them into her ass getting it ready for my cock. While I would love to go in dry and tear her shit up and really show her what rough is, I don't want to piss her off. I'm so close to being done. I just need to finish this and I'll be able to walk away finally free.

Once I know she's ready, I guide my cock to her ass and push in slowly.

"Oh my God!" she yells. "Pull my hair!"

And so I do. I grab ahold of her hair and fist it around my hand while pushing my dick all the way in.

"Hard! I want it hard!" She wiggles her ass, wanting more, and once again I give her exactly what she wants.

With her mane wrapped around my fist, I pull her head back to the point that it's got to be painful and begin fucking her ass with abandon. Harder and harder I pound into her. Does it feel good? I would be lying if I said it doesn't. I am a man after all, fucking a woman in the ass. Of course it feels good. The problem is every time I come it's tainted knowing this isn't my choice. I have never had sex by choice. Thinking about Gloria taking my virginity at fifteen years old pisses me off. I keep pounding this bitch, remembering my stepmom threatening me, telling me if I didn't fuck her she would destroy my dad, and then spending the next several years dreading every time my dad went away knowing she would be showing up to my room.

Once I turned sixteen, she began forcing me to fuck other women. I thought maybe she would stop wanting me, but she didn't. She had no problem continuing to make me fuck her even though she knew all the women she was pimping me out to. The memories become too much and I try to shake the thoughts from my head. If I think too much my dick will go soft.

"Caleb, make me come." Norma's words bring me back to the now remembering this shit is about her. It's always about the woman. They don't care if I get off. They're using me. That's what women do. They use.

I bring the hand that isn't grabbing her hair down to her clit and begin rubbing it in circles while I continue to fuck her ass. I can feel my body trying to release, but I focus on something else to stop myself from coming. I can't come before her. I need to end this shit on a good note. Thankfully her second orgasm hits and she's coming once again, allowing me to come as well. I release into the condom and slow my thrusts to a standstill. I untangle my fingers from her hair and slowly pull my dick out of her ass.

She turns around and smiles. "Thank you. That was so good."

I nod and head to the bathroom to get cleaned up, grabbing my clothes from the floor so I don't have to walk out naked.

My phone goes off in my pocket and I check it.

Diego: Great opportunity for you has come up. Call me when you get this.

I flush the condom, get dressed, and say goodbye to Norma for the last time. She, of course reminds me she'll check on my grades and make sure everything is going okay—her way of reminding me she's in control. Once I'm in the lobby, I dial Diego.

"Hey man, where are you?" he asks.

"Heading to your place now. What's up?"

"Cooper and the guys are here and want to talk to you. I'll see you when you get here."

We hang up and I head straight to his place.

I knock and let myself in like I've done a million times. I'm so thankful he's giving me a place to stay. I had no idea there was a room in the back of his house. The guys are all sitting in the living room watching a basketball game, drinking beer and eating what looks like take out from a local Chinese place. Eating healthy is a huge part of training, but most fighters will give themselves cheat days to stay sane. This must be theirs.

Cooper is the first to stand to say hi. "What's up, man?"

"Nothing much." I give him a handshake.

I glance over and see Kaden—Cooper's trainer—and sitting next to him is Bentley.

"What's going on?" I ask anxiously.

"You're out of college for the summer, right?" Diego asks.

"Yeah, I'm considering taking a couple classes over the summer, but nothing major until August. Why?"

"Could you transfer to a different college?" Bentley chimes in.

"I guess I could if I had to." I'm not sure what all the questions are about my schooling, but I'm getting kind of nervous.

"Diego told us you're in the transition of moving out. We're heading to Miami to do some promo shit and then moving to Las Vegas to train at my dad's gym," Cooper says.

I nod, but I'm still not sure where he's going with this.

"Kaden and I both decided to purchase a home over there, which leaves Bentley living on his own. He found a three-bedroom place and plans to use one room for an office, but he's looking for a roommate for the third bedroom, and when I mentioned it to Diego, he thought you might be interested. What do you think about moving to Las Vegas and rooming with Bentley? You can also train at the gym there free of charge."

Are these guys fucking serious? It's like they're handing me my dreams on a silver platter.

"Umm...that sounds awesome, but I only have a few grand to my name. I don't know how much the rent is, but I would need to get a job, and even then, with training and college, I don't know how many hours I would be able to work..."

Bentley raises his hand to stop me. "Bro, chill. I'm good with paying whatever. I just want a roommate since these two pussies have decided they need to grow up and buy a house and shit. Pay or don't pay...I don't care. Just keep your space clean, if you eat my food, let me know, and if you have a female over, try to keep her quiet."

This shit is too good to be true, but I'm not about to look a gift horse in the mouth. I could tell him he won't need to worry about me bringing any females over, but I would imagine that would raise questions, so instead I just say okay and thank him.

Coopers adds, "We're leaving the day after tomorrow. A bunch of the guys from the gym are flying out as well. We'll be in Miami for a few days and then we'll head to Las Vegas. You're more than welcome to join us in Miami."

I look to Diego to make sure this is all legit and he's okay with this. I trust him to steer me in the right direction. He nods and smiles, and I silently scream *fuck yes!* I'm getting the fuck out of here.

One

CALEB

Present Day

IT'S DECEMBER IN LAS VEGAS, AND WHILE MANY WOULD think it would be hot because well...it's Las Vegas and Las Vegas is in the desert, it's actually not. It's freezing cold outside. I jump into my blacked out Dodge Ram, turn the key into the ignition, and put the heat on full blast. *Fuck, it's cold!*

I go through the local coffee shop drive thru to pick up a couple hot coffees before heading to the gym. The coffee serves two purposes: one, to warm me up, and two, to wake me up. I didn't get in until almost four this morning from work and I'm exhausted. I was only supposed to work until two, but between the call-outs and the private parties at the club, the owner, Matt, needed me to stay late. I'm definitely not complaining about the hours because more hours means more money in my bank account, but when you have to get up at seven in the morning to head to the gym to train for a fight, the sleep I'm lacking feels more important than the money.

I know I should quit my job. My dream has finally come true and I have a contract with the UFC, but what people don't realize is, while a contract is definitely a step in the right direction, it doesn't mean instant stardom or money. I am lucky my roommate Bentley barely lets me pay a dime to live here. I had no idea how expensive it could be to live in Las Vegas. The problem is I know it won't be long until he moves out and I'll have to find my own place and pay real rent. Luckily, I have been busting my ass and saving for the last several years since we moved out here, and I actually have a very good amount of money saved up.

Bentley and I have been roommates for the last seven years, but a lot of shit has recently changed. First off, he and his girlfriend, Kayla, who is one of my best friends, had a baby girl in June. Her name is Faith and she's the cutest baby in the world.

I'm not going to lie; it took a little while to warm up to Kayla. I don't trust women, but living with her allowed me to get to know a female who isn't trying to use a man for his money or dick, and over time a friendship developed. She has also taught me women are human and make mistakes. Not every lie is vindictive and I need to remember that about my mom and sister. They didn't lie to be vindictive, not like my stepmom did.

Bentley and Kayla are planning to get married soon which means they'll be moving out to get their own place, leaving me in this expensive ass three-bedroom place by myself. Bentley has told me several times I can stay and he will keep paying the rent. *Rich fucker!* But we both know I can't allow him to do that.

I pull up to the gym and grab my coffee and the other coffee I picked up. I swing the door open and head straight to the office, handing Liz the hot cup.

"Ooohhh! For me? You are the best!" she says, taking a long sip. She closes her eyes and moans dramatically. "This is so good! I needed this coffee fix."

Liz is the office manager here at Cooper's Fight Club, and married to Cooper. She's another female I've gotten to know and adore. Those two women are definitely proof that not all women are gold digging, untrusting bitches. Once in a while I actually wonder what it would be like to meet a woman like Kayla or Liz. Then I remember my past. I can't see myself ever trusting a woman enough to want to be intimate with her.

A while back Cooper's dad passed away and left the gyms he owns to his son. All this took place shortly after Cooper found out he had a baby with Liz he knew nothing about. Remember the mention of our trip to Miami? Yeah, well, what happened in Miami didn't stay in Miami. Without realizing it, Liz and her best friend Kayla wound up in Las Vegas as well—Liz pregnant with their daughter Bella—and a few years later they reconnected at a UFC fight, fell in love, got married, and recently had another baby. Their son's name is Nathan, and he's almost as cute as Faith.

After Cooper's dad died and left him the gyms he decided to take a step back from fighting to run the gyms and focus on his wife and kids. Bentley is doing the same thing...well, not running the gyms. He has decided to be a stay-at-home dad. Kayla is a physical therapist at the gym, so Bentley is still around a lot, but he's no longer fighting competitively. Yep! A lot of shit happens in seven years.

As for me, not much has changed since I moved here. I transferred to a local college and a few years ago graduated with my degree in business and finance. I haven't heard from my dad or Gloria since I moved and I prefer to keep it that way. While I miss my dad, I know it's for the best. I still find it hard to believe Gloria let me go so easily. For the first few years after I left, I held my breath waiting for her blackmailing to begin again, but it never did.

In the last few years I have won several fights and received a UFC contract, which I am on cloud nine about. I work at the club at night, train during the day with Kaden—who took me and our friend Alex on, after Bentley and Cooper decided to take a break—and chill with my friends. Life is actually really good.

After giving Liz her coffee, I head to the locker room to change. As I'm turning the corner, I run straight into Hayley. My coffee slushes around inside the cup and some of it flies out of the small slit in the lid, not much but enough to stain her shirt.

"Oh, shit! I'm sorry," I say, looking around for something to help her wipe up the coffee on her shirt.

She looks at me nervously, biting down on her lower lip. It reminds me of her face after the first and only time we kissed, when she realized I couldn't give her anything more. The truth is we never even should have kissed that night.

"Let's play a game!" Hayley shouts over the music. We're at the club I work at celebrating Kayla and Bentley going out for the first time after having

Faith.

"A game? What are we, five?" Kaden asks. Everybody laughs at his question, but of course all their drunk asses agree to play.

"Caleb, truth or dare?" Kayla asks me. I know I have to pick dare even though I don't want to. If I pick truth, she'll ask me a question I won't want to answer. She's always asking why I never bring females home. I can't put myself in that position to have to lie to her.

I glare at her but go along with it. "Dare."

Kayla looks over to her left, and following her line of vision, I see her glance at Hayley and then smirk. Don't do it Kayla...but she does.

"I dare you to kiss Hayley."

Hayley glares at her, clearly embarrassed. "You don't have to..." Hayley turns to me and says. But without letting her finish, for the first time ever, I let my hormones control my actions as I pull her to me for a kiss. Her lips are soft and warm and she tastes like the sweet liquor concoction she has been sipping on all night. My tongue seeks entrance and soon we are full on making out in front of everyone in the middle of a nightclub. I can almost enjoy it, but then it hits me. Once again I'm kissing a woman against my own free will.

No, I'm technically not being forced and I wouldn't compare it to what Gloria did to me, but we aren't kissing out of love or even lust. I'm kissing her because somebody dared me to, and just like that it's as if I'm being manipulated and used all over again. It's like ice water being splashed on me. I end the now tainted kiss abruptly slightly pushing Hayley away from me. She gives me a confused, embarrassed look that turns sad, probably wondering if she did something wrong...

Since then Hayley has made it clear on several occasions she likes me, but I've continued to ignore all her advances. I know it's been seven fucking years since I left Boulder and my past behind, but I can't find it in me to be with a woman of my own free will. Every time I think about it, I feel like in some way or another it's being forced on me. I don't know how to change the way I feel.

And let's say I do find a woman that I choose to touch. How do I know I can trust her? How do I know she won't want me for all the wrong reasons or that she won't cheat on me? I think about my sister and mom and stepmom, and how I trusted each one of them in a different way and what did they do? They all lied. I think about all the women I watched cheat on their husbands. I don't know how to truly trust a woman, and I can't imagine being with someone without trusting her, but then I think about Kayla and Liz, and while neither of them are perfect, I don't believe either of them would do anything to deliberately hurt Bentley or Cooper. I trust both of those women as much as I am capable of.

And even if we get past all that trust bullshit, how do I tell her that I lost my virginity at fifteen years old to my stepmom who then blackmailed me into learning how to please a woman so she could pimp me out to cheating wives? Who the fuck wants to deal with that kind of baggage?

Attempting to shake myself out of my thoughts I see Hayley still standing there, staring at me, and fuck if she isn't a naturally beautiful woman. I first look at her eyes because they're wide open. They are light brown and remind me of the Werther's caramels my mom used to buy me at the store when I was younger. Then my eyes drift to the rest of her face and notice she has cute freckles lightly spattered across her nose. She doesn't wear tons of make up like most women do in Las Vegas. She looks like she has a bit of clear lipstick on because her lips are shiny. It makes me want to taste them. Forcing myself to look away from her face, I look at her hair. It's brown with shades of lighter brown and blonde mixed in.

Her head is tilted just a little to the side, and my eyes go back to her mouth, which is curved downward. Her frowning does something to me. I want to make her smile. Is it crazy that I want to kiss that frown right off her face? Why is she just standing there staring at me? *Shit!* Remembering I just spilled coffee on her, I grab a towel off the towel rack and go to clean her shirt. My hand hits her breast and she jumps back, her face turning red with embarrassment. *What the hell am I doing?*

"I am so sorry!" I say once again, this time for touching her without permission.

She lets out a soft giggle and it's got to be the sweetest sound I've ever heard.

"It's okay," she says, taking the towel from me. She grabs her water bottle and pours some water on the towel and proceeds to dab the wet towel onto the stain. "I just wasn't expecting you to do that." Her face is bright red as she looks down at the spot to avoid looking at me. She's so adorable.

When she removes the towel, the area is soaking wet and I can see right through her white button up shirt to her white lacy bra. From the cold water, her nipple is poking through, and for the first time in

God knows how long, my dick is twitching of its own free will. I bring my eyes back up to her face and try to discreetly adjust myself. I'm obviously not discreet enough, though, because Hayley looks at my face, down to my hard-on, then back to her soaked shirt.

If it's even possible, her face goes redder and I can't help but laugh at the awkwardness of this entire situation. How did I not notice how fucking adorable this chick is? She pouts at my laughter and covers her wet shirt and pointed nipple with the towel, making me laugh even harder.

"Are you laughing?" Kaden comes over and pats my shoulder trying to assess the situation.

He glances back and forth between Hayley and me. "You must be hilarious because I don't think I have ever heard Caleb laugh."

Hayley's eyes go wide and she mutters something along the lines of, "I need to go find a new shirt," as she hightails it away from us with the towel still covering her chest.

"What was that about?" Kaden asks, watching Hayley as she walks away.

"Nothing. I spilled my coffee on her by accident. Ready to go workout for a little bit?"

He studies me for a second. "Yeah. If you want to be ready for the fight in a few months we need to start training hardcore. You ready for that?"

"I was born ready."

We begin warming up and a few minutes later I notice Hayley walking out of the locker room with a new shirt on. She walks over to

Stephen, another fighter, and begins feeling his fingers. He must have hurt them somehow while training. I know she's the onsite doctor here at the gym ,so it's her job to touch the fighters to see what's wrong, but something I've never felt before hits me as I watch her touch him— jealousy maybe? I'm not sure. Then he says something to her causing her to break out in a full grin. Her head goes back and she laughs. She might have been giggling with me, but it wasn't anywhere close to the reaction he's getting from her. She might be adorable with her shy giggles, but when she laughs...she's downright fucking beautiful.

Kaden catches me watching her and clears his throat. When I force my eyes off her and look at him he's got a smirk on his face looking like he's about to comment.

I ignore him and walk to the ring ready to train. I don't know what the hell is wrong with me but I need to focus on fighting. Sure, her laughter does something strange to my insides, and yeah, she looks hot as hell with her body full of curves and toned legs that go on for miles in her high heels and skirts. And on top of all that I know from experience, she can kiss. Everything about Hayley is a complete turn on, but at the end of the day she is still a woman, and like I've said before and will continue to say, women, for the most part can't be trusted, and I doubt Hayley is an exception.

We get into the ring and get our gloves and gear on, when I hear someone call out my name. I scan the area and see Marco running over to me. Marco is twelve years old and part of the Youth MMA program Cooper is running for kids who want a safe place to practice and train. As often as I can, I teach the class. Cooper and Liz's almost six-year-old daughter, Bella, is part of the program as well. She swears one day she'll become a UFC fighter. I don't doubt it. That little girl is beyond determined.

Earlier this year, Marco started coming into the gym. He wanted to be a part of the class, but his mom couldn't afford it, so Bentley opened up a scholarship program for kids whose parents don't have the money to pay. It allows them to train at a discounted rate. In Marco's case, he trains for free.

The truth is, nobody has ever seen Marco's mom except for me. After getting excuse after excuse, I followed him home one day and saw he lives in section eight housing in a shitty area. When he went to school the next day I knocked on the door and found a woman who looked like the weight of the world was on her shoulders.

She confided in me that Marco's dad was killed in a drive-by years ago. She recently had another baby by some other guy and is between jobs. I could tell she was strung out on drugs but knew better than to bring it up. The sure-fire way to piss off a drug addict is to call them out on it. She would most likely just lie anyway. I had her sign for Marco to join the program and told her if she needs anything to let me know, not because I want to help her but because I want to make sure Marco is okay. She is another example of an untrustworthy woman, choosing drugs over her own children.

Since she signed the papers, Marco has practically lived at the gym. When there aren't classes I let him clean and sweep just like Diego did for me. It keeps him off the streets and out of trouble. Before he started coming to the gym he used to hang out down at the skate park.

He enjoys skateboarding but says he loves fighting.

"What's up?" I say, fist bumping him.

"Wanna join us?" Kaden asks. The guys know all about Marco's situation and treat him like he's one of us.

Marco looks conflicted for a second, but shakes his head no. "No, I can't. I have stuff I have to do today, but just wanted to let you know I won't be able to make the training camp today."

A red flag immediately goes up. Marco has never missed a class. Ever. That kid is the first one here and doesn't leave until he has no choice. For him to miss a class, something is up.

"I'm gonna miss you in class. What's going on that you can't make it?" I ask nonchalantly trying to get him to open up. He reminds me a lot of myself. He keeps to himself and doesn't speak more than necessary.

His refusal to look me in the eyes tells me whatever he is about to say will be a lie.

"I have to help take care of Chloe. I just wanted to tell you."

Chloe is Marco's little sister. She's only a few months old. I know he helps watch her, but he's never missed a class to watch her. I let it go for now. Calling him out on this won't help the situation.

"Okay, buddy. If anything changes, come back, okay?"

"Okay," he says with a frown marring his face. It breaks my heart what this kid goes through. Yeah, my situation was shitty as a teenager, but I never had to worry about when I would eat next. I had name brand clothes, the newest cellphone, and was given a new car almost every birthday. I chose to walk away from it all the day I left, but for

Marco, he doesn't get a choice. He's never been given a choice.

He leaves out the door and I rip my headgear and gloves off, throwing them to the side.

"Where are you going?" Kaden asks.

"I'm following him. Something is up. That kid doesn't miss class."

Not waiting for a response from Kaden, I run to the locker room to grab my wallet and keys and run out the door to find out where Marco is really going.

Two

HAYLEY

I'M RUNNING SO LATE THIS MORNING AND I HATE RUNNING late. The water heater in my house broke last night, so I was forced to take an ice cold shower this morning. I tried to call around to find someone to fix it, but with Christmas so close these people want to charge an arm and a leg. So much for the holiday spirit! I still need to buy a couple more presents. I have no idea what to buy my sister, Hannah. She is seriously the hardest person to shop for.

On my way to the gym I received a call from Cooper letting me know one of the fighters thinks he might have sprained or possibly broken a couple of fingers and would like me to check it out before he goes to the hospital. His text throws me off and I completely forget to go through the drive thru to grab a coffee. Oh well! I'll have to run back out later when I have time.

I make it to the gym in record time, run straight to the locker room to throw my purse and keys into a locker, fill up my water bottle with cold water, and head back out to find Stephen, the fighter with the possibly broken fingers. I barely make it out of the locker room when I run into a wall. Okay, not a wall, a solid man whose body feels like a wall. Warmth spreads across my chest and it's not from the unrequited lust I feel for this man. Nope, it's from the warm coffee that just spilled all over my blouse. Coffee, that isn't even mine. Coffee, that I almost want to lick off my blouse in hope I will get even a little bit of caffeine running through my exhausted body.

I look up from the stain covering my chest and into the most beautiful blue-grey eyes of Caleb Michaels, the man who I have a huge crush on. I know what you're thinking. What woman in her thirties has a crush? Well, most women in her thirties are married with kids, so they don't have to crush like a damn teenager. Not me, though. After spending my teenage years studying my ass off to get into a good college, I then studied my ass off to get into a good medical program. It has always been my dream to get a degree in sports medicine. I love sports and I love healing people so it just made sense. I did make the mistake of dating once in college. I was so busy with school, the guy ended up cheating on me with my roommate. I told myself I wouldn't date again until I could devote the right amount of time to a man.

I finally graduated and was fortunate to get a job working at Cooper's training facility right away. The hours are great and I'm able to work with athletes every day doing what I love. I get to travel to fights and it's seriously amazing. I couldn't ask for a better job. The only downside is that between all my years of school and now work, I'm thirty years old and still single with no kids. And if that isn't enough, the guy I like doesn't even know I exist. Well, I think he knows

I exist, but he definitely doesn't reciprocate my feelings.

Although, there was that time at the club when he was dared to kiss me...*Hol-y shit!* It had to have been the most intense kiss of my life! I thought maybe he felt something as well, but after the kiss was over, he walked away without looking back.

Caleb looks around for a moment and grabs a towel, bringing it right to my chest. He starts dabbing my boob with it and I'm shocked he's actually touching me. My memory flashes back to the time we were all over Cooper and Liz's place. The guys had stayed home to watch Bella and Tristan—our friend Ashley's son—while the women all got drunk and had a girls' night at my place. Somehow we ended up back at Liz's place, and Caleb was there, looking sexy as hell in his own brooding way, sitting on the couch watching a UFC fight. In my intoxicated state I walked over to sit down next to him and patted his leg...

"Sorry, to ruin your little fight party." I sit next to Caleb and pat him on his leg. He stiffen slightly before he jumps up from his spot on the couch like he's on fire.

"I have to get to work," he says, and without saying goodbye to anybody, he hauls ass out the door.

Then there was the ski trip where he didn't want to even sleep in the same room as me...

We had just arrived at Bentley's amazing vacation home in Breckenridge. Caleb asked where everyone was sleeping and within seconds rooms were called. Bentley and Kayla went to the master suite, Cooper and Liz went off to another room and even though Ashley and Kaden are just friends, they're really close, so they had no problem sharing a room. That left Caleb and me and unfortunately only one room left.

"I don't mind sharing if you don't," I said.

Caleb looked around the room and saw there was only one bed, which meant sharing a room also meant sharing a bed.

"Sorry, I can't do this." He grimaced.

"I promise not to attack you in my sleep." It was my attempt to make light of the situation. He wasn't having it though.

"No, I'm not going to be forced to share a room with you. Sorry."

Geez. I get he doesn't want to share a room with me, but damn. I'm not forcing him to do anything...

Needless to say, he ended up sleeping on the couch during our stay and has pretty much avoided me since then.

I glance at him, embarrassed. One, for realizing how ridiculous I must look for hitting on him when he's made it clear he doesn't want me, and two, for being completely turned on by his touch.

He must suddenly realize he's rubbing all over my breasts, because he pulls back and begins to apologize profusely. I can't help but nervously laugh. The guy who doesn't want to touch me is not only touching me but also unintentionally feeling me up like we're back in high school.

"It's okay," I say, unable to make eye contact with him. This is so embarrassing.

"I wasn't expecting you to do that," I add, referring to him feeling me up. I grab my water bottle and try to blot the stained area, hoping to make it a little easier to get out later. The stain doesn't seem to be coming out at all so I give up and remove the towel from my chest. When I notice Caleb hasn't said a word I finally get the courage to look at him and when I do I see what looks like lust in his eyes...but it can't be. This guy has made it clear he doesn't want me.

I follow his gaze to find my traitorous nipples are poking through my soaking wet blouse! Jesus, I don't think this situation could get any more embarrassing...until I look back at Caleb and see him adjusting what now looks like an erection in his boxing shorts. I can feel my face heating up and then Caleb laughs. He. Fucking. Laughs. I don't know what he thinks is so funny, but it's definitely not any of this.

Kaden comes over just in time and asks why Caleb is laughing. He says something about me making Caleb laugh, and before Caleb can explain and further embarrass me, I mumble about needing a new shirt and get the hell out of there.

"Can I borrow a shirt?" I blurt out when I find Liz in her office.

She looks up at me with a confused expression. I shake my head not wanting to get into it, but of course she isn't having it.

"Everything okay?"

I let out a frustrated breath. "My shower almost froze me to death, Caleb spilled coffee on me and then felt me up, and then saw me turned on, and I might be wrong, but I think my getting turned on, turned him on."

She bursts out laughing, grabs a gym shirt, and throws it to me. "Well, I guess you got your wish."

"Oh, shut up! I need to go change and find Stephen to check out his hand."

I turn to leave and can hear her continuing to laugh from her office. She is getting entirely too much pleasure out of this situation.

As I exit the locker room, I spot Stephen and check out his hand. I don't think his fingers are broken but I'll need to take an x-ray to make sure. We go back to my office, and after running the x-rays, my suspicions are confirmed. Not broken, just significantly bruised. I put a splint on his fingers and tell him to take a couple of days off to let them heal.

As I'm walking back out, I see Caleb rushing out of the locker room. Kaden is watching him with a worried look. As Caleb exits the gym, Ashley enters. Ashley and I have become good friends over the past several months. We met through Liz a couple years ago. She's a single mom, an elementary school teacher, and just an all-around good person. With Kayla and Liz both having new babies at home, and both happily taken, we've started hanging out together since her son is no longer a baby and neither of us are taken.

"Hey sexy momma," I say, waggling my eyebrows at her. She laughs and shakes her head, walking over to me with Tristan following behind. Kaden comes over to say hi as well, giving her a one armed hug and a kiss to her temple. It's completely innocent, but I see the look in Ashley's eyes. It's the look of a woman who wants more. Since Kaden is single and has become good friends with Ashley we all hang out quite often. I've asked Ashley on more than one occasion why she and Kaden aren't dating, but she always says the same thing—she doesn't want to lose him as a friend. It's rumored Kaden isn't the settling down type, and over the years I've been working here, I've seen him with various women, but since he started hanging out with Ashley, I haven't seen him around any other woman but her.

Caleb is single as well, but is more of a loner. I haven't seen him hanging around a single woman in the time I've been working at the gym. Whenever Kaden, Ashley, and I hang out, we invite Caleb to join us, but he always says no. I try not to take it too personal.

"What's up with Caleb?" Ashley asks Kaden. "He almost plowed through me on his way out."

Kaden leaves his arm dangling over Ashley's shoulder and pulls her in closer to him, not noticing—or ignoring—the blush that creeps up Ashley's face. We'll definitely be talking later. "He's worried about Marco. He told him he couldn't make it to class today, so he's following him to see where he's going."

Poor Marco. It's no secret the type of home he comes from. When he first started coming here he was so shy and quiet, but several months later and he has grown on all of us, especially Caleb. If you didn't know better you would think Marco was a mini-Caleb. He follows him around and copies everything he does. They are both so serious all the time. It really is adorable.

"Oh, well, Tristan is here for the MMA boot camp. With school out for the holidays Cooper and Caleb are doing a mini-training camp for the kids. My parents are going to take him afterward and keep him for the rest of winter break."

"Let's go see what's going on with the camp," Kaden says, leading her to the backroom where the kids classes are all held.

"Hey, Hayley," Ashley calls back to me. "Dinner tonight?"

"Sure! I'll bring dessert."

"Sounds good!"

Three

CALEB

I FIND MARCO AS SOON AS I WALK OUT THE DOOR, ONLY HE isn't walking anywhere—he's standing in the parking lot talking to some shady-looking motherfuckers. There are two of them and both are covered in ink. Now, I'm not by any means against tattoos. I have several of my own, and because of that, I know ninety percent of the time they have meaning behind them. Staring at these guys talking to Marco, I can tell right away they're in a gang. They both have the same tattoo of what looks like a local gang symbol going up their neck and, when I look closer, I can see the tear drop tattoos on their cheeks, the universal code for how many people they've killed.

A third guy approaches from an expensive Mercedes, looking out of place. He's dressed much nicer than the other two guys in a suit, but peeking out from under the collar is the same tattoo as the other guys, telling me he is some type of leader. He hands Marco a brown package, and before Marco can leave, he grabs him by his shirt and pulls him closer whispering something to him. Marco nods nervously and then walks away.

The three guys stay in the parking lot discussing something but I don't wait around to see what they are doing. I'm about to jump in my car but think it might be more discreet to follow by foot. Without letting Marco know, I follow him, staying close enough to see him but far enough back he doesn't catch on. He walks several blocks to his neighborhood looking around. I can tell by his body language he's scared. He's gripping the bag in both hands and when he looks around, it's like he wants to make sure nobody's going to steal the package from him.

It doesn't take a genius to figure out what's going on. I seriously hope my suspicions are wrong, but when he stops walking at a house a couple streets over from his and pulls a cell phone out of his pocket, one I know damn well he can't afford, I have a sinking feeling in my gut.

My suspicions are confirmed about two minutes later when a guy walks over to Marco, looks around, and then takes the package from him. He opens it up, takes something out, dabs it on his wrist, and then licks his wrist. *Fuck.* Marco just handed this guy cocaine.

The guy nods once and then hands Marco an envelope, which I'm sure contains money. He says something to him I can't hear and then walks away. Marco opens the envelope and then calls someone. He starts walking down the street and ends up in front of an old warehouse a street over from his house. A few minutes later, the two guys from earlier pull up, take the envelope from Marco and hand him some money. Marco pockets the money, takes another brown envelope from the guys, and then they part ways. I follow Marco until he's at his house and wait until he's inside before leaving. The only reason I can think of why these guys aren't dealing themselves is they are under surveillance, so instead of handling the exchange themselves, they're using Marco, a twelve-year-old fucking kids, as a middleman.

I head back to the gym in a daze. I always knew there was a possibility of something like this happening. The kid lives in a neighborhood surrounded by druggies and those who deal the drugs to them. His own mom is a fucking druggie. I just hoped him hanging out with me would keep him away from that shit as long as possible. I join Kaden and Cooper in the kids' class. The boot camp is a blast. The kids have fun and learn a lot about self-defense, but the entire time I can't take my mind off Marco. I don't know how to handle this situation. I don't even know who to talk to about any of this.

After all the kids' parents pick them up I head to the mall to pick up a couple last minute Christmas gifts. I purchase a couple new Disney movies for Bella that Liz mentioned she wanted, some light-up musical toy for Nathan since he's five months old, and a shirt that reads, "My uncle is better than yours" for Faith. Since Kayla and Bentley live in the same apartment as me I know Faith has way too many toys, and Kayla will get a kick out of the shirt.

I take them to the wrapping station in the middle of the mall and make a donation to the school's local band for them to wrap them for me. As I am heading out, my phone dings with a text from Kaden.

Kaden: Going to Ashley's for dinner. Hayley will be there...Wanna go?

My thoughts go back to her this morning—her reaction to me touching her, her nipples getting hard, her face turning red, and then her cute-as-fuck embarrassed giggle over it all. Every time he asks me to join, I always say no. I don't want to give her any reason to think there's a chance with us, but for some reason I find myself wanting to go, wanting to see her giggle some more, wanting to see if I can bring the same smile to her face Stephen did.

Me: Sure. What time? Need me to bring anything?

I get ready for his smart-ass remark, but it doesn't come.

Kaden: 5 p.m. Just bring you.

After taking a shower and getting dressed, I search the kitchen to see if we have a bottle of wine I can bring with me. I don't want to show up empty handed. I find red wine in the cabinet and then walk out to the living room. Kayla is sitting on the couch bouncing Faith on her legs and singing the ABCs to her while Faith makes noises she thinks are mimicking her mom.

"Where are you going all dressed up?" she playfully asks, still in her singing mom voice.

"I wouldn't call a shirt and jeans dressed up...I'm going to Ashley's for dinner." I glance down at my clothes. I'm in a collared shirt, which I don't usually wear, but still...Do I usually dress so crappy she's considering this dressed up?

Kayla's eyes widen out of shock. "Just you and Ashley?"

"No. Kaden will be there and so will Hayley, I guess. Mind if I take this wine?" I try to sound as chill as possible not wanting her to question my motives.

"Sure."

"Wanna go?"

Her smile widens and she shakes her head slowly. "Nope, you enjoy your double date, my friend."

"It's not a double date. Kaden and Ashley are only friends."

"Yeah, until they both get their heads out of their ass and admit they want more."

I laugh at that. "Kaden settle down? Highly unlikely."

"You never know. Cooper and Bentley both settled down."

"Yeah, but the difference is, Bentley has always wanted to settle down and Cooper was pining over Liz for years. Plus, they have a kid together. I don't think Kaden will ever settle down."

"And what about you?" She quirks a single brow. "Will you ever settle down?"

I don't like how serious this conversation is getting, so I say something to deflect. "Not a chance in hell. The only woman I trust is taken, and plus...Bentley would *try* to beat my ass." I give her a wink and Faith a kiss on her forehead, and walk out the door before she can say anything else. She laughs as I close the door behind me.

As I walk down the stairs to my car, I start to feel uneasy. Is that what this is? Was I tricked into a fucking double date? The thought pisses me off. Once again I'm being forced into something I didn't ask for. Did Hayley put Kaden up to this?

I pull out my phone and text Kaden.

Me: Hey...is this a double date?

Kaden: No...just dinner with friends.

Me: Okay, fine. I'm on my way.

Kaden: <insert middle finger emoji>

Me: You're a dick.

While I want to cancel and not take the chance that Kaden might be lying to me, I decide to go. Kaden has never lied to me before and I don't think he would start now. If he says it's just friends hanging out, I believe him.

I arrive at Ashley's house twenty minutes later, and both Kaden and Hayley's vehicles are in the driveway. I barely make it up the sidewalk when the door swings open. Kaden is standing there with his arms crossed over his chest and a knowing smirk on his face.

"After your texts, I thought for sure you were gonna bail."

"Shut up, man." I push the wine into his chest for him to grab and follow him into the house. The aroma of Italian food hits my senses and my stomach growls loudly as I walk to the living room to sit down. I can't even remember the last time I had a home-cooked meal. Hayley hears it from the couch where she's watching television and laughs, not quite like the laughter I saw Stephen bring out of her but close.

"Hungry?" she asks, keeping her eyes on the show she's watching.

"Yeah, it's been a crazy day. I forgot to eat."

"I saw you run out earlier. Everything okay?" She turns her attention from the show to me. The way she looks at me reminds me of Kayla. Like she genuinely wants to know what's wrong. No hidden agenda. It makes me want to be honest with her. I sit next to her on the couch since Kaden is sitting on the loveseat with Ashley.

"Yes...No...Shit, I don't know."

She gives me a confused look that encourages me to keep talking.

"You know Marco, right?"

She nods, smiling. I've seen her talk to him, and she's clearly fond of him and he of her.

"I followed him home today because he said he couldn't make it to class, and I think he's selling drugs for some guys."

"Holy shit!" Kaden yells, overhearing our conversation.

"Are you sure?" Ashley asks.

"Yeah, I think so. The guy looked to be trying out the product and then gave him an envelope of money. I have no idea how to handle this."

"Damn," Hayley weighs in frowning. "Marco is such a good kid, too. What are you going to do?"

"I have no clue. His mom is in a bad place. I'm afraid if I tell the authorities it will mess up things for her."

"You have to do what's best for Marco. I see kids all the time in bad situations, and as much as I don't want to report it, I have to," Ashley says sadly. It makes sense she would feel this way. She teaches at a school close to where Marco lives. It's a poverty-stricken area, so I can imagine the shit she sees and hears from the kids.

"I need to think about how to approach it." I need to handle the situation with care. Marco trusts me and I don't want to do something to lose that trust.

"Just don't think too long," she says before getting up to go to the kitchen.

Dinner is served and the food is delicious. We eat while making light conversation. We discuss what we're all doing for the holidays. Ashley is going to her parents' house for Christmas. Tristan's grandparents picked him up after MMA class today to spend some time with him, and since Kaden's parents are in Hawaii for the holidays he's joining Ashley instead of flying back to Colorado to visit them. Hayley says her family lives here in Las Vegas, so she's joining them and her sister for Christmas. When Hayley asks what I'm doing, I tell her I'll just be home hanging out with Kayla and Bentley. She doesn't need to know most of my family is dead, and the one person who is alive, I haven't talked to in over seven years.

I do notice that hanging out with Hayley today seems different than before. She hasn't once tried to come on to me—she hasn't tried to touch me, or even flirt. Thinking about it, since the day at Bentley's house in Breckenridge when I refused to share a room with her, she hasn't tried anything. Not that she was so forward before. Just a touch here, a flirtatious smile or comment there, but now...nothing, and for some reason it makes me want her. It makes me want to make her want me. I am one fucked up son-of-a-bitch.

After we eat dessert I say goodbye and wish everyone a Merry Christmas in case I don't see them beforehand. Hayley decides to leave at the same time so I walk her out.

"Have a good Christmas, Caleb." She gives me a bright smile. Fuck! That smile has my dick twitching. It makes me want to cover her lips with mine, to feel her smile against me. It makes me want to take her right here on the hood of her car. I don't know what the hell has gotten into me today.

"You too, Hayley," I say before she shuts her door, turns on the ignition, and drives away.

Four

HAYLEY

TO SAY I WAS SHOCKED CALEB WAS ACTUALLY JOINING US for dinner was an understatement. I had already made the decision to stop pursuing him weeks ago at the ski resort, but that doesn't mean his presence doesn't affect me. When he showed up in a navy blue collared shirt that made his stormy blue eyes pop, hair still damp and wild from the shower, and in jeans that fit his ass perfectly, I couldn't decide if I wanted to first run my fingers through his messy hair, grab his ass, or run my hands down the washboard abs I know are hidden under his shirt.

A while back Kayla decided to surprise Bentley with a trip to a resort overnight and thought she could play matchmaker by having Caleb and me babysit together. I showed up to their apartment at the same time Caleb was walking out of the bathroom in nothing but a towel. I honestly thought I was going to orgasm right there on the spot.

His body was not only covered in sexy as hell tattoos, but he was also sporting a nipple ring. *A fucking nipple ring!* It took everything in me not to run straight to him to lick the nipple ring, and while licking it, I could have run my hands down his rock hard abs. I wasn't aware of the restraint I was capable of until that moment.

Of course he nearly freaked out and hurried to his room. He could cover himself all he wanted, that visual was engrained into my brain—and vagina—and not going anywhere anytime soon. Needless to say, Caleb's sexy-as-sin body has become the focal point of most of my self-inducing orgasms these days.

So when he walked in to Ashley's house, I thought it would be best to watch the television and not him. If I stared at him too long I couldn't be held responsible for the things that would come out of my mouth. I thought I was in the clear but then he sat next to me and I could smell his cologne—not too strong, just a light, fresh, clean scent—and it took everything in me not to lean over and give him a good sniff.

After he told us about Marco, I could see how much he really cared about him. The worry on his face was heartbreaking. Dinner and dessert thankfully went smooth, and I was really proud of myself for remaining cool around Caleb. I think he was more comfortable around me today as well and that confirmed what I already knew—he isn't into me. But it also gave me hope we could be friends. Caleb is a good guy, and I would rather have him as a friend than not at all.

After getting home, I text my sister to let her know I will be over to mom and dad's house Christmas morning first thing. The guy she's dating is joining her, so she begged me to be there when they arrive. It'll be Dad's first time meeting one of our boyfriends, which is making her nervous. Hannah is a lot like me. While she is three years younger, she's my best friend. She focused on school and college and then law school. I seriously missed the hell out of her while she was away at law school and was so excited to learn she would be moving back to accept an amazing job offer here in Las Vegas as a defense attorney for a prestigious law firm. Once she was settled into her job, she started dating, and after quite a few duds, she met Gavin.

They were at a mediation meeting—he was council for the other side—and they hit it off. They waited until the case was resolved and then went out. They've been together for about four months now and are inseparable. Because our parents were vacationing with my aunt and uncle in New York, they haven't met Gavin yet and will be meeting him on Christmas. I am definitely curious to see how they act. It's like a trial run for when, or I guess I should say, *if* I ever bring someone home.

After showering and pouring myself a glass of wine, I snuggle up on my couch to get caught up on *The Bachelor*. It's one of my favorite shows. It's so hilarious watching the women get all catty with each other, fighting over one man. I also love to watch their one-on-one dates. They are always so romantic. I would give anything for a guy to take me on a date like the ones they go on.

My phone dings with a text from Cooper reminding me the gym will be closed the next few days for Christmas, and will open back up afterward. I text him back wishing him and Liz a Merry Christmas and decide to go to bed.

As I walk through the house turning the lights off and double-checking the locks I feel the loneliness that surrounds me. It seems like everyone is with someone besides me. Even Ashley and Kaden have each other. Sure, they're only friends, but they hang out so often they might as well be together. I wonder if Caleb ever feels lonely. Does he lie in bed at night and wish someone were next to him?

After brushing my teeth and washing my face, I lie down in my dark room and turn the television on, turning it down to almost mute. The light and sound makes me feel a little less alone. Cuddling up in my down blanket, I think about how I got to this point. Back in high school when I was so hell-bent on studying and getting good grades, I told myself college was where I would meet someone. The problem was, while in college I got cheated on and so I told myself it would be best to wait until after I graduated. Medical School came and went and I was so busy studying I didn't have time to date anyway. Jeez... when was the last time I even had sex? There was that one guy I met at the party Kaden threw. How long ago was that? It must have been well over a year ago. I seriously need to get laid.

My issue is at thirty years old I want more. While a one-night stand would definitely scratch my itch, I really want my house to be less quiet. I was so excited when I purchased this home. With four bedrooms and two and a half bathrooms, I envisioned finally having a family. The backyard is perfect to set up a swing set next to the underground pool. I can see myself having play dates and barbeques.

While volunteering at a local YMCA last year, there were people from DCF encouraging us to sign up to be a foster parent. I filled out the paperwork and got approved, thinking if I don't meet Mr. Right I can always adopt. I haven't fostered anyone yet, though. I think I keep hoping I'll meet someone and we'll choose to create kids together. Now if I could just find someone. The question is, how do I meet someone if all I ever do is go to work and home? I need to get out more often. Maybe I'll ask Ashley to join me one night. Hell, maybe I should just woman up and go out by myself.

I make a promise to myself that after the holidays I'm going to try to meet a guy. I'm never going to meet anybody if I don't try. And then I remember the dating site Ashley once mentioned. Maybe I can meet a guy on there. I roll over to the middle of the bed and stretch out wrapping my body around the body pillow and wish that one day there will be a warm body next to me.

Five

HAYLEY

CHRISTMAS WAS OVERALL A GREAT HOLIDAY. MOM MADE Christmas breakfast while we watched the Disney parade on television. It's a tradition I look forward to every year. Her cinnamon buns were mouth-watering delicious like they are every year. Dad and Gavin hit it off and watched football the rest of the day while Hannah, mom, and I cooked Christmas dinner and made cookies. I love that, even though Hannah and I are older and there are no kids running around, mom still makes cookies with us every year just like she did when we were little.

After dinner, Gavin got down on one knee and proposed to Hannah. It was a sweet proposal and the ring he gave her was beautiful. She, of course said yes, and the rest of the evening was focused on when they plan to get married and where they plan to live. I'm thankful Gavin's family mostly live local so they're planning to make roots here. They even talked about looking for a house in the same neighborhood as mine.

Of course Mom and Dad had to point out several times throughout the night that I'm three years older and still single with no kids. Hannah came to my rescue, insisting I'm still young and have plenty of time, but I know they're right. It just solidifies my plan to take the initiative to meet Mr. Right.

It's been three days since Christmas and I'm back to work. I joined the dating site Ashley recommended and actually have a date tonight with a guy name Greg. He's a few years older than me and owns a construction company locally. We agreed to meet at a restaurant in the area. I don't know this guy, so I figured it would be safer to meet somewhere public instead of him picking me up.

I'm about to leave when Alex, one of the fighters, comes over and asks me to take a look at his ankle. It's been bugging him a lot recently. I tell him to head into my office and I'll meet him there. I grab my purse from the locker room so I don't have to grab it afterward and see Caleb and Marco fighting in the ring. I'm glad to see Marco here. If he's here ,he's safe. Caleb is showing him how to do a move correctly and Marco is watching with complete rapture. Caleb catches me watching and grants me a slight smile. I give him a small wave and head to check out Alex's ankle.

"Which ankle is it?" I ask Alex. He points to his right ankle, so I grab it gently and place it on the medical bed to examine it. I feel for any tension and when I hit a certain spot, he jumps in pain.

"I take it, it hurts there." I smile at Alex before touching it again, making him jump in pain.

He smiles back a boyish grin. "Hey now! What did I ever do to you?"

"Oh, don't be a baby. I just had to make sure that's where it hurts."

I've known Alex since I started working here, but never paid attention to how cute he is. While he isn't hot like Caleb, he definitely has that whole boy next door look going for him.

"It looks like you just sprained it. I don't think it's fractured and it's definitely not broken. Keep it up and alternate between cold and hot compressions. I want to see you back in a couple days to make sure it's healing okay."

"Thanks, Doc." He gives me a wink as he carefully jumps down on his good ankle.

I lock up my office and head out the door when I see Marco leaning against the outside window staring at his phone and looking around nervously.

"Hey, Marco. What are you up to?"

He looks around again and quietly says, "I'm about to go home."

Something tells me this kid shouldn't be alone right now.

"I'm going to grab a bite to eat and could use the company. Want to join me?" I know I'm supposed to be going on a date, but I'll have to call or text him to cancel. It's not exactly the first impression I wanted to make, but the look I see in Marco's eyes tell me he needs me more.

He looks conflicted, but after a few moments, nods. "Okay, yeah, sure."

As we're heading to my car, I notice a couple of guys heading toward us. They don't look like they belong to the gym and it hits me they might be the guys Caleb mentioned Marco has been associating with. I try to rush us to the vehicle, but the faster we walk, the faster they do, and before I can unlock my doors and get us in, they make it to my vehicle.

"Yo, Marco. We've been looking for you," scary guy number one says. Marco's face pales, looking more scared than any kid should ever look. I pull him behind me and raise my chin, praying I don't pee my pants when I confront these guys.

"What do you need him for? Isn't he a bit too young to be hanging out with you?"

"He wasn't too young to take what doesn't belong to him," scary guy two spits out.

I keep Marco behind me. "Well, you shouldn't be dealing with a child. Do I need to call the police?"

"Lady, this shit ain't your fucking business. I suggest you worry about yourself," scary guy number one says, getting in my face. He places his hands on my shoulders roughly, attempting to shove me out of the way to get to Marco, but I plant my feet firmly in the ground, refusing to let him get to him.

"Bitch, you need to move out of my way." He's too strong and my body begins to sway against my will. I don't want him getting to Marco, but I'm not going to be able to go up against these guys.

I consider yelling for help, but suddenly his hands are off me and he's practically flying into the side of my vehicle. When my heart slows down, I realize Caleb has scary guy number one up against the side of my car, and scary guy number two doesn't even try to help. I don't blame him. Angry Caleb looks downright frightening.

"What the fuck do you think you're doing putting your hands on her? Did she say you could put your hands on her?"

Six

CALEB

TO SAY CHRISTMAS WAS A CLUSTERFUCK OF EPIC proportions would be an understatement. The morning started out great. Faith woke up to a million presents under the tree from Santa. Kayla, Bentley, and I watched her rip apart the paper, not even caring what was in the boxes. I swear she loved the wrapping paper more than the items inside. Unfortunately when Kayla asked Bentley to grab her camera it all went downhill fast. Bentley found a prenuptial agreement she was hiding that her shitty lawyer mom put together and shit hit the fan. He left, then she left, and after a few hours, she came back in tears and spent the rest of Christmas day crying on my shoulder.

This isn't the first time Kayla has fucked up. She hid her pregnancy from Bentley in the beginning and moved back to Florida to live with her parents. I hate that she did that, but I know she was scared and quickly owned up to it. I think the reason Kayla and I became close was because I watched how protective she was of those she loves, especially Bella and Liz. Liz and Kayla are best friends and for years she helped her raise her daughter. I guess I choose to see the good in her. I choose to trust her to an extent, probably more than I trust any woman, but I also don't have to sleep with her or marry her. I know she's been through a lot of shit and has pretty crappy parents. I don't like some of the choices she's made, but my job is to be her friend and let her and Bentley figure their shit out.

When I think about how I'm able to open up and trust Kayla, and even Liz, it makes me wonder if maybe I could one day open up to a woman who isn't engaged or married to one of my friends. I think it's definitely easier to let a woman in that you know doesn't have a chance of hurting you. Kayla and Liz can't do anything to me. They can't use me or cheat on me—I'm not vulnerable to them. I just can't imagine being in a situation where I ever feel so out of control ever again.

And if Kayla and Bentley's shit wasn't enough to fuck up Christmas, I got a call from my father's attorney requesting to speak to me in person. While he's an old friend of my father's, I don't know what the fuck he could want from me, and after seven years, I can't imagine there is anything left to say. The fact that my father couldn't even call me himself and had to have his lawyer call me instead speaks volumes. If he wants to talk, he can call me his damn self.

It's been three days since Christmas and since Kayla has finally got it together long enough to go to work, I decide I'm going to go train for a little bit. After a couple hours of working out, Marco shows up. I ask him how his Christmas was and he just shrugs his shoulders. Something is definitely going on with this kid. Yeah, shit has always been rough for him, but he never used to let it get him down like this.

I offer to spar with him and show him some new moves and he lights up. While we're working out I notice Hayley observing us. She doesn't have the look of lust like she used to, though, and for some reason once again it's making me want her. I'm pretty sure a therapist would have a field day with my fucked up logic. Her smile is more friendly and less flirty and without thinking about it I smile back at her. She gives me a small wave and I can't help but watch her as she walks away. I would be blind not to notice how sexy she is. How did I seriously not notice her before?

"Do you like her?" Marco asks, taking me away from staring at her perfect ass as she enters her office.

"Huh? Like who?" I ask, confused.

He nods toward where Hayley just was and grins.

"We're just friends," I say before throwing a punch to his gut to make him block.

"Really? Cause you look like you wanna give her some cooties," he sings while waggling his eyebrows before busting out laughing. I throw another punch to his stomach and he drops to the ground laughing and singing some stupid song about kissing in a tree.

I jump on top of him and start grappling with him. He gets serious and tries to throw me off when his phone rings. He taps out and gets up to go check it.

"Hey, I gotta go," he says, frowning down at his phone.

"Where do you need to be?"

I notice he once again doesn't make eye contact. "I gotta go help my mom out. I'll see you tomorrow, okay?"

"Yeah, okay. If you need me you know my number. Right?"

"Yeah, I do," he says distractedly, gathering up his stuff quickly.

I take a quick shower to rinse off then head to the parking lot to go home. While checking my texts I see one from Kayla.

Kayla: Bentley and I made up!! We're getting married New Year's Eve!! You're a groomsman!

As I'm texting her back, I look up before crossing the street and see Marco and Hayley near her car, only they aren't alone. The two guys I saw Marco talking to the other day are also there, and one of them appears to have his hands on Hayley while Marco is hiding behind her.

I throw my phone in my pocket and run over to them. When I get closer I hear him threatening her and everything goes red. Without even thinking, I grab the fucker by the back of his shirt and throw him up against the car.

"What the fuck do you think you're doing putting your hands on her? Did she say you could put your hands on her?" I scream into his face. He looks shocked, and out of the corner of my eye, I can see his pussy friend trying to decide if he should intervene. He takes a step back. *Good choice, motherfucker.*

"I don't know what the fuck is going on here, but whatever it is, you don't ever put your hands on a woman without her permission. Got me?"

He nods like the scared pussy he is, and I release him. Now that my hands aren't on him, he gets his balls back. "Marco owes us and we will be collecting. You heard that, Marco? You can run, but you can't hide."

"What the fuck does he owe you?"

"That's between Marco and us, *loco*," he says, walking away. I don't take my eyes off either of them memorizing everything I can about them. I have a feeling this won't be the last time they come around here. Just before they get in their car, the other guy looks right at Hayley. "You are a pretty little bitch. Maybe you can help Marco give us what he owes us. I might be willing to make a deal." He winks at her and gets in the car.

Whatever she said to them, put her on their radar, and guys like that don't let shit go. That wasn't just a comment. That was a threat, one they will most likely try to make good on.

I look over at Hayley and Marco and they both look terrified. I want to find out what the guys said to her and what Marco owes them and I will soon, but I want them both to calm down first.

"Where are you guys going?" I ask.

Hayley's body visibly relaxes and Marco comes out from behind her. "We're going to get some dinner...Umm...Would you like to join us?" Hayley asks nervously, making me realize I need to work on how I act toward her. I don't want her feeling like she can't even speak to me.

"Absolutely. Let's take my truck."

She doesn't argue. After locking up her car and getting into my truck we head to a local bar and grill Hayley suggests. While we're driving there, her phone rings. She gives me an apologetic look and accepts the call. I can only hear her half of the conversation, but it's obvious she was supposed to go out with some guy and is canceling last minute.

"Hey Greg...I'm sorry. I was just about to call you...I'm going to have to cancel...Yeah, something came up...Sure, I'll call you when I know I can make it...Okay, bye."

For some crazy reason the thought of Hayley on a date with another guy forces my fists to tighten on the steering wheel. It makes me want to lock her up and keep her for myself. Only she isn't mine.

Once we are seated and the waitress takes our drink orders I reach into my pocket and take out a twenty-dollar bill, handing it to Marco.

"Why don't you go get change and play some video games?" I nod toward the game room in the corner.

His eyes widen in shock, breaking my heart. The kid has probably never played a video game. He looks down at the money and back up to me unsure.

"Go on, and don't come back until you've spent it all."

"Thank you!" he says, before he takes off running to the video arcade room.

"What did they say to you?" I ask Hayley, getting straight to the point. I need to know how bad this is.

"Nothing really. They wanted something Marco took that didn't belong to him. I told them they shouldn't hold a child accountable and they told me to mind my own business. The one guy tried to get around me to speak to Marco, and when I wouldn't let him, he called me a bitch. That's when you walked up."

"It's got to be the drugs...or money."

"I'm terrified for him, Caleb. Those guys were scary." It's definitely not what I should be thinking about right now, but my name coming from Hayley's mouth is like an instant jolt straight to my dick. I have never felt like this before, and I have no idea where it's coming from, but it's been happening more and more lately. It's like the minute she stopped outwardly wanting me, I can't stop thinking about her.

"I'll talk to Marco and see what's going on. Whatever it is we'll figure it out."

Hayley's phone dings and when she looks down at her phone she frowns.

"Everything okay?"

She looks back up and I notice a light blush spreading across her cheeks.

"Yeah, as you kind of heard in the truck, I was supposed to go out on a date tonight. I joined some stupid dating site in attempt to meet someone. Anyway, I canceled when I saw Marco outside. I know it was rude of me to cancel last minute, but he's being kind of mean about it."

Does this woman not realize how beautiful she is? Why would she think she needs a dating site? Every guy around her that's single practically drools over her, and she definitely doesn't need to put up with some asshole who doesn't understand life happens.

"Maybe it's not too late to meet him. I can stay with Marco... Then he won't be so mad." I have no idea why the hell I'm even suggesting that. The thought of her leaving us to go on her date makes me sick.

She frowns but quickly replaces it with what looks like a fake smile. "That's okay. I already told him we could reschedule."

I want to ask her why my suggestion made her sad but then Marco comes running back, out of money, and sits down, grabbing on his drink, and my mind immediately goes back to Marco and keeping him safe. There's no way I'm letting anything happen to this kid. The waitress comes over, and after we order, I figure now is as good a time as any to ask Marco what's going on.

"Marco, can you tell us who those guys were and what they were talking about?"

He instantly looks nervous, bouncing his eyes back and forth between Hayley and me.

"You can trust us, Marco," Hayley adds in a soothing voice that makes me want to see how well she can soothe my dick. *What the fuck is going on with me?*

"Umm...Well...The guy you put up against the car is Hector and the other guy is Santos. I ran an errand for them to make some money and my mom borrowed the money I owe them. She promised to pay it back. She said she just needed to buy Chloe diapers. But she hasn't given me the money back yet, and Hector and Santos want the money because their boss Antonio needs it."

Fuck. His mom took the money he owes these guys, probably to buy more drugs. This isn't good. I can easily pay them back, but this isn't just about money. Guys like them don't like to be stolen from. This is about pride, about sending a message. They will definitely be sending a message.

"Okay, how much do you owe them?"

"Two thousand dollars."

Holy shit! What the hell are these guys doing trusting a fucking twelve-year-old with that kind of money? Hayley hasn't said a word.

She looks scared as shit for this kid. I don't know much about Hayley, but I know she comes from a good family, and while I do as well, I also come from a home where my stepmom runs a strip club, which is shady as fuck, and used to pimp out her teenage stepson. Oh, I didn't mention that before? Yep, my dad met Gloria at a strip club and decided to marry her and then fund her opening her own strip club. I used to see some crazy shit go down at that club when I would have to go see her.

Then working at the clubs on the strip, watching the deals go down every night, you learn real quick how fucked up life can be. I've stood in on too many deals to count at the clubs. To make extra money I've taken private bodyguard jobs to escort guys into business meetings. You have no idea how corrupt Las Vegas truly is until you've sat in a few of those meetings.

The difference is, those meetings were with legitimate businessmen—even if they are corrupt—not fucking gang members hanging out on the streets. The men I've dealt with aren't hiring twelve year old's to deliver their drugs for them.

"We're going to go by the bank and I'm going to give you the money to give to those guys, okay? But Marco, you can't keep running errands for them. They aren't good guys."

"I know but the money they pay me helps my mom. It gives Chloe her formula and diapers. My mom doesn't have a job right now."

"We'll figure it out. Just promise me, no more running errands for them. Got it?"

"Okay," he agrees, but I can see the fear in his eyes. There's more to this than he's telling us.

After we're done eating, I run by the bank just before it closes and take out the money. I drop Hayley off at her car and take Marco to his house. I'm not stupid enough to just give the kid the money.

"I want you to call or text those guys and tell them you have their money. I'm going to wait here while you give it to them."

"Okay."

After a few minutes, the guys pull up and get out of the car. We're parked in front of Marco's house and I tell him to stay in the car while I get out to deal with the guys.

The guy Marco said was named Hector walks up to me first. *"Que pasa, loco? Where's Marco?" What's up?*

"Here's three grand. The two grand he owes you and one more for your trouble." I take the envelope of money and shove it into his chest. "Leave Marco alone."

"Hey now, nobody forced him to do anything. He needed money and we offered him a job."

"Yeah, well, consider his employment terminated as of now."

"Whatever you say," he says with a smarmy smirk.

I walk back to my car knowing this shit isn't over but not sure what else to do. Marco gets out and I walk him up to the door. I can hear the baby screaming inside, so I follow him in. The house is fucking gross and smells like piss. The baby is on the floor on a blanket, red-faced, screaming and crying her head off without her mom anywhere to be found.

Marco goes straight to her, picking her up with expertise as he tries to soothe her. His mom walks out looking strung out on drugs just like the last time I saw her. Before she sees I'm here, she yells at Marco.

"Where the fuck have you been? I need you to get some formula for the baby! And I'm fucking exhausted from dealing with Chloe. It's your turn to watch her..."

Before she can finish, I clear my throat indicating they aren't alone. She doesn't even have the audacity to look apologetic that I just witnessed her treat her kid like absolute shit. She walks by me to her room and slams the door shut.

Marco goes to the cabinet and pulls out a can of what I imagine is formula since he pours some into a bottle, heats it up, and feeds it to the baby.

"I bought some last night, but she was asleep when I got home and wasn't awake yet when I left this morning," he says, like it's perfectly normal for that bitch to speak to her kid like that. I'm speechless. I'm watching a twelve-year-old act like a father to a baby when he's still a fucking baby himself.

"Hey, I'm going to take care of this, Marco. I promise you."

"Please don't report my mom. If you do, they'll take away my sister. They'll put us into foster care. Some of my friends went there and told me it's really bad. Please don't do that," he begs.

I don't even know how to respond to any of this. This is all so over my head, but there has got to be an answer.

"Okay, buddy. Let me think about it for a little bit and I'll figure it out." I take some money from my pocket and hand it to him. "Don't show your mom this. It's a hundred dollars. Use it to feed your sister and you. If you need money, you come see me. Okay?"

"Okay, thank you." He burps his baby sister and then lays her down on the couch, patting her to sleep.

Seven

HAYLEY

IT'S NEW YEAR'S EVE, WHICH MEANS IT'S ALSO BENTLEY AND Kayla's wedding night. We're all standing at a local chapel on the strip listening to them say their vows to each other. Once Kayla decided she wanted to marry Bentley after almost losing him to her ridiculous insecurities she decided not to waste any more time. If she could have she would've married him the minute he said yes. Yep! You heard me right. She proposed to Bentley the second time around and of course he said yes. She wanted to get married immediately but agreed to New Year's Eve to give her brother, Zach, time to get here for the ceremony.

"You may kiss the bride," the Ordain Minister says and they kiss. Because of the small ceremony Kayla insisted on, Liz and I are her only bridesmaids and Cooper and Caleb are the groomsmen. Everybody claps and then we take off to Kayla and Bentley's new home for their reception-slash-house warming party. As an engagement present, Bentley surprised Kayla by purchasing the home of her dreams, which is also right down the street from Liz's house. I look over at Caleb and he gives me a small smile. He looks sexy as hell dressed in slacks and a button down dress shirt, but I still prefer him in nothing but a towel hanging from his hips. It's like he knows what I'm thinking when he raises a brow and gives me a cocky smirk.

I shake my head and walk over to him. "Heading over to the house?"

"Yeah. You?"

"Yep, I guess I'll see you there." I'm about to walk away when he grabs me by my elbow, forcing me to stop in my place in shock. Caleb has never willingly touched me.

"Hey, do you think maybe we could grab a bite to eat one day?"

"Like as a date?" I don't want to assume anything.

He contemplates my question for a second. "Umm...As friends."

It's a good thing I didn't assume. "Friends...Yeah, sure. Just let me know when."

His phone dings, alerting him of a text message and he frowns at whoever is texting him. He puts it back in his pocket and looks back up at me.

"That was Marco. He didn't realize the gym was closed and needs me to meet him there to give him some money. I'm trying to figure out how to help him without turning his mom into the Department of Children and Families. I'm looking into some rehab facilities that run off private donations to those with kids who can't afford it, but even then she would need someone to take care of them unless she can do outpatient or something."

"That's really sweet of you. He's lucky to have you in his life. If you need any help, please let me know."

"Thanks."

We both head out to our cars and go our separate ways, him to the gym and me to the party.

A little while later he arrives at the reception looking completely distracted.

"Hey, is everything okay with Marco?"

"I'm not sure. Marco is acting off. I think something is going on at his house. I'm going to head over there after the party and check on him."

"Do you want me to go with you?"

"No, I appreciate it, but I would rather you not be in that area. It's not a good neighborhood."

"Okay, well, if you need anything let me know."

"Thank you, I will."

I give him a smile and reach for his arm to give it a friendly squeeze before I remember he's not keen on me touching him. I pull back just in time, give him another smile, and walk away. God, he must think I am so weird.

Walking over to the kitchen to grab a drink, I spot a bunch of people dancing outside in the backyard on the makeshift dance floor. I make myself a Malibu lemonade and head out back to watch the drunken silliness.

"Get over here, Roberts!" Alex yells over the music. I shake my head. "C'mon! Now!"

I can't help but laugh. He is definitely one of *those* drunks.

After he begs some more, I give in.

After taking another sip of my drink, I put it on the table and walk over to join him on the dance floor. The music is pumping, so I sway my hips to the music. Alex stands behind me and dances up against me. I look over and see Caleb watching us. He almost looks... pissed? But that can't be right. He wouldn't care who I'm dancing with. The song changes to a slow song and the deejay tells the newlyweds to get on the dance floor to join in. Caleb's eyes still haven't left mine. He walks my way and I'm frozen in place. I hear Alex saying my name, but I tune him out, only focusing on Caleb.

"I'm cutting in," Caleb says to Alex, his eyes never leaving mine.

A second later I'm in Caleb's arms swaying to the tune of Jason Derulo's *Marry Me*. Knowing he doesn't like me to touch him, I have no idea what to do with my hands. He notices and frowns. Then, taking my hands in his, places them around his neck, as he pulls me closer to him. He wraps his arms around my waist and settles his hands at the small of my back. We dance for a few minutes in a comfortable silence staring into each other's eyes. I can't help but think how natural it feels to be in Caleb's arms, like this is exactly where I belong.

Unfortunately his phone vibrates in his pocket ending the moment too soon. He looks down at his phone and then back up at me. With what looks like a silent apology, for what I don't know, he gives me a small kiss on my cheek and whispers, "It's Marco. I have to go. Thank you for this dance."

As he walks away, my heart pounds against my ribcage from his closeness. His words do crazy things to my body, and when his lips brushed across my cheek, I wanted to grab his face and not let go. But I know he needs to be there for Marco, so without saying a word, I watch him walk away.

Eight

CALEB

SEEING KAYLA LAUGHING AND SMILING MAKES MY DAY. That woman deserves her happily ever after, that's for damn sure. It has taken a little while but Bentley and her are finally in a good place, and as their best friend, it makes me damn happy to see them like this. The wedding was nice and simple just like Kayla wanted. The reception at their place is a whole other story. There are decorations everywhere including a huge sign announcing their marriage. There's catered food aligning the walls inside, and outside there's a deejay playing music. The kids have all left and it's just drunk adults left celebrating their wedding as well as New Year's Eve.

Grabbing a beer after talking with Hayley, I head outside to find Kaden or Cooper when I see Alex and Hayley dancing close on the makeshift dance floor. I have never wanted to dance with a woman as much as I do right now. She has her head thrown back in a laugh at something he said and it reminds me of the other day in the gym. I want to be the guy making her laugh.

The music shifts to a slow song and throwing caution to the wind, go for it. It will be my choice to ask her to dance. She looks over at me and gives me a small smile. She is absolutely stunning and I can't even take my eyes off her.

"I'm cutting in," I let Alex know. He nods and walks away. As I try to dance with Hayley, I notice she isn't putting her arms around me. I don't blame her. Every time she's attempted to touch me, whether on purpose or on accident, I made it clear her touch wasn't welcome. I need to change that.

Taking her delicate hands in mine, I bring them up and wrap them around my neck and then wrap mine around her perfect waist. We dance to some song about getting married, but the only thing on my mind is how for once in my life the touch of a woman feels good. Her small body fits perfectly in mine. We don't talk, but it's not awkward. Looking into her eyes is like finding water in a desert. I suddenly feel replenished.

My cell vibrates in my pocket. I want to ignore it, but the fear that it might be Marco makes me grab it out of my pocket to look. Sure enough, it is.

Marco: I need you to come to my house.

Knowing I just left there from dropping him off and giving him some money, it must be important. I look at Hayley and wish I could ignore the text and continue to dance with her, but also know Marco can be in trouble. I try to relay to her I'm sorry.

Before I can walk away I give her a kiss on her cheek. It's warm and a bit flushed and it makes me want to kiss her in other places. "It's Marco. I have to go. Thank you for this dance." Before she can respond, I walk out needing to get to Marco.

Arriving at Marco's place, I see a couple cars along the road in front of his house I don't recognize. This shit can't be good. I jump out of my car and can immediately hear screaming from inside. Without knocking, I go right in and take in the sight in front of me. Marco's mom is on the floor naked, on all fours being fucked from behind by one guy, while another guy is holding Marco back from trying to stop it from happening. I can also hear the baby crying in another room. I assess the situation and don't see any guns drawn. They probably didn't think it would be needed since Marco and his mom would be helpless against them.

I take one look at Marco's pleading eyes, the tears silently falling, and I lose it. I grab the guy fucking his mom by the neck, pulling him out of her, and push him up against the wall. I start punching him in the face repeatedly, hoping to knock him out. In my peripheral vision I see the other guy drop Marco from the wall and stalk toward me. Leaving the guy bleeding against the wall, I turn toward him to find out I was wrong about the gun. He grabs the gun from the front of his pants and shoots me in the shoulder.

The pain is unbearable, but I can't go down without a fight. I should have called the police. I should have called someone, but I didn't. So now I'm here and need to try to at least save Marco and his sister before I bleed out. I walk up to the guy with the gun and knock it out of his hand before he can shoot me again. We start rolling around on the floor grappling. Both of us are getting punches in and I just pray I can hold on long enough to beat the shit out of this guy to the point he will black out so I can call the cops.

Unfortunately before that happens the door swings open and two more guys I don't recognize walk in.

"Go shut that fucking baby up!" the guy booms and Estella, Marco's mom, runs to the room to calm the baby down. They grab me by my arms and I know I don't stand a chance. There's too many of them. They begin punching me in my ribs over and over again. When my legs give out on me, they throw me to the ground and begin kicking me, and then I hear a gunshot and everything goes black.

Nine

HAYLEY

THERE IS NO WAY I'VE BEEN ASLEEP MORE THAN A FEW minutes when my phone goes off. I attempt to ignore it, keeping my eyes closed so I don't get dizzy. I didn't get ridiculously drunk tonight, but I definitely drank enough to have a hangover in the morning. I ended up taking a cab home after the ball dropped, leaving my vehicle at Kayla's house. I'll have to ask someone to take me to get my car in the morning. I was hoping Caleb would return, but he never did. I hope everything is okay with Marco.

My phone rings again. Whoever is calling must really need to get ahold of me. Looking at my cell phone, I see it's four in the morning and Kayla is the person who keeps calling me. Jeez! I was actually asleep for almost three hours.

"Hey! Everything okay?" For Kayla to be calling me on her wedding night, something has to be wrong.

"No, it's not. Caleb is in the hospital. We don't know the details, but it's not good, Hayley."

This wakes me up. I grab some clothes on the dresser that I didn't get around to putting away yet and quickly get dressed. As I'm looking around for my keys, I remember I have no car. *Shit!*

"Hey can you swing by and get me? My car is at your house!"

She tells Bentley to pick me up. Luckily my house is on the way to the hospital so they don't have to go out of their way. We hang up and I go outside to wait for them so they don't have to stop for too long.

We get to the hospital and Bentley goes to the nurse to get answers on Caleb. We don't know anything about his family, but Caleb having no emergency contact listed other than Bentley is a good indication they aren't in the picture. The nurse tells us to have a seat and she'll come out to update us as soon as she can.

A few minutes later she begins explaining Caleb's condition as Cooper and Liz come running through the door out of breath along with Kaden and Ashley.

"Is he okay?" "What happened?" Liz and Cooper ask at the same time.

"The nurse is about to tell us right now," Bentley says, turning back to the nurse and indicating for her to continue.

"Mr. Michaels is currently in the ICU but stable. We're prepping him for surgery. He was brought in a couple hours ago, but we needed to stabilize him and assess his injuries. He experienced two gunshot wounds, one to the shoulder, and one to the chest. Luckily the one to the chest didn't hit any major arteries."

I gasp hearing he's been shot. Immediately my mind goes to those guys going after Marco.

"He was beaten pretty badly. We think he has several broken ribs and his leg appears to be broken. We'll know more once he's finished being prepped and taken into surgery. Please stay out here and once we know more we'll let you know."

"Thank you," Bentley says. I can't help but wonder how this happened. He left clearly worried about Marco. It had to have had something to do with those drug dealer guys from the other day.

While waiting to hear something, I decide to seek answers. I can't get this horrible feeling out of my head. If this has something to do with Marco, is he okay? Just as I make the decision to find a police officer, I see Marco come in and with him is a police officer holding his baby sister. Marco isn't crying, though. He looks numb. His baby sister is crying loudly and he's attempting to soothe her.

"Marco, what happened?"

"My mom is dead and they beat up and shot Caleb."

Oh God! I knew it! I knew this had something to do with Marco. Trying to remain calm, I put my hands out to take his sister from the police officer.

"Are you a friend of the family?" the officer asks.

"I'm a friend of Marco's. I'm a doctor at the gym he works out at and the gentleman who was at his house, Caleb, is a friend of ours," I say, pointing to everyone around me.

The officer hands me Chloe. "We need to get them both checked out to make sure they're okay."

Marco and I sit down and I rock Chloe, trying to calm her. Marco rubs her back trying to soothe her as well. The nurse comes over and hands me a bottle of formula. After thanking her, I feed the precious baby. With her belly full, I burp her, and within minutes she passes right out in my arms.

A few minutes later, the nurse calls Marco and Chloe back, and I go with the officer to have them checked out. Once the doctor confirms they're both healthy and not injured in any way, the police officer takes Marco's statement.

In a nutshell, the men came to Marco's house to get money from his mom. When she said no, one guy forced himself on her while the other guy held Marco back. Caleb tried to save them and was beaten and shot. Marco's mom went to the room to quiet Chloe down because her crying was making the men mad, but she never came back out of her room. When the police got there and Marco went in to let her know the cops were there, he found her dead. She overdosed on drugs in her bedroom.

It's absolutely heartbreaking to listen to his recount of what happened, to hear what he witnessed. Once he's done we go back out to the waiting room and I sit next to Kayla.

"Have you heard anything on Caleb yet?"

"No, not yet. Are the kids okay?"

"Yeah, the doctor said neither of them were physically hurt." I don't have to say anything for her to know what I mean. Marco is going to need to see a therapist. He's going to need a loving and supportive home and somebody to talk to. Luckily his sister is too young to remember anything.

"I'm assuming this is Marco's sister?"

"Yeah, she's a sweet thing, isn't she?"

I see the officer standing in the corner and want to ask him some questions. "Would you mind holding her for a few minutes. I want to speak to the police officer."

"Absolutely."

I carefully hand her Chloe and then look over and see Marco is sleeping. I can't even imagine the nightmares he will have. Walking over to the officer, I reintroduce myself.

"Excuse me, I was wondering if you have contacted the Department of Children and Families?"

"Yes, ma'am. Somebody is on their way."

"Did you catch the guys who did this to Caleb?"

"We have them in custody. Because the neighbor called so quickly after hearing the first gunshot we were able to catch them leaving the scene. We're compiling evidence now, but we should have enough to put them away for a long time."

"Good. I hope they rot in prison. Thank you, officer."

I head back to Marco and, putting my arm around him, hold him close. He may have had a shitty mom, but losing her can't be easy, and to be the one who found her, my heart is breaking for him.

Within an hour a sweet woman from DCF arrives. Marco moves closer to me when she says she needs to place them in an emergency foster home for the night.

"Can he please stay with me?" I beg. The kid has been through enough. "I'm actually an approved foster parent."

"What about Chloe?" Marco begins crying. I completely forgot about Chloe. My only thoughts were taking care of Marco. It doesn't surprise me that even after everything Marco has been through his number one concern is the welfare of his sister.

"I can take her as well. I just don't have a crib or diapers or anything for a baby." I begin to panic, mentally making a list of everything I would need.

"We can take her," Kayla says. "We actually have an application in to foster since it's the first step to adopt. We recently submitted it and it might even already be approved. Because of the holidays I haven't checked."

"Okay, I'll need a copy of both your driver's licenses and social security cards. I'll call my supervisor and check on your fostering statuses."

"Thank you," I say, continuing to hold Marco close, letting him know I'm not leaving his side.

I look over at Bentley and Kayla cooing over Chloe and can't help but wonder if maybe this was God's way of intervening on these children's behalf—taking a tragedy and giving them their own little miracle.

While waiting to hear back from the DCF worker, a doctor comes out and lets us know Caleb is out of surgery. Looking at the time, I see it's just after seven in the morning. Marco is asleep with his head on my shoulder and Chloe is still asleep in Kayla's arms.

"We feel everything went good. He has three broken ribs, which caused internal bleeding. We were able to stop the bleeding without any further complications. Unfortunately, broken ribs can't be fixed, they will have to heal over time, but he's wrapped up. The gunshot wounds to his shoulder and chest were clean, so we just had to stitch him up. His leg was broken in two places, so he's in a cast. He suffered a head injury as well, but other than having a concussion there is no swelling in the brain, which is a good sign. He's in recovery now and we'll continue to monitor him. Once they get him settled, you can go back two at a time. Do you have any questions?"

"Will he get back full use of his shoulder and leg?" I know in hindsight it's not important, but Caleb's world revolves around fighting. I know he's going to want to know.

"The specialist will be in to speak with Caleb once he wakes up. He'll be able to answer that question better."

"Okay, thank you."

Just as the doctor is leaving, the DCF worker returns, smiling softly.

"Okay, good news. You both are active on the fostering list, so I was able to approve both of you to take them home. We will have to do home visits in the next few days so I'll be in touch."

Marco wakes up and looks around to find Chloe, then turns to the worker. "Does that mean Chloe and I can stay together?"

"How would you feel if you stayed with me and Chloe stayed with Bentley and Kayla? You know how they have Faith, right? So they have all the baby stuff already for Chloe."

"Can I still see her?"

"Of course you can, sweetie!" Kayla chimes in. "You can see her whenever you want. Let's just take this one day at a time until we figure out what's going to happen."

"Would you rather go with Kayla and stay with Chloe?" I ask him.

"No, I know they're good with Faith. I would rather go with you. Can we stay and wait for Caleb?"

"Absolutely," I tell him, and his body visibly relaxes.

"Thank you," I tell the worker. She lets me know she will be in touch and leaves.

"Family of Caleb Michaels," a nurse announces.

"I want to go see Caleb, please!" Marco begs the nurse. He's so worried about Caleb.

"I'm sure we can make that happen," I tell him.

"I'm sorry but only family right now," the nurse says sympathetically.

"She's his fiancée," Bentley says before I can even think of a lie to get us inside.

The nurse doesn't look convinced but doesn't argue.

"Is he your son?" she asks, pointing to Marco. Without hesitation, I tell her yes.

"Okay, he can come with you guys since he's a minor and in your care."

"Thank you."

"C'mon." Bentley puts his arm around me and walks us toward the nurse. "I'll go with you, future Mrs. Michaels."

Ten

CALEB

HOLY SHIT! MY HEAD FEELS LIKE IT'S ABOUT TO EXPLODE. I hear a faint beeping sound and try to remember where I am and why I feel so hung over. The overwhelming smell of antiseptics hits my nose causing me to almost choke. Then the memories all come crashing back.

Marco…His mom being raped…Getting the shit beat out of me…Getting shot…Everything going black…FUCK!

"Well, good morning, Mr. Michaels. Welcome back. Your fiancée and son were just here. They stepped out to get a drink of water but should be back any second. How are you doing?"

Fiancée? Son? What. The. Fuck.

I rack my brain trying to think if I could have possibly missed getting engaged. I sure as fuck know I don't have a son. I look around and see Bentley sitting in a chair shaking with silent laughter. Then, when Hayley and Marco walk in, he smiles wide and laughs out loud.

"Well, how are you?"

"Umm...I think I'm okay..." I wiggle my fingers and they work. Then I start touching various parts of my body to see if I am in fact okay. When I move my arm too far over, I feel a sharp pain in my shoulder and chest. It's kind of hard to breathe now that I'm thinking about it.

"Oh fuck!" I scream louder than I realize when I attempt to move my hand to my shoulder.

"Be careful. You were shot, Mr. Michaels. The doctor will be in momentarily to explain your injuries and what he did during surgery." The first thing that comes to mind is fighting. If I'm in this much pain there is no way I'll be fighting anytime soon.

After checking my vitals, the nurse gives me more pain meds before she leaves the room.

"Fiancée and son?"

Bentley cracks up laughing, again. "Don't look so scared, bro. I had to say Hayley was your fiancée to get them in here, so Marco could see you. The kid was worried."

Am I crazy that for a second I almost thought it wouldn't be such a terrible thing to be engaged to Hayley? Yeah, I must have been hit in the head. It's the only way to explain these absurd feelings.

The doctor comes in and explains I suffered a concussion, have three broken ribs, and a broken leg that they put a cast on and will have to remain on for about six weeks before getting it checked. My shoulder is in a sling so it can heal from the gunshot wound, and I was shot in the chest. Jesus, it's a fucking miracle I'm alive.

"Do you have any questions?"

"Will I get full rotation of my shoulder back? Will my leg be healed one hundred percent? I'm a fighter."

"It's definitely going to take some time. If you were working a desk job I would say you'll be fine, but as an athlete, you will most likely need to attend physical therapy for your shoulder and leg. Unfortunately only time will tell."

"Okay, thank you."

After the doctor leaves, I let out a slew of curse words. Fighting is my fucking life. Without it, who am I?

"I'm sorry," Marco says. And that's when I remember him and Hayley have been in the room the whole time.

"Come here, Marco."

He comes forward nervously. My cursing having him scared.

"Don't ever apologize for what happened last night. Do you understand me? I would have done it all over again if it meant protecting you."

Marco's eyes well up with tears and he throws himself at me for a hug. My chest burns and my ribs ache, but I don't outwardly react. Marco needs a hug and I don't want him to see the pain I'm in.

"Hey, buddy. It's okay," I say, trying to calm him.

Then I ask Bentley, "Have you guys been here this whole time?"

He looks at me incredulously. "Of course we have. Coop, Liz, Kaden, Ashley, and Kayla are out there as well."

I choke up at the realization that all these people have been here waiting to see if I'm okay. I've felt so alone for so long, but the fact is these people have been here for me for years.

"As you can see, I'm okay. Take Kayla home and tell Cooper and everyone else I'm good. Get some sleep and call me later."

"Wait! Does that mean Chloe is leaving? I have to kiss her goodbye!" Marco says, frantically turning to Bentley and Hayley. Why would Chloe be here? And why would she be leaving without Marco?

Hayley crouches down a little to soothe Marco. "Hey, it's okay. We can go say bye to them. I'm sure Chloe is tired and wants to sleep in a comfortable bed. We can go visit them later, I promise." Why the hell does Kayla have Chloe?

Marco calms down and says okay. Bentley and Hayley share a look before she says she's going to take Marco to say bye to his sister.

Marco gives me one more hug. "I'm glad you're okay, Caleb."

"Thanks, buddy."

Bentley waits for the door to close before he speaks. "Marco's mom overdosed. Marco found her dead in her room after the cops showed up."

"Holy shit." I don't even know what else to say. I know how Marco feels to an extent. When my mom died, it hurt, but we knew it was coming.

"There's more..." I wait for him to continue. "Apparently there are no living relatives so Kayla and I are fostering Chloe and Hayley is fostering Marco so they aren't sent away and completely separated. Marco was given the option to come with us but wanted to stay with Hayley."

Wow, the fact that Hayley would do that for a kid she barely knows speaks volumes about the kind of person she is. I know Kayla and Bentley have talked about adoption, but Hayley is single with no kids or significant other. That's a huge commitment on her part.

"That's really awesome of you guys. Marco is a great kid, but you know that. I'm glad he won't be alone and his sister will be taken care of."

"So what are you going to do for the next six weeks?"

"What do you mean?"

He looks down at my leg. "Once you get out of here...You can't walk up the three flights of stairs to the apartment. You know you can stay with us or Cooper and Liz, or even Kaden. We can set up the couch for you..."

Shit! I didn't even think about that. All my friends have two-story houses and none of their guest rooms are on the first floor. There's no way I'm staying on one of their couches for the next six damn weeks.

"He can stay with us," Marco says. I look over at Hayley and Marco standing back in the doorway.

Hayley looks nervous. "Umm...Yeah...You can stay with Marco and me if you want." Then she turns to Bentley. "Marco said goodbye and we're going to come by later so he can see where Chloe is staying. Kayla is getting Chloe situated in the car and will meet you outside."

"Okay, cool. Caleb, if you need a place to stay you can stay with any of us. I'll give you a call in a little bit."

We bump fists and he leaves.

"Do you want to stay with us?" Marco asks again sounding hopeful.

Hayley still looks nervous. "My house is a single story and I have two guest rooms that aren't being used. You can stay in one and Marco can stay in the other." I'm about to argue, but she must know it's coming, because she speaks before I do. "Please don't argue, Caleb."

I want to say no. I want to argue. I want to run the fuck away from this woman who is slowly making me feel shit I shouldn't be feeling. Maybe six weeks in the same house with Hayley can be a good thing. I'm starting to catch feelings for her, feelings I don't know what to do with. I can't find a single thing wrong with her, so maybe living under the same roof with her will reveal her faults and flaws and then I can drop these feelings bullshit like a bad habit. My brain goes back to a time when I trusted Gloria—reminding me where that got me.

Fifteen years old

"Is it okay if I spend the night at David's house?" I ask my dad.

"I think it would be best if you wait until I get home. I'll be back the day after tomorrow. I don't want to make Gloria stay at the house alone."

When my parents were married my dad never went out of town for business, but since my mom passed away a lot has changed. My dad recently married Gloria, who is young enough to be his daughter. He goes out of town for business several times a month, and she never goes with him. Shortly after they met, they married and he bankrolled her new business, a strip club.

Opening a strip club makes sense, since I'm pretty sure that's where he met her. He hasn't actually said that, but between the way she dresses, the friends she has over, and the conversations I've heard, I'm almost positive she was a stripper until she got ahold of my dad's money.

I have my bedroom door closed but can still hear Gloria and her friends downstairs drinking and listening to music. Recently, the more drunk she gets, the more hands-on she gets, and the last woman I want touching me is my dad's wife, even if she is closer in age to me than her husband.

When he first started going away she would let my friends come over and we would all hang out. She was actually really cool. She would convince my dad to buy me the latest video games and electronics. She would let me and my friends drink some alcohol with her and her friends. We would order food in and watch movies together. It was like having a friend. While she didn't feel like a stand-in mom, she did kind of feel like a sister in a way. After losing my sister and mom, it was nice hanging out with someone, especially with my dad gone all the time.

Then one night everything changed. She and her friends were completely wasted and came on to me after my friends went home. They asked me if I was a virgin and when I said I was they offered to help me change that. I laughed it off to their drunkenness and went to my room, but since then she's acted differently around me. When my dad isn't looking, she'll rub her ass against me or touch me as she walks by. When we watch a movie she'll get closer, putting her feet into my lap. It's just weird.

When my dad said he was going out of town this morning she made a comment about not wanting my friends over this weekend when she usually encourages me to invite them over. I don't understand why she even cares. While I've been in my room all night, I can hear her friends and her getting drunk once again. I was hoping to get out of here, but it doesn't look like it's going to happen. Putting my ear buds in my ears, I press play on my playlist, attempting to get some sleep.

I feel the bed sink and turn over taking my ear buds out. The music has stopped and when I glance at the clock, it reads two in the morning. I've been asleep for about three hours. A hand glides down my stomach inching its way toward my dick. Before it lands on it, I grab the hand, bringing it to a stop.

Squinting my eyes to adjust to the darkness I see Gloria lying in my bed.

"What are you doing?" I hope I'm misunderstanding her being in my bed, trying to feel up on my junk.

"I want you, Caleb." I should have seen this coming...

"You're married to my dad."

She scoots toward me and continues where she left off, grabbing my dick and squeezing it.

I jump up off the bed and switch the light on.

"Don't do this shit. You got it made with my dad. If I tell him what you're doing he'll throw you out on your ass."

She deviously smirks, shaking her head. "You aren't going to tell him...because if you do, I'll tell the Feds what I know, and your dad will end up spending twenty years in prison."

I know exactly what she's talking about. I have heard her and my dad talking about a shitty choice he made that made him millions but was illegal, something to do with insider trading. If she rats him out I'll either end up as an orphan or be stuck with her, and my dad will spend the majority of his life in prison. He's been through enough between losing my sister and my mom. I can't let her do this to him.

"What do you want?"

She smiles smugly knowing she's won.

"You."

And once again another woman has been added to the list of women I can't trust.

"Caleb...are you okay?" Hayley asks, concern laced in every word.

I scrub my hands over my face shaking off the memory of the day I learned how vindictive and untrustworthy a woman could be.

"Yeah, I'm sorry. What were we talking about?"

"I said my house is a single story. You and Marco can both stay with me. Don't argue with me, please."

I hate that it feels like she's telling me what to do. I wouldn't be surprised if once I am moved in, she finds a way to manipulate me. Unfortunately, I'm not really sure what other choice I have at this point. It goes against everything in me to trust this woman, but instead of saying no, I say okay and hope she shows her true colors sooner rather than later.

Or maybe she'll prove my theory wrong...And for some reason, deep down, I really hope she proves me wrong.

Eleven

HAYLEY

IT'S BEEN TWO WEEKS SINCE I BROUGHT CALEB HOME FROM the hospital. Well, not his home, my home. I have a four-bedroom house, so Caleb and Marco are each sleeping in one of the guest rooms. I enrolled Marco in school and hired a tutor to help him in case he needs to get caught up on anything. I also set it up for him to see a therapist on a weekly basis. He needs somebody to talk to after everything he has been through. I had to go through DCF to find an approved therapist and I really like the one they assigned. Marco seems to like her as well.

Cooper insisted I take a few weeks off, paid of course, to be here for Caleb. According to him it's still working since Caleb is a fighter at the gym and I'm the doctor on staff. Caleb was in a lot of pain when we first arrived home. He spent the first week pretty much sleeping, eating, and reluctantly having me help him use the bathroom. He was on some strong meds, but the last couple days he's been starting to come around. He's sitting up more, watching ESPN, refusing the pain meds, and playing games from his bed with Marco and me like Scrabble, Monopoly, and Yahtzee. It's become part of our routine, playing a game together before Marco goes to bed.

The door swings open and Marco comes barreling into the house with a big smile on his face. Is it weird that the feeling of this pseudo-family makes my heart melt?

"Hey, sweetie. How was your day?"

He pulls a piece of paper out of his new backpack I purchased for him for school. We went by his house to see what he could bring from his mom's place before they cleaned it all out, but there was nothing but a few photos that were worth taking. I took him shopping and bought him all new clothes that fit him.

"I got an A on my math test," he whisper-yells, trying to stay quiet in case Caleb is asleep, even though I've told him repeatedly this is his home and he can talk at whatever level he wants.

Tears prick my eyes at how happy he is. I didn't know Marco well before all this happened, but anybody who knew him at all saw the sadness that resided in his eyes. Looking at him right now, it's like looking at a completely different kid. I pull him into a hug and tell him congratulations. It would be so easy for him to rebel. Nobody would blame him after everything he has been through. But instead he's focusing on the positive and shining bright.

"That's amazing, buddy." We both look up and see Caleb leaning against the wall with one of his crutches under his arm, smiling at Marco. He looks a lot better. Most of his bruising is now light yellow or completely gone, his leg is in a cast, but with his ribs starting to heal, he can use crutches when he needs to. Well, right now only one crutch, the one with his good shoulder.

"Want to see it?" Marco asks.

"Absolutely!"

Marco brings the test to Caleb and Caleb makes a huge deal out of it telling him the problems look really complicated. "I think this calls for a celebration. What do you want for dinner tonight?" Caleb asks him.

Marco looks unsure, like it's a trick question. While he's now smiling and dressing nicely on the outside, inside holds too much insecurity from years of abuse from his mother. He eats every meal like it's his last, never gives his opinion unless we beg, and asks constantly what he can do to help out of guilt. The therapist told me it's going to take time for Marco to be comfortable with just being a kid. He's never been given the chance to behave like one before.

"Umm...Can we...maybe...order in Chinese and...umm...maybe invite Kayla and Bentley over so I can see Chloe?"

Caleb looks to me to confirm it's okay with me, and I nod in agreement. I'm so proud of Marco for actually answering this time.

"Sure, buddy. Why don't you go do your homework and I'll text Bentley now?"

Marco says okay and heads to his room.

"He's come a long way," Caleb says softly to me.

"Yeah, he has. Karen from DCF has asked me if I'm interested in adopting him."

Caleb's face looks shocked. "What did you say?"

"Well, I know you and Marco are close, so I wanted to make sure it's okay with you first. I don't want to overstep."

"Of course you can adopt him. You'll make a great mom to him. I can already tell. What about Chloe?"

"Okay, good," I say in relief. "I just wasn't sure if maybe you wanted to. I agreed to foster him when you were in surgery. Oh, and Kayla said she's looking into adopting Chloe. I considered adopting them both, but I know it would mean a lot to Bentley and Kayla since she can't have any more kids." When Kayla was giving birth to her daughter there were complications and the obstetrician had no choice but to perform a partial hysterectomy to save her life. Unfortunately that meant she wouldn't be able to ever get pregnant again.

"Marco needs a mom like you. I know he'll be in good hands when I'm healed and move out. I'm glad for Bentley and Kayla. They're awesome parents."

The thought of Caleb moving out makes my stomach sink. I know he's only here because he's hurt, but these last two weeks have felt like my house is finally a home. Marco is coming around, finally laughing and watching television, and the house is no longer quiet. The thought of Caleb leaving saddens me, but at least I'll still have Marco. With Caleb's leg being stuck in a cast for at least six weeks, I decide to enjoy his company while he's here and not dwell on him eventually leaving.

"Thanks," I say, forcing a smile.

"I'll go text Bentley and Kayla and invite them over for dinner."

"Sounds good."

Dinner with Kayla, Bentley, and the babies went well. Kayla and

Bentley have decided to officially start the process to adopt Chloe but insisted on making sure it's okay with Marco. He said okay but then asked what would happen to him.

"How would you feel about me adopting you?" I asked him.

"Really?" he asked excitedly. Then he turned to Caleb. *"Would you be adopting me, too?"*

Caleb's face sunk at his question. "Unfortunately the state frowns upon people who aren't together adopting a child together, but with Hayley working at the gym, we'll still get to hang out a lot."

Marco scowled and if not for the sad situation causing these two to both be upset, I would laugh at how adorable they both looked. Hanging out so often together has caused their facial expressions to mimic one another. They might not be related, but they are very similar in their mannerisms.

"Okay," Marco whispered, not comfortable enough yet to argue with something an adult said, even though he clearly didn't agree.

After putting Marco to bed, I come out to the living room to watch some television. Caleb is sitting on the couch with his casted leg straight out in front of him texting someone with a frown once again on his face.

"What's wrong?" I ask, sitting next to him on the couch.

He looks up and gives me a shrug. "My apartment is due to renew in a couple weeks. I'm going to have the guys move my stuff to storage. Once I'm out of this cast I'll have to find a new place to live. I don't need a three-bedroom apartment for just myself."

"I have a two-car garage and it's basically empty. Just have them put it all in there so you don't have to pay for storage."

"You sure?"

"Completely."

"Okay, cool. Thanks."

Caleb sends a few more texts and then puts his phone away.

"I guess I'll just head to bed," I say, standing, unsure of what to do. Caleb is usually in his room at night, not out here, and I want to give him his space.

"Wait! Want to watch something out here with me?"

"I was just going to watch *The Bachelor*, but we can watch something else…"

"No, *The Bachelor* is fine. I'm used to all those girly shows thanks to living with Kayla."

"Okay." I sit back down and grab the remote to put on the latest episode.

Twelve

CALEB

I DON'T KNOW WHY I ASK HER TO STAY AND WATCH TV with me. I don't even know why I'm sitting out here on the couch. I've been able to get up for days, but I usually stay in my room to avoid her. Before I got hurt I had asked her if she wanted to grab dinner sometime as friends but quickly thought it might have been a mistake. Now, instead of grabbing dinner, we're living together. I've been here for two weeks and haven't found a single thing wrong with this woman. She has taken to parenting Marco with natural grace. She bought him new clothes, signed him up for tons of school shit, and is home every day when he gets home. She cooks every meal and every single one tastes amazing. I even look forward to our nightly routine of playing games together before Marco goes to bed. She has given me plenty of space and hasn't once tried to hit on me. She even wants to adopt Marco. When she brought it up, clearly nervous I was considering the same thing, I didn't have the heart to say I was considering it. I know he deserves a permanent place to live, so I was looking into what needs to be done. I didn't imagine she would also be considering it.

I know she'll let me and Marco hang out, so I let it go. She'll probably make a better parent than me anyway. She isn't tainted with the past I have.

We're watching some ridiculous show about a guy who has ten women all fighting over him. I look over at Hayley and see the hearts in her eyes over this shit.

"Do you really think you can meet your spouse on a show like this?" I ask, sounding as negative as my thoughts are.

She gives it some thought for a few seconds. Her cute nose scrunches up making me want to lean over and kiss it. "I'm not sure, but based on my results on the dating site Ashley had me join, it probably can't hurt. Those guys who message me are crazy! At least on this show they have to do a background check."

She cracks up laughing at herself and so many thoughts run through my head. First, I go back to my thought of wanting to kiss her nose. I decide to ignore that shit. Next, I think about the fact this beautiful woman seriously thinks she needs a dating site to meet a man. Is she crazy? Then again, she wanted me, and I turned her down. Nope, she's not the crazy one...I am. My final thought is a feeling I only recently experienced, jealousy. Like when I saw Hayley dancing with Alex—my blood boils thinking of all these jackasses messaging her wanting a date. I'm not a hundred percent sure I can trust this woman, but I'm going to figure my shit out soon before some dumbass on a dating site scoops up the woman I'm pretty sure I'm slowly falling for.

"You're still on that dating site? Haven't you ever heard of catfishing? You should stay off that shit. A beautiful woman on a dating site is just asking for trouble."

Her eyes go wide and I backtrack realizing I just went off, and on top of that, called her beautiful. Fuck it! Let the chips fall where they may...

"Umm...Well technically I haven't gone on a date yet using the site since I had to cancel my first one the night we went out to dinner with Marco. I didn't like the way he acted about the whole situation of me having to cancel, so I never messaged him again."

Good.

I just nod, trying to be cool. We go back to watching the show and the guy is going on a one-on-one date with one of the women who won the date because they had the most in common according to some quiz.

"Do you really believe these women tell the truth?"

"Of course! They can't lie on television. Everybody would know they're lying." Wow, she is so gullible. I can't help but chuckle at her seriousness.

"How would anybody know they're lying? I've seen plenty of women lie and get away with it. I bet you could lie to me right now and I wouldn't even know."

"Okay, you're on!"

"We're going to need some alcohol for this. Go grab a bottle and then we'll play a game."

She jumps up from the couch and goes to the kitchen to grab some liquor while I watch her cute behind sway in her tight tank top and tiny little cotton shorts that reads *Will squat for tacos* across the back of her ass. She always wears them around the house at night and swears Taco Tuesday is a real holiday. And so far every Tuesday she's made tacos.

"All I have is a bottle of Patron Silver. Is that okay?"

"Sure." I take the bottle and pour two shots into the glasses she brought over.

"Okay, so what's the game?"

"It's called two truths and one lie. You'll tell me three facts. Two of them will be the truth and one of them will be a lie. If I figure out which one is the lie you have to take a shot. If I can't figure it out, I have to take the shot."

"Okay," she says smiling. "Hmmm...Let me see..." She's so cute as her eyes shoot up to the ceiling and her finger taps her chin in concentration trying to think of what to say.

"Okay, I visit New York yearly, I love fuzzy socks, and I hate exercising.

"Your lie is you hate exercising."

She smiles big. "Nope! Drink up! My lie is that I visit New York yearly. Other than going to Breckenridge and to the different sports arenas for the UFC fights, I have never been anywhere, like on vacation. I would love to go to New York one day."

I down the shot of Patron and think how awesome it would be to take her to New York. I was there a while back for a photo shoot for the UFC and there's so much to do and see.

"See?" I tell her. "It's hard to tell when someone is lying."

"I guess," she says softly. "But I wouldn't want to purposely mislead someone I'm trying to be with. If those women lie on *The Bachelor* they're basing their relationship on a lie. They must know it won't work out in the end."

My heart speeds up at her words. She's too good to be true. She is so damn sweet and innocent. I grab another shot and down it, letting the alcohol numb my brain...and my heart. She's confusing the shit out of me.

"Hey! I didn't even give you any truths or lies. You aren't supposed to drink yet."

"Sorry, go ahead. Try again."

"Okay, I love to gamble at the slot machines, I love to cook, and I love to play candy crush on my phone."

"I have no clue what candy crush is, so I'm going to go with that one for your lie because we live in Las Vegas and your cooking is good as fuck."

She giggles and pours me a shot. "Drink up! My lie was that I love to gamble at the slot machines. I have never even gambled before."

I shoot the shot back welcoming the burn in my throat. "How is that possible? Haven't you lived in Vegas your whole life?"

"Yep, but I never went gambling. I also have never been to a strip club or to watch the fountains at the Bellagio. I spent so much time studying and going to school I guess I forgot to take advantage of where I live."

Before I know what I'm saying, I blurt out, "That's going to have to change. When my leg is out of this cast we are hitting up the strip clubs, a casino, and the fountains all in one night."

She laughs and pours herself a shot. "Okay, so now it's your turn. Tell me two truths and a lie."

My cellphone rings right then and my dad's attorney's name shows up on the caller ID. He called before I was put in the hospital and a couple more times, never leaving a voicemail. I might as well answer this shit and get it over with. I show her my phone is ringing and answer it.

"Hello."

"Hey, Caleb! It's Jason Caldwin, your father's attorney."

"Yeah, I know who you are. What's up?"

I see Hayley trying to act like she's not listening next to me. I want to stand up and walk away, but I can't with my gimp leg.

"Caleb, we need to speak. It's about your father."

"I haven't spoken to my father in over seven years. If he wants to talk to me he can call me himself."

"He can't do that, Caleb. He passed away last month. I have been trying to get ahold of you. Gloria handled the funeral since I couldn't get you to answer but there is the issue of the will. I need to meet with you in person so we can go over the details."

Holy shit! My dad is dead. The man who chose his pedophile pimp of a wife over his son is dead. My last words to him were *I'm out of here.* I should hate him but my heart hurts. It shouldn't hurt, but flashbacks of life before my mom died flash in front of me. Camping, sports events, concerts, him taking my sister and me to the park on Sunday mornings to let mom sleep in. I want to hate him, but knowing he's dead, all I can feel is pain.

I don't even realize I've dropped the phone or that there are tears pouring down my face, when Hayley moves toward me and grabs my phone to talk to Jason. I don't know what is said. It's all a blur. She sets the phone down and looks unsure of what to do. Can you blame her? The crazy mixed signals I have sent...Not wanting her to touch me. How do you comfort someone without touching him? And then I lose it. The lump in my throat that feels like it's going to close up and choke me to death suddenly releases and I cry.

Before I can question it I'm laying in her lap bawling for the loss of the man I once looked up to while Hayley runs her fingers through my hair massaging my scalp. She doesn't say a word, just lets me let it all out. When I finally stop crying, I don't wait for her to ask if I'm okay. I don't know what makes me do it, but I tell her everything I've kept to myself.

"My dad is dead. I haven't seen him in seven years."

"Why haven't you seen him?"

"My stepmom raped me when I was fifteen." I hear Hayley gasp at my words, but she doesn't say anything.

I can't look at her. I don't know what makes me trust her in this moment, but I don't question it.

"After she forced herself on me and took my virginity, she had sex with me for several years while my dad was away on business. Then she pimped me out to a bunch of unhappily married women. I have never had sex of my own free will. When my dad caught us together she blamed me and he chose to believe her. I left and never looked back."

I give her a few minutes to absorb everything I just gave her. When she doesn't say anything but continues to play with my hair, I know she's waiting for me to continue.

"It's why I hate being touched. It's not that I don't want to be touched. I just want it to be my choice. I spent years being forced to touch women I didn't want to touch."

Her fingers stop moving, so I turn my face toward her stomach to look at her. I keep my eyes closed, afraid of the disgust or pity I'll see. After counting to three, I look into her eyes, only I don't see disgust or pity, I see a beautiful woman smiling at me.

"Well that's good to know. I thought it was me, like maybe I smelled bad or had bad breath. I'm glad to know it's you not me..."

I burst out in laughter. I word vomit all over her and she lightens the mood by cracking a joke. I can see why she's such good friends with Kayla and Liz. She is good.

"Are you okay?"

If that ain't a loaded question...

I left out a heavy breath. "I don't know. I hate that I never had a chance to make him believe me, but at the same time, I'm mad that he chose not to believe me. Now he's dead and his attorney needs me for the will. I don't know if I can handle flying back there and being in the same room as that cunt."

"Well, how about this? Marco has a three-day weekend coming up. You'll need help getting around, so why don't we fly there together? We can stay at a resort just outside of Boulder at one the ski resorts and take Marco to see snow."

Damn this woman and her positivity, how did I not see how amazing she is before now? Oh, that's right...because I pushed away all women lumping them into the same compartment as the women who have lied to me in the past.

"You would do that for me? After I continually ignored you and pushed you away?"

"How about we start over? Let's be friends. You're going to be here for several weeks anyway. Let's start over."

Friends? Fuck that! I don't think I want to be friends with Hayley. I want to be more than friends, but I guess friends is a good place to start...

"Okay, friends."

She gives me a full-blown thousand mega-watt smile that could seriously light up a dark room and all I want to do is grab her by her neck and pull her face to me and kiss her. But I don't. Instead, I smile back.

"I think this calls for another shot," she says. I sit up and we both take a shot. Then we go back to watching *The Bachelor*. While she swoons over the guy, I point out all the lies women are telling, making her laugh.

Thirteen

HAYLEY

IT'S FRIDAY AFTERNOON AND I STOP INTO THE GYM TO SEE a few of the fighters before Caleb, Marco, and I head to Boulder to meet with his father's attorney to discuss his will. The night Caleb confided in me I wanted to find his stepmom, Gloria, and beat the shit out of her. I wanted to make her pay for what she did to Caleb, but I knew Caleb wouldn't want my pity, so I made a joke to make light of the conversation and it worked. We even became friends that night.

I'm getting all my files situated when Alex comes walking into my office without knocking and plops into a seat in front of my desk.

"Hey Alex, how's your wrist doing?" I ask, coming around my desk, and taking his hand in mine to check out his finger function.

"It's good, Doc. Thanks."

"So what brings you by?"

"I haven't seen you around lately. How's Caleb doing?"

"He's good. He's healing."

"That's good. I was wondering if maybe we can go to dinner

sometime." Before Caleb and Marco moved in with me, I would have said yes, but now I feel like I need to focus on Marco and I'm not sure how I feel about dating with Caleb staying with me.

"Can I think about it?"

"Sure. How about you take my number and call or text once you decide."

"Okay," I say, handing him my cell phone to input his number in. I hear his phone ring and he laughs guiltily.

"Now I have your number as well." He winks at me as he hands me back my phone. With a kiss on my cheek, he heads out the door.

"What was that about?" Liz asks, standing in the doorway as soon as Alex leaves.

"What?" I ask, not sure what she's talking about.

She sits in the seat Alex was just sitting in.

"Alex kissing you on the cheek..."

"Alex kissed Hayley on the cheek?" Kayla asks, walking through the door without knocking and dropping into the seat next to Liz. Apparently today is drop in on Hayley day...

"He asked me out to dinner. No big deal."

"And what did you say?" Kayla asks.

"I said I would think about it."

"Uh huh," she continues.

"Uh huh, what?" I plop back down into my seat.

"How are things going with Caleb?" Kayla asks. Of course Liz leaves the interrogation to her.

"Things are fine. He's healing. His father passed away so we're going to Boulder today to take care of his dad's will. He and I have actually become friends." I'm trying so hard to sound nonchalant.

"And how many times have you ogled his fine ass body when he's come out of the shower?" Kayla asks. Both she and Liz laugh and I shake my head. They will never let me live that down.

"He makes sure to change in his bathroom. I'm sure the last thing he wants is me seeing him without clothes on. How's Chloe?" I ask, hoping to change the subject.

Kayla smiles big and pulls out her cell phone to show us pictures of Chloe and Faith. "They are so precious!" I say, looking at the cute pictures.

"Karen, with DCF says it shouldn't take long for the adoption to go through."

"I'm so happy for you guys." And I am. I'm glad she's getting the chance to be a mother to Chloe as well. She's mentioned so many times feeling broken because of her hysterectomy. Seeing her being given the opportunity to adopt Chloe and provide a good life for her makes me so happy.

"Why do you look so sad?" Liz asks. Oh, now she wants to jump in and be observant. Fabulous!

"I'm not sad. I just don't think having a baby is in the cards for me. Don't get me wrong. I love and adore Marco. He is an amazing kid. I feel absolutely blessed to have him in my life..."

"Hey," Liz says, coming around the desk to give me a hug. "You have plenty of time to have a baby and when you do, Marco will make a great brother. You'll meet an amazing guy who will want Marco in his life and you guys will have beautiful babies."

Kayla comes around my desk and we end up in a group hug.

"Hmm...Anything special I'm walking in on? I can join if needed," Alex says from the door, waggling his eyebrows. We all laugh.

"No, but I need to get going. We should all do something soon. Poor Caleb is stuck in the house with just me."

"Stuck isn't the word I would use," Alex says smiling at me.

"Weren't you just in here, lover boy?" Kayla asks, putting her hands on her hips.

"Yeah, but I just thought I would see if Hayley has thought about what I asked."

I need to give him some credit on his persistence.

"You just asked her!" Liz laughs. I love that my girls always have my back.

"Okay...Okay..." Alex puts his hands up and backs away. "Think about it, Hayley!" he yells before Kayla closes the door on him. We all crack up laughing.

"Just for the record, I am team Caleb," Kayla says. Liz laughs and agrees.

"You both are crazy! First you need to get Caleb in the game then we can pick teams. Okay, I really need to get going. Dinner soon?" Both ladies nod as we walk out to the gym floor.

I say goodbye and head out to my car. About halfway through the parking lot, I get this weird feeling like I'm being watched. I quicken my steps and once in my car press the lock button. I glance around but don't see anything that looks alarming. I chalk it up to paranoia. Caleb got a call from the detective of his case earlier this week letting him know the four men who were arrested were denied bail, which is great, but the problem is none of those men were Hector or Santos. They are still out on the streets because they weren't there when everything went down. The guys who were at Marco's house are the enforcers, sent to scare someone into paying. Apparently Marco's mom was in some major debt from buying drugs. Because Hector and Santos are both still free, Caleb insisted I put a tracker app on my phone and requested I let him know if I'm going anywhere other than to the gym.

While driving I think about what Kayla said regarding the adoption and decide to call Karen and find out the process of adopting Marco. I want to make sure nobody can take him from me. She lets me know the process is a bit longer for a single mom, but everything should go through smoothly. I hate that Caleb won't be on the paperwork, but I need to still go through the steps to ensure Marco is mine legally.

I get home in time to see Marco getting off the bus and wave to him. While he's walking toward the house I get the feeling of being watched again. I look around and don't see anyone but the few parents walking back to their houses with their children. I am definitely paranoid!

"You ready to go see some snow?" I ask Marco, handing him a bag of snacks for the trip.

"Yes!" He beams at me and then goes to his room to put his backpack away.

Caleb comes hobbling out from the room with his crutches. Luckily when the guys broke his leg it was only the lower part so it's not a full leg cast. He can use crutches instead of needing a wheelchair. Unfortunately they also broke his ribs and shot him in the shoulder and chest so his crutches only get used for short distances. We will be taking a wheelchair with us to the airport. Thankfully Bentley offered to charter a private plane for us to Boulder so Caleb wouldn't have to deal with his broken body on a public plane.

"Ready to go?"

Before I can answer, Marco answers for me. "Yes, sir!"

Once on the plane, I give Marco a present. I picked up an iPad for him this week so he wouldn't be completely bored on the plane and at the attorney's office. As soon as I give it to him, ready to go with apps, he goes crazy with excitement.

"This is mine?"

"Yep! All yours. I downloaded some games and if there's any other games or apps you want just let me know."

He gives me a hug and thanks me. I don't think I'll ever get tired of his hugs.

The stewardess takes our drink orders and Caleb jokingly asks if I would like some Patron to finish our drinking game that got stopped from his phone call.

"Oh no, I'm good. Root beer is just fine."

We're seated on opposite sides of the plane so he tells me to come sit next to him so we can talk.

"How was work?" For a second I wonder if someone said something to him about Alex asking me out, but I doubt it.

"It was good. How was your day?"

"I spoke to the manager with the UFC. They're suspending my contract until I'm healed. I have no idea how long it's going to take to be at a hundred percent and ready to fight again."

"I'm so sorry. Kayla is going to work with you, right?"

"Yeah, once I'm ready. I just feel so restless. Fighting is all I have ever known."

"The weeks will fly by and you'll be healed before you know it."

We get to Boulder and have a rental SUV waiting for us. Caleb sits in the back letting his leg sprawl across the backseat, and Marco sits in the front with me. We arrive at the resort, have a late dinner, and get situated. We decided to meet with his father's attorney first thing in the morning to get it over with, which will give us the rest of the long weekend to enjoy our time with Marco.

Caleb obviously can't ski with his broken body and after our last group trip where I fell on my ass a hundred times before giving up, I have no desire to, but we're bringing Marco to the ski resort so he can do snowboarding lessons and go tubing while Caleb and I hang out and watch him. I'm sure Caleb will have a lot to figure out after meeting with Jason, his father's attorney.

"Time for bed, buddy," Caleb announces after Marco's show finishes. We both get up to tuck him into bed. Somehow it has become part of our routine for both of us to say goodnight to Marco together once he's in bed. I try not to think too hard about what will happen once Caleb is healed enough to get his own place and it's just me saying goodnight to him. I think the only reason he hasn't yet is because he can't drive with the cast on, which makes it difficult to find an apartment.

After we both give Marco a kiss on his forehead, we head to the main room. The hotel suite only has two rooms. but Caleb has insisted he can sleep on the couch. I grab a bottle of water from the fridge on my way to my room.

"Hey, wanna watch something? I don't think they have *The Bachelor* here, but I'm sure we can find some chick flick of some sort."

I laugh and join him on the couch. "Sure, you pick."

"Okay, grab a bottle of liquor and two glasses. You can't make me watch a chick flick without alcohol."

After skimming through the channels he stops on *Friends With Benefits* and looks to me for approval. I smile and he presses play.

About thirty minutes into the movie we're both cracking up and I've noticed Caleb has moved closer to me. We've had quite a few shots and I'm feeling warm and fuzzy. I need a breather from his closeness so I have him pause the movie for a two-minute bathroom break. When I return, he's glaring at my phone like it just insulted him.

"What's up?"

"Nothing."

He pats his leg, indicating for me to lay my head on his lap. I do what he asks and he presses play and then runs his fingers through the strands of my hair just like I did for him that night he confided in me. He has turned this into our go-to position when watching TV at home. We watch the movie in mostly silence, laughing at certain parts, and I sniffle trying to hold back tears at other parts. I am such a sappy romantic!

At one point Caleb wipes the tear falling down my cheek. I look up at him and he is silently laughing at my tears. I don't know when it happened, but we seem so much closer than we were when he first moved in. It makes sense since we're always together. Eating together, hanging out with Marco, watching television shows after Marco goes to bed. Everything feels like it has shifted. We went from barely acquaintances to friends in such a short time.

"Do you think it's possible?" I ask when the movie ends. "To have sex without the emotions?"

I regret the question before I ever finish it, but Caleb answers before I can take it back.

"No, it's not possible." *Did he feel something for these women he was forced to have sex with?*

Almost as if he hears my silent question, he adds, "I hated every one of the women I had sex with. I felt the contempt and disgust run through my veins for years. You can't have sex without emotions. I have never had sex that I enjoyed. "

While my experience is limited to a few guys, I can honestly say for the most part they were all decent in bed. Sure there wasn't huge sparks, but I can't imagine hating the person I'm intimate with.

My cell phone dings with a text, so I check it. It's Alex. When I go to check the text, I notice one I missed from earlier. Did Caleb see the text? Is that why he was glaring at my phone?

Alex: Have you thought any more about dinner?

Alex: Just one date...

I put the phone down and turn to Caleb, moving a bit closer. "Maybe if you have sex with someone by choice you might enjoy it." I give him a small smile hoping he catches my drift. The alcohol is definitely giving me liquid courage.

"Maybe...Have you ever had no-strings attached sex?"

"Once. It was okay. I didn't really know him though. I think it would be better if I at least got to know him first."

"Like Alex?" I cringe when he says his name instead of his own. That's not where I was trying to go.

When I don't say anything, he says, "We're friends...You can tell me."

Friends...Right...And it's obvious that's all we'll ever be.

"Maybe. I don't know," I say, grabbing my phone and suddenly feeling exhausted.

"I'm going to bed. I'll see you in the morning." I don't bother looking back before I close my door and climb into bed without changing my clothes. I don't know why I thought Caleb would want me to be the person he has sex with by choice. I told myself I was done trying to be more with Caleb, but it's almost impossible not to have feelings for him when we live together and I see what an amazing person he is. The more I get to know him the more I want to be with him. Maybe saying yes to Alex would be a good idea. I can get Caleb out of my head and focus on another man. I would rather have Caleb as a friend than as nothing at all.

Me: Okay. One date.

Alex: How about dinner on Tuesday at 6?

Me: Sounds good. We can leave from the gym.

After I'm done texting with Alex, I decide to sneak in a quick orgasm. Being so close to Caleb has gotten me completely turned on with no chance of a release. I move my hand down to my shorts and panties, and pull them down to my knees. Separating my pussy lips, I put a finger into my warmth and find I'm already wet. Using my juices, I add another finger and move them to my clit. With my other hand, I pull my shirt up slightly and pinch my nipple. Closing my eyes, I imagine Caleb is the one with his hands on me...

Fourteen

CALEB

JESUS! WHY DO I FEEL LIKE A TEENAGE FUCKING BOY WHEN I hang out with Hayley? Between being turned the hell on and unsure of what to say, I feel lost as fuck around this woman. She's the only person I have told about my past life and she doesn't treat me any different than she did before she knew. We've become close the last couple weeks. I thought Kayla and I were close, but hanging out with Hayley has made me realize Kayla's and my relationship was one-sided. I wasn't ready to tell her about my shit, so instead I was there for her through all of hers. For me to tell Hayley everything, I know somewhere deep down I have to trust her. Maybe it's the way she treats Marco or the way she no longer flirts with me, but I want this woman in a bad fucking way.

When she went to the bathroom and I saw Alex's text come through, I wanted to chuck the phone across the room. His text confirms what I already knew, guys aren't blind to Hayley. I can't believe she hasn't been scooped up yet.

And then when she asked me about sex without emotions, I wanted to take her and throw her down onto the couch and show her every foreign emotion I'm feeling right now. But I remembered I have ribs that aren't healed yet and a cast on my leg. I'm not in a position to throw anyone anywhere.

I took my frustrations out on her and asked about Alex. I shouldn't have brought him up...or I should have asked her not to go out with him. He's a good guy and would treat her right. I know this, but fuck if I don't want her for myself. I clearly suck at this conversational bullshit because she practically ran from me and into her room for the night.

I need to go speak to her. I hate the way we left things and I don't want it to be awkward between us. Grabbing my crutches, I make my way to her room and knock lightly. I hear a noise and assume she's telling me to come in, so I open the door.

The room is mostly dark, but from the door opening there is now light filtering through and before she realizes I am there I see the most beautiful, erotic sight of my life. She has her shirt up, shorts down, eyes closed, and she's fingerfucking herself. What makes it even better? My name graces her lips as her orgasm hits her full force.

"Mmmm...Caleb," she says, her body bowing. I quickly and quietly close the door not wanting to embarrass her. I might have been on the fence before, but I've made my decision.

I want this woman and I'm coming for her.

THE NEXT MORNING WE ARRIVE AT THE ATTORNEY'S OFFICE

at nine o'clock on the dot. It was rough sitting across from Hayley, watching her eat her muffin with the same fingers she had in her pussy last night. I wanted to make a comment, let her know I saw, ask her if I could help her out next time, but I was afraid of how she would respond.

Once we're seated in the waiting room I look over and see Gloria. Can you say instant turn-off? She's dressed to impress in her name brand clothes my father's money has paid for. She has a face full of makeup and her hair is done to perfection. She's aged over the last several years, but she's still young, and I want to throw up just looking at her. Hayley sees me stiffen but doesn't say anything.

"Hello, Caleb. It's nice to see you, again," Jason says, shaking my hand.

"Hey, man. These are my friends Hayley and Marco."

"Nice to meet you both. Why don't we get right to it? Marco, why don't you stay out here with Veronica, my secretary?"

Hayley hands him his new iPad she bought for the trip and gives him a smile, reassuring him it's okay. "Stay here and don't move. We'll be right over there if you need anything. Okay?"

"Okay."

Gloria stands as we walk toward the room eyeing me like the vulture she is. Once we all sit down, Jason begins. "Because your father insisted you are present for the reading of the will, Gloria is hearing all of this for the first time as well."

At the mention of her name, Hayley's face whips around to look at Gloria, and if looks could kill Gloria would be in hell right now courtesy of Hayley. Feeling the need to calm Hayley, I take her hand and place it on my thigh and begin rubbing my thumb over her fingers trying to calm her down. It seems to work for the most part, but now with her hand on my thigh I can feel my dick twitching, and in this room, with Gloria sitting on the other side of me, this is the last place I want to be turned on. Suddenly, flashbacks of Gloria touching me surface and I have to swallow down the bile I feel building in my throat. I want to push away Hayley's hand, but I don't want her to think it's her I don't want to touch.

"Go ahead," I choke out, trying to get this ball rolling. The sooner we get this over with, the sooner we can get the fuck out of here and take Marco to see snow.

"Okay, first of all, I have a letter here from your father. It was given to me about three years ago. He came in to make some changes to his will and also brought this letter in. He said you are to be given this letter and he asked that you read it after I go over the details of the will."

Jason hands me the envelope with my name scrawled across the front in script that I recognize as my dad's handwriting. It feels like it weighs a hundred pounds in my hand. I place it on the desk and nod for him to continue. He turns on a recorder—I'm assuming to record this is being done properly.

"I would like for it to go on record, I am Jason Caldwin, the attorney of Adam Michaels, and I am here today with Caleb Michaels and Gloria Michaels to read the living will and testament of Adam Michaels. It is sworn before me that this is the only will and will be upheld in the court of law. I would also like for it to be noted Adam Michael was in good health and sound mind when he created this will.

Adam Michaels leaves any and all assets to his son, Caleb Michaels, including but not limited to all bank accounts, stocks, bonds, houses residing at the addresses named below, all vehicles, as well as the two businesses he owns outright named *Assets*."

"What the hell are you saying?" Gloria shouts, cutting Jason off. I'm in shock—my father has left me everything, including the clubs he built for her. What the hell happened while I was gone?

"What did he say about me?" she shrieks.

Jason clears his throat and continues to read. Judging by his calmness he already knew this was coming.

"I, Adam Michaels, leave a separate bank account to my estranged wife, Gloria. In the bank account, she will find twenty thousand dollars to start her life over with. She may also keep the Porsche SUV, which is in her name. She has thirty days to move out of the house I am leaving to Caleb."

Hol-y shit. It takes everything in me not to laugh at the look on that miserable bitch's face as she realizes the jokes on her and my father didn't leave her shit. I am now dying to open the letter from my father.

"I will take this to court!" she yells at me. She's now standing and is too close for comfort. I breathe in and out slowly to calm myself.

"Gloria, you have the right to do as you wish, but maybe spending the generous sum he left you on an attorney isn't the best idea. I can assure you this will uphold in the court of law," Jason states matter-of-factly.

Gloria is so mad she's practically shaking. I stand and shake hands with Jason and thank him. I have a lot to think about. Jason hands me a large envelope telling me everything I need to know including accounts and passwords are in here and to let him know if I have any questions.

As I attempt to grab my crutches to hobble away, Gloria grabs me by my arm, but before I can say anything, her hand is ripped away.

"Listen here you nasty bitch. I know all about you. If you ever lay a hand on Caleb again I will throw your ass out a window. Do you understand?"

Hayley says the words so quietly I don't even think Jason can hear from his desk, but her tone is made clear, and I think I just fell for this woman even more.

Gloria looks shocked, clearly wondering if Hayley really knows all about her, but she recovers quickly. "You will be hearing from my attorney." And with those words, she's out the door.

Hayley runs out after her and I think it's to go for round two, but when I get to the waiting room she's sitting next to Marco smiling and asking him something about the game he is playing. She wanted to make sure Gloria didn't get anywhere near him. My heart constricts, thinking of my own mom and how protective she was over me. I miss her so damn much. Hayley is an amazing woman and Marco is lucky to have her in his corner.

"All right, you two. Ready for some snow?" I ask, tucking the letter from my dad into my back pocket.

"Yes!" Marco says, pumping his fist into the air.

"Let's go!"

We spend the rest of the weekend having fun at the ski resort. Marco takes snowboarding lessons and after a few hours is flying down the slopes. He's really good. It's obvious he's a natural athlete. Hayley and I watch from the sidelines and every so often she heads indoors to read her romance book by the fireplace. I hate that I can't join Marco on the slopes, but decide once I'm healed, I'm going to take him back here to do some snowboarding with him.

By the time we fly back to Las Vegas, it's late. Luckily Hayley left her vehicle at the airport so we can head right home. While she's getting the luggage into the trunk I see a sheet of paper sticking out of her windshield. I grab it and open it up: **DROP THE CHARGES OR ELSE...**

I look around but don't see anybody. Since the four men who attacked me weren't granted bail this has to be from someone on the outside, most likely Hector or Santos. I'll turn this into the police station tomorrow. For now, I decide not to tell Hayley. I don't need to worry her.

Fifteen

HAYLEY

IT'S BEEN A MONTH SINCE CALEB FOUND OUT HE'S RICH. Not only is he rich, but he's also the owner of several businesses and homes. His ribs are pretty much healed and while he hasn't been able to drive himself anywhere because of his cast, he's been making phone calls like crazy, having his friends take him places as well as taking a cab when necessary. It is only a matter of time until he finds a new apartment and moves out. I haven't brought it up, but I'm sure it's coming.

During these last several weeks things have been good between us. We've established a great schedule with Marco—he's thriving in school and at home. We spend a lot of time together, the three of us, sometimes going to the movies or out to dinner. We have Kayla, Bentley, and the babies over a lot as well. Marco loves to see his sister, and Kayla is beginning to work with Caleb on rehabilitating his shoulder. Caleb's shoulder is nowhere near back to the way it was before but he hasn't lost hope. From the outside looking in, one would think we're a family, and the truth is, I have to constantly remind myself when we're together that we aren't.

Last weekend was Bella's Birthday party so the three of us attended the party at her favorite park. Marco was nervous and told us it would be the first party he's been to. Even though he's older than Bella and Tristan, he still enjoys hanging out with them. He's a good kid. He had a blast at the party, but I could see the sadness when he told me he's never had one. I shouldn't have been shocked to learn he never had a party of his own, but I still was. Even though his birthday just passed in December, I make a mental note to throw him a half-year party this summer once school is out. It will be warm outside and we can invite his friends over and have them all go swimming.

At night Caleb and I spend time together just the two of us. We usually watch a show or a movie, but rarely pay attention it. We talk about our day, what's going on with Marco, how he feels about his dad leaving him everything. He's a complete open book when we talk. The only thing it seems we don't talk about is when he plans to move out. He did mention needing the time off to get his dad's estate in order. He seems to have turned a corner—so much more upbeat than he was before.

One night I nervously asked him about the letter his dad wrote. He hadn't brought it up yet and I was curious what it entailed.

"You don't have to tell me if you don't want to. I just want you to know you can talk to me about it if you ever want."

Caleb hobbled over to the room and came back with the letter in his hand. "I read it when we got back from Boulder. He knew everything."

I was flabbergasted by his words. His dad knew but didn't say or do anything? He chose his wife over his son?

"Did he explain why he chose her over you, yet left you everything?"

"Yeah, do you want to read it?"

"Do you want me to?"

He nodded and handed me the letter.

Dear Caleb,

If you're reading this I have passed away without getting the courage to speak to you. I have written this letter because I am a selfish man who couldn't face his own son. I am currently in the middle of divorcing Gloria and I would like to say I am truly sorry for what I did to our family. The day in your bedroom when you begged me to believe you, I should have taken your side. I didn't know for sure but I had a feeling Gloria was up to no good. I just had no idea how bad it was. After you left and I confronted her she admitted everything including blackmailing you and then having sex with you. I was so scared to end up in prison, I let her get away with what she did to you. I know nothing I say will make up for what she did and what I did to you by not believing you and choosing to believe her. You were so young, still underage, and it was my job to protect you. I'm so sorry I never protected you from her. I'm sorry I couldn't be the dad you deserve.

I have left everything I own to you. I have filed for divorce but it will take time and so I made sure to change my will in case something happens to me before it's finalized. Please don't let Gloria threaten you. She can't do anything to you. Everything I am leaving you is yours. The clubs actually make real good money. If you don't want them, sell them. Just please accept everything I am giving you. Is it guilt money? Sure! But do you deserve it any less? Hell no!

In case she gives you any trouble, please feel free to use this letter as a witness testimony to what she did to you. I also have a tape recording of her admitting what she did in my safety deposit box. Jason should have given you the key.

Please know I have watched you over the years from afar. I have watched you fight your way to the top. You are pursuing your dreams and I am so damn proud of you. You walked away with nothing but your dignity and pride and created a life for yourself. Take the money I left you and use it for good.

I love you, son.

Dad

I handed it back to him and tried to wipe the tears from my eyes before he could see. He reached over and wiped them for me.

"How do you feel about all this?"

"I feel like I am ready to move forward."

And he has moved forward. He laughs more and is way more social than before. It seems like the weight has been lifted from his shoulders and he is finally free. I hope now that he's put it all behind him, he will one day be able to date a woman. Caleb is an incredible person and deserves to be happy, even if it's not with me.

During the last few weeks I have been on a few dates with Alex. I haven't spoken to Caleb about it and for some reason that makes me feel guilty. It's not like I need his permission to date, but because we're at a good place in our friendship and I don't want to rock the boat, I haven't actually told him I have gone out with Alex. He hasn't made any indication he would even care who I date. I usually leave from the gym to meet Alex and we only go out when I know Marco is with Kayla or doing something with Caleb. The truth is I don't feel a huge spark with Alex. While he is sweet and nice, he just doesn't do it for me.

Today is Valentine's Day and I'm going to dinner with Alex. I know I shouldn't lead him on, but it's been awhile since I actually had a date for this holiday. Caleb has been gone all day, so hopefully I'll leave before he gets home. Marco is at Bentley's parents' house for the night spending time with Chloe while they babysit Chloe and Faith so Bentley can take Kayla out. Alex insisted on picking me up and I couldn't say no. I've tried to muster up the courage to tell Caleb all afternoon but have chickened out.

"Hey, want to grab a bite to eat? I didn't even realize it's Valentine's Day. The restaurants seem to be all booked, but we can go to the diner you love." Caleb is sitting on the couch, looking down at his phone. He must have gotten home while I was in the shower.

He looks up from his phone taking me in from head to toe. I'm suddenly self-conscious about my outfit. I am wearing a tight red dress that shows every one of my curves and I've paired it with black peep-toe heels. I normally don't dress up, but with it being Valentine's Day, Alex insisted on making reservations. I even straightened my hair after getting my highlights redone this morning along with a fresh manicure and pedicure.

"Going somewhere?" Caleb asks, looking confused.

Of course that's when Alex knocks causing Caleb to get up to answer the door. For a guy with a broken leg, he can move quickly when he wants to. That's when I notice his cast is off. He has a walking boot instead of the cast, which means he can now walk without crutches.

"Hey, man," Alex says, walking in. He's holding roses in one hand and shakes Caleb's hand with the other, completely unaware of the now thick tension in the room.

"What's up?" Caleb asks, darting his eyes from Alex to me.

"Nothing much. Taking Hayley out for Valentine's Day," Alex says to Caleb before he turns to me. "You look beautiful, Hayley." He hands me the flowers and gives me a kiss on my cheek. I thank him and excuse myself to go put them in water.

While I'm filling the vase, I feel a warm body come up behind me. I know instantly it's Caleb. Nobody makes my body react like his does. Before I can turn around, he presses his front up against my back. His hands lay flat on the counter caging me in, and his cool breath is so close to my ear, I get the chills.

"How long have you been dating Alex?" he asks softly.

"We've just gone on a few dates." I don't know why I feel the need to downplay it.

He moves one of his hands to turn off the water since the vase is now completely filled and is overflowing. I am stuck where I am. I've never felt Caleb this close.

"Is that who you want, Hayles?" Oh, did I mention since we've been hanging out the last several weeks he has started calling me Hayles? And did I mention every time he does, my panties go wet? Well, he does...and they do!

"He's nice," I say because it's the first thing that comes to mind.

His closeness is causing my mind to go blank.

"Nice," he repeats and then chuckles without humor. One of his hands comes off the counter and moves my hair to the side, and then I feel his lips touch my neck as he gives me a chaste open-mouthed kiss right on my pulse point.

His hands move to my hips and he turns me around, not backing up at all. I can feel his cock up against the thin material of my dress pushing against my stomach.

I look up and into his glaring eyes. I'm not sure why he's mad, but I wait for him to say something else since he's holding me against the counter.

His face moves closer and I think he might be about to kiss me when he keeps going, lining his lips right up to my ear.

"Enjoy your *nice* date." Then he let's go of me and saunters out of the kitchen to his room. I didn't realize the warmth his body radiates until he's no longer touching me, causing my body to suddenly shiver. I want the warmth of Caleb back.

I put the flowers into the vase and try to compose myself as I walk back to the living room.

"Ready?" Alex asks. I want to cancel this date. I want to feign illness and find Caleb and his warmth. I want to stop trying to be into a guy who doesn't turn me on at all. But I'm not that woman, so instead I plaster a smile on my face and say, "Yep," and follow Alex out the door, leaving my warmth behind.

Sixteen

CALEB

WHAT'S THAT SAYING...YOU DON'T KNOW WHAT YOU HAVE until it's gone? I'm pretty sure that's how it goes and that's exactly how I feel right now. I'm lying in my bed in my bedroom with the door shut because I couldn't watch Hayley and Alex leave for their date.

These past six weeks with Marco and Hayley have been nothing short of amazing. I haven't been this happy and content since my mom and sister were both alive. We have somehow created our own version of a family and every day I look forward to the moments we spend together. Whether it's the three of us, or just Hayley and me, I am falling hard...Fuck it! Let's be honest...I *have* fallen hard!

I know realistically I could have moved out a couple of weeks ago. I could have found an apartment on the first floor, but I made excuses to myself not wanting to leave. I have been busy getting my father's affairs in order during the day and enjoying my afternoons and evenings with Marco and Hayley. If I'm honest with myself, I don't want to leave either of them.

I've kicked Gloria out of my dad's house and put it on the market and sold all of his vehicles, donating all the profits to the charity Bentley and I started. It is another jump up from the one he started to help pay for the MMA classes Cooper runs. We're working together to build a sports complex next to the gym for kids to come to instead of going home alone. They will be able to participate in a variety of sports and have a safe place to go to instead of running the streets. We're still in the planning stage but it's going to be cool as hell once it's done.

My next step is to deal with Gloria's strip clubs since Gloria didn't take Jason's advice and has made it clear she is going to take me to court for ownership of the clubs. Turns out she owns two clubs, one of which is right here in Vegas on the strip. I've shut them both down for renovation with paid leave for all the employees while we go to court. I could have closed them down, but I felt bad leaving so many people without an income. Plus, I had Liz take a look at the books and my dad was right, they turn a nice profit. Until it gets sorted out, the court has put a freeze on all things club related. Because Jason was the attorney for the will I need to find a new attorney to represent me in court.

I have also been attending physical therapy with Kayla for my shoulder. I won't be fighting in the upcoming UFC fight anymore, which sucks, but I do plan to fight again in the future. No longer needing the money definitely changes my outlook on life. I can see myself taking a step back from fighting for a bit. I have spent so many years focusing on my dream I didn't realize how much I was missing from life. I'm enjoying my time with Marco and Hayley.

There's been so many times I have wanted to take things further with Hayley, tell her how I feel, that I want more with her, but felt it was best to wait until I'm no longer handicapped. So today when the doctor took my cast off and put me in a removable walking boot jokingly saying, "Happy Valentine's Day," it hit me that today would be the perfect day to tell Hayley how I feel.

I tried to find a restaurant to take her to, but of course they were all booked for the holiday. I definitely didn't think this through. Then as quick as this was all handed to me, it was taken away when she walked out of her room in a sexy-as-hell red dress and fuck-me heels. I almost came in my pants from just looking at her. The way the dress swoops down just low enough to show the outline of her amazing breasts, and how it's formfitting enough to show her perfect curves that I want to grab ahold of in bed as I make love to her while she's wearing nothing but those damn heels.

Then it hit me, she didn't know I planned to take her out, which means the dress wasn't for me. So who is it for? And like the devil himself heard my question, there was a knock on the door, and on the other side was my friend Alex. Shit! How the fuck did I not see this coming? I tried hard to think if Hayley had mentioned Alex before and I am pretty damn sure she hasn't. Other than the one night I saw his text, he never got brought up again.

I wanted nothing more than to slam the door on his face, but Alex is a good guy, and he didn't do anything wrong. If I'm being honest neither did Hayley, but she could have mentioned dating him during one of our nighttime conversations. *Did she purposely keep this from me?*

When she went to put the flowers in water I watched her fine ass sway to the kitchen and wanted to tie her up in my room and never let her out. Needing to know if my feelings for her were one-sided, I cornered her in the kitchen. I know she felt something for me before, but she hasn't acted on those feelings in months. Maybe she no longer wanted me. But when I pressed my body up against hers I knew damn well she wanted me just as bad as I wanted her. And when she described Alex as *nice*, I knew I had her.

I'm not going to lie. I'm new to this dating shit. I have no idea what to do. I've had sex hundreds if not thousands of times over the years, every single time not by choice. I had a girlfriend once. I was thirteen and we went to the skating rink. I asked her to be my girlfriend, she said yes, we kissed on the lips a few times, wrote a couple notes back and forth, and a few months later I was taken out of school to watch my mom die.

Now I'm in my room while Hayley is on a date and I have no clue where to go from here. I know Kayla is probably on a date with Bentley, but fuck it, she's the only person I can ask about all this.

"Hello?" she answers the phone on the second ring.

"Are you busy?"

"Caleb? What's wrong?"

"Are you busy?" I ask again.

"No, Bentley and I are picking up the kids from his parents' house. They were going to keep them overnight, but Faith is teething and is super-fussy, so we decided to call it a night after dinner. Everything okay?"

"Did you know Hayley is dating Alex?" My question comes out a lot harsher than I intended, but of course Kayla doesn't miss a beat. It's quiet and then I hear laughter over the phone.

"Yes, I know they've gone on a few dates, but I don't think she is really into him."

"I don't know how to do this, Kayla." We've had a few discussions since I opened up to Hayley. Kayla always knew something was up, but I confirmed her suspicions one day during physical therapy. She knows I haven't been with anyone since my last night in Boulder when I fucked Norma before moving to Las Vegas.

"Well, I'm assuming you aren't referring to not knowing how to have sex..." She laughs and tries to play it off with a cough successfully lightening my mood.

"I watched her leave with Alex on a date. Shit, Kayla. I didn't think it was possible to feel so jealous of another man."

"Well, you have to tell Hayley that, silly."

"That's it? Just tell her how I feel? What about the fact I'm living here still?"

"Hayley is a grown woman, Caleb. You both put Marco first. Just tell her how you feel and see where it goes. I have Marco for the night, so maybe tell her when she gets home from her date."

"Okay..."

"And Caleb? You can't hold it against her if she's slept with Alex. She doesn't know how you feel."

Oh, fuck! I didn't even think about the fact she's probably slept with Alex. Would I hold it against her? No, I wouldn't. But it still sucks thinking about the fact he has had his hands all over the body I should have claimed months ago.

"Yeah, yeah, I get it," I say before hanging up.

I consider texting Hayley there's an emergency to get her to come home but decide against it. I'll just wait until she gets home and speak to her then.

After about an hour I say *fuck it!* And shoot her a text.

Me: You should come home.

Hayley: Everything okay?

Is everything okay? Technically it is...but also technically it's not because she's out on a date with another guy. I don't want to worry her, so I go for vague.

Me: Yeah, but we need to talk.

Hayley: About what?

Me: About the fact that I saw you calling out my name while fingering yourself in Boulder, yet you're on a date with a guy who isn't me.

Straight forward much? Yeah, but if I'm going to go in, I might as well go all the way in. I stare at my phone, waiting for a response that never comes.

Seventeen

HAYLEY

ALEX AND I ARE AT DINNER, AND I SHOULD BE FOCUSING ON him, but instead my attention is on Caleb...His lips touching my neck, my earlobe, and the way his body touching mine sent shocks of pleasure straight to my core. We're finishing up our dessert when Caleb sends me a text telling me to come home because we need to talk. At first I was worried it might be something serious and then my curiosity got the best of me. When I asked him what we needed to talk about I didn't expect the text he sent.

Luckily Alex was in the bathroom because having to explain the wine that shot out of my mouth and all over the table would have been awkward. I can't believe Caleb saw me that night in the hotel room. My eyes were closed and thinking back I thought I heard something, but I was so caught up in imagining it was Caleb getting me off I didn't even think about it.

I don't even know how to respond, so I put my phone away knowing I'm going to end things with Alex. I should have ended things sooner.

"Is everything okay?" Alex asks, sitting back down.

"Yes...No...I'm not really sure. Caleb needs to talk to me. I need to go home tonight. I'm sorry." I leave out the part about him letting me know he watched me finger myself while calling out his name.

Alex's look of disappointment solidifies my decision to end things tonight. I don't want to lead him on.

"Alex, I have had a lot of fun with you, but I don't think it's going to work out."

He gives me a small smile and nods. "Yeah, I kind of figured that when I picked you up tonight."

I raise a brow in confusion.

"Hayley, I knew you had a thing for Caleb but I still took my chances. I saw the way you acted around him. It's obvious something is going on between you two. And by the daggers he was shooting at me tonight, I would say it's no longer one-sided."

"I'm so sorry. I honestly don't even know what's going on."

"It's okay. You're an amazing woman. I can't blame the guy for wanting you." He gives me a wink and it gives me a sense of relief things aren't ending on a bad note.

Alex pays the bill and drops me off at home. As he walks me to the door like the perfect gentleman he is, I notice a car sitting a few houses down. It's an expensive vehicle, and while this is a nice neighborhood, this car looks to be worth more than even the houses are worth. It clearly doesn't belong here. I look closer and notice two dark shadows inside. This horrible feeling of being watched again comes over me, but I shake it off.

Alex gives me a small kiss on my cheek and says goodnight before walking back to his car. I wait until he takes off before I go to unlock the door. As I place my key up to the lock, the door swings open and I am met with Caleb's beautiful blue-grey eyes glaring at me.

"You didn't text me back," he growls.

My eyebrows shoot up making it clear I am not okay with how he is speaking to me. He closes his eyes briefly and when he reopens them, his eyes have lightened a bit taking the grey away. He's no longer towering over me, but has slouched a bit calming down.

I look back to make sure Alex is gone and notice the expensive car still sitting down the street. Maybe I should tell Caleb—it's probably nothing but what if it's something?

We're both standing in the doorway with the door open but he moves over to let me inside the house. When I walk through and turn around to face him he's right up against me. His mouth is so close to mine, it takes all my willpower not to reach up and kiss him. Then I remember about the car.

"Hey, without being obvious open the door back up and look down the street to the right. There's a car sitting on the side of the road. I don't think it belongs there."

His eyes widen and he swings the door open. "I don't see anything."

I look outside to where the car was, only it's gone. I know I wasn't seeing things. "It was just there. It looked like two people were just sitting in the car. It gave me a bad feeling, like I was being watched."

Caleb closes the door again. Grabbing my hand, walks us to the couch, and then gripping my sides, pulls me into his lap. I'm so shocked he's not only touching me, but that he has pulled me on top of him, I'm having trouble speaking.

"Is this the first time you've felt like you were being watched?"

I think about it for a second and remember when I was at the gym recently and had the same feeling. "No, I felt it before but didn't really think much about it. Do you think someone could be following me? Who would do that?"

"I found a note the day we came back from Boulder warning me to drop the charges. You need to be careful. Please don't leave the gym by yourself. Have someone walk you out. Don't be on your phone while walking to your car. Pay attention around you. Hector and Santos, the guys who were threatening Marco, are still out there, and remember how they threatened you before...insinuating they would accept you as payment. I'd hope they aren't stupid enough to come around with the trial coming up and their friends all in the spotlight but you never know." I didn't even think about the fact that Hector and Santos weren't the ones arrested because they weren't there the night all that shit went down. Because the cops have nothing on them but Marco saying they sell drugs, they can't arrest them. They need more evidence to build a stronger case against them.

"Okay, I'll be careful," I promise.

Suddenly feeling shy sitting on Caleb's lap, I lift up to climb off him, but he grabs my hips to keep me in place. He doesn't say anything for a good minute. He just rubs circles into my flesh with his thumbs while searching for something in my face, I don't know what. I look down and notice when Caleb pulled me on top of him, my tight dress had nowhere to go but up and my panties are visible.

I try to get off Caleb once again to pull my dress down, but before I can, he glances down to see what I'm looking at and then licks his lips at the sight in front of him. This whole scene is so confusing. Caleb has never wanted me. Whether it was when we kissed once at the club or when it was just a small pat on his leg, he always made it clear I'm not who he wants. I know a lot of it has to do with what his stepmom did to him. He's told me so himself that he needs to be in control, but over the last few months if he wanted me, he would have done something about it, right? Until today I thought Caleb didn't view me as anything more than a good friend, but now his actions are telling me otherwise.

I need to just let him take the lead. If he needs to be in control I need to let him be. The thought of Caleb controlling me causes the area between my legs to clench.

He feels my thighs tighten and raises a brow. "You didn't respond to my last text."

Oh my God, he is actually going to bring that up. Okay, then. "What would you like me to say? Apparently you saw it all, so you know I was getting off while thinking about you." My neck and face warms at my admission.

Caleb studies my face for a few seconds before he whispers, "I want you." Those three words make me want to jump this man. They make me want to take his dick and put it in me and ride him, but I choose to stay silent only nodding once in case those three words are asking for permission. I need him to know he can have me.

Gripping my ass with his hands, he picks me up. My ankles link together around his waist and he walks us to my bedroom never taking his eyes off me. He lays me on the bed and steps back, bringing his hands to his face. He scrubs his hands up and down his stubble...out of confusion? Frustration? I don't know. I have no idea what's going on in his head.

"I have no clue what to do with you," he finally says. I'm not sure what he means by this. He's told me he's had sex with hundreds of women, surely he knows what to do.

"Do you like it soft or rough? How do you want it? Do you like it missionary or from behind? Fuck! I'm going to mess this up." I see the frustration in his eyes. It's never been in his control. He's always been told exactly what to do. He doesn't know what to do if someone isn't telling him, yet he needs this to be in his control. My heart breaks for this grown man who looks completely lost.

I sit up and pat the bed next to me, giving him a small smile. He crawls up the bed and lies next to me, so we're both lying on our sides facing each other. "I want it however you want to give it to me. We don't have to have sex tonight. Let's just take it slow. You lead and I'll follow."

He nods slowly and swallows loudly. Taking my face in his hands, he brings his body closer to mine so we're lined up against one another just barely touching, and then brings his lips to mine for a small kiss. He doesn't take it any further, leaving his lips on mine, and I let him figure out what happens next. This is definitely a test to my restraint.

After pulling back, he drags his thumb across my bottom lip and smiles. "That's the first kiss I have had willingly since I was thirteen." My heart cracks, but I keep myself composed. I remind myself he doesn't need my pity.

He brushes his lips against one once again, only this time his tongue pushes against my lips seeking entrance. I part my lips slightly, welcoming him. My one hand is propping my head up and my other is holding the sheet to remind myself not to jump him.

Our kiss deepens, and it feels like it goes on for hours. His tongue entwines with mine. He tastes like the mint toothpaste I always see on his bathroom sink mixed with Patron. He must have had a drink while I was out. I think back to my date. It seems like it ended days ago, yet it couldn't have been more than an hour ago. At some point Caleb's hand moves from my face to my ass, and he tugs me toward him. We're close enough that I can feel his hard length pressing up against me. I don't make any move except continue to kiss him back, and he is an amazing kisser.

Caleb's lips break apart from mine and then he rolls me to my back hovering over me. He looks lost in thought for a moment, almost like he's in pain, but then he seems to snap out of it, coming back to me. My lips feel numb from the excessive kissing we've been doing. His hands are resting on either side of my face, as he peppers small, wet kisses all over my face, on both my cheeks, on each of my eyelids, my nose, and my chin. Then he moves to my neck, kisses the same throbbing pulse point he did earlier tonight in the kitchen.

"I love the way you taste," he whispers into my ear causing my legs to tighten. Because he's situated between my thighs, he feels them tighten and chuckles softly. He goes back to kissing my neck, and then kisses my exposed collarbone and shoulder. I'm so turned on, I'm afraid I'm going to combust.

I think he's going to go to my breasts next, but he doesn't. He bypasses them altogether and goes straight to my feet. On his way down, he sees my dress back over my waist, so he pulls it back down over my panties. He takes each of my heels off, throwing them to the ground and then kisses my big toe. I want to pull it back out of embarrassment, but I don't. I remind myself he needs to be in control.

"I love this color on you," he says, pointing to the blood red nail polish that matches my dress. He nibbles on each toe then moves his way up to my calf, giving it a small kiss before placing my leg back down on the bed. I have no idea where he's going to go next, but I've realized once I allowed him to do what he wants how nice it feels to just let him be in control. All I have to do is lie here and enjoy his touch.

He sits up on his heels and that's when I notice he's not wearing his walking boot. He peels his shirt over his head leaving his amazingly hard body on display for me. I've seen him without his shirt on briefly at Kayla's place but it wasn't long enough to enjoy it. Since he's lived here, he's always come out of his room or bathroom dressed.

Caleb's body is as close to perfection as it can get. He's in great shape from working out but not overly muscular. He has a tattoo going across his chest that reads *Mi vida loca*. Another one on his arm of a woman and surrounding her are clouds and roses. On his side, just under his left peck, says one word: *Trust*. His right nipple is pierced and

I want so badly to grab it and pull on it with my teeth. He has perfect washboard abs I would love to run my tongue down. Just below his abs, his grey sweatpants hang low resting on his perfect hips. I have never wanted anybody as much as I want Caleb.

He crawls back up my body, but instead of taking things further he lies down next to me, wrapping his body around me and pulling me close to him. He grabs my leg and pulls it up and over his thigh intertwining our legs together. He gives me another soft kiss on my lips and one more on my neck before he speaks.

"I think I could make out with you forever." His comment is so innocent, I can't help but laugh. This man, who is obviously a sex god, is perfectly content with just making out.

I point to the words on his chest. "What does this mean?"

He looks down like he needs to see the words before answering. "It means 'My crazy life.' I got it when I first moved out of my dad's house. I went right from under his roof to living with Bentley in Las Vegas. I got a job as a bouncer, the same club I was working at up until I got hurt. I went out with a bunch of guys who all worked at the club one night. I listened to them talk about their problems and realized how fucked up my life was compared to theirs. I met this Hispanic woman that night. After having a few drinks I vaguely told her about what happened between my dad and me. She told me that life can be crazy and all I can do is embrace it, but don't ever let it own me. I got the tattoo the next day. The problem was, I did let my crazy life own me. I got the tattoo to remind me of what she said, but instead I looked at it and allowed it to keep me from living my life. Every time I looked at it, I was reminded of what my stepmom did to me and what I had to do to all those women."

His story is so completely heartbreaking, yet when you look at him, all you see is strength. You would never know how vulnerable he really is.

"What about the other ones?"

"I got the tattoo of the word trust to remind me to trust, but also to remind myself not to trust too easily. My mom and sister both lied to me, and then I trusted my stepmom and I shouldn't have. I'll never make that mistake again."

I want to ask him about his mom and sister but mentally put it aside for later.

"This one," he says, pointing to the one of the woman, "is of my mom. I decided I needed something positive on my body to counteract the negative shit, so I had her picture tattooed on me. She's surrounded by flowers and clouds because she's in heaven."

He brings his shoulder forward to show me another tattoo on the back of his shoulder. It's of a young girl who is surrounded by the same clouds and flowers as his mom. "This one is of my sister, Colette. This was the last picture I have of her alive."

I gasp at his words. How did she die?

It's like he hears my question because he goes on to answer it. We lie in bed for what feels like hours while he rubs circles on my arms and my waist while he tells me stories of his sister and mom from when they were alive. He tells me about his sister lying and being raped and killed, and of his mom's death and how she didn't tell him she was dying until right before she died. He tells me how everything changed after they both passed away. I can't even imagine going through half of what Caleb has been through. He's stronger than anybody I've ever met.

After he's done telling me his stories, he asks about my family. I tell him about my sister, her recent engagement, and how she's my best friend, about how my parents are still married and how close we are. We've lived in Las Vegas our entire lives. I feel guilty because even though my family isn't perfect, we have never been through anything of what he's been through. He notices my hesitancy while talking and grabs my chin for me to look at him.

"Hey, don't feel guilty for having a nice life. Never feel bad for all the good in your life." I continue to tell him how my mom would like to meet Marco. I haven't seen any of them in weeks because they went on a last minute trip to Seattle to visit friends of theirs. Since my dad retired last year, they've been spending their time traveling. I can't wait for them to return to meet Marco. Caleb tells me we should invite them all for dinner. Eventually we fall asleep in each other's arms.

Eighteen

CALEB

WHILE LAST NIGHT DIDN'T EXACTLY GO AS PLANNED, I would like to think it went even better. I never felt such intimacy with a woman before, and the fact that it was all felt without even having to be sexual speaks volumes about our connection. It goes against everything Gloria tried to instill in me. I look down and see Hayley's face mashed up against my chest. Her arm is thrown over my stomach, and her tanned sexy legs are still entwined with mine. She's snoring lightly. I notice she's still in her tight red dress from last night. I almost feel bad that we fell asleep without her changing, but looking at her dress bunched up at her waist, giving me a view of her ass cheeks, makes it worth it.

She stirs awake, rolling onto her back and stretching, and wipes the sleep out of her eyes. She's absolutely beautiful inside and out, and I want her to be mine. She looks down, and when she sees her dress is bunched up, she grabs the blanket and pulls it over her, taking away my great view, which causes me to frown.

She sees my reaction and giggles. "Don't pout." She leans in to give me a kiss but hesitates and backs up, unsure. She doesn't feel comfortable being the one to initiate anything because of the times I have rejected her. I want to tell her it's okay, but the truth is I don't know if it is. I don't know how I feel about not being the one in control. Last night I almost made love to her, but then I had a flashback of a time I was with another woman and I stopped. I don't want anything Hayley and I do to be tainted with my past.

Leaning forward, I pull her in for a kiss. It quickly builds, becoming more intense, when her phone rings ruining the moment. I give her one last chaste kiss on her cheek before heading to the bathroom.

"I'm going to take a shower. Wanna grab breakfast?"

"Sure, let me just call Kayla back. It's probably about Marco since they kept him overnight."

After I get out of the shower, I grab a towel to dry off and head back out through Hayley's room to go get dressed and put my walking boot back on. She's talking to someone on the phone but stops when she sees me. In the past a woman eyeing me made me feel sick. I used to hate the thought of another woman using me for sex, but when Hayley does it, I don't get the same feeling I used to get. I want her to look at me. I want her to want me. It's a foreign concept, but one I welcome.

I give her a small smile and head back to my room. After getting dressed, I hear her shower running so I grab my cellphone to see if I have any missed calls or emails. There's an email from Jarred Harms, the prosecutor assigned to my case, letting me know we need to meet to go over my testimony before we go to court. They have scheduled a court date. He also lets me know two of the men they caught are only being tried with aggravated assault and after they filed an appeal were granted bail. The other two men are being charged with rape and attempted murder, so they'll remain in jail until their hearings. I reply that I can come by next week sometime. I also make note to get an alarm system installed in here. With Hector and Santos around, and now the other two guys out on bail, it worries me to have Hayley and Marco out of my sight.

There's a knock at the door and when I open it, it's a young man holding an envelope.

"Are you Caleb Michaels?"

"Yes."

"Sign here, please." I sign, take the envelope from him, and open it up. It's the court documents pertaining to Gloria's lawsuit. It says I have thirty days to respond or give up my rights to the clubs. I knew these would be arriving soon, but it still pisses me off. I would burn those clubs to the ground before giving her ownership of them.

"What's wrong?" Hayley comes out in tight black jeans that mold to her curves and a loose off-the-shoulder cream sweater that makes me want to kiss her exposed skin. Her hair is wet from her shower and pulled into some sort of side looking braid thing. She looks just as gorgeous as she did last night in a completely different way.

"Gloria is suing me for the clubs. I need to hire an attorney." I sit on the couch and she walks over to sit next to me.

"Do you want the clubs?"

I have given this question a lot of thought, so I already know my answer. "Yeah, I do. Liz and I looked over the books and they turn a nice profit. While Gloria has done some shady shit behind the scenes, I've met a lot of the staff and many of these women and men need this job. I can put an end to the illegal shit she has going on and can make a steady income from these clubs. I would need to hire a new manager for the club in Boulder since I don't want to have to fly out there often and don't trust Gloria, as well as find a manager for the one here once I'm healed and start training again, but I think it would be good."

"Then you should do it. I'll have to check out these strip clubs once they reopen. Why don't we have my family over for dinner and I can ask my sister what she thinks since she's an attorney. Maybe she can even represent you."

"That would be great, thanks." I grab her by her hips and pull her into my lap. Now that I've had a taste of this woman, I can't get enough.

"Was that Kayla on the phone?" I ask, situating her so she's straddling me.

"Yes, she dropped Marco off at school. He loves spending time with Chloe. I'm so glad Kayla and Bentley are getting approved to adopt her."

"They're good people. So are you. You choosing to bring Marco home and making the choice to adopt him is one of the most selfless acts I've witnessed. Providing him this home, a room to call his own, clothes, food...You are amazing."

She nuzzles her face into my shoulder, shaking her head. I pull her back up to look at her. "What's wrong?"

"Nothing, it's just...it doesn't feel selfless...Sometimes it feels like I need Marco more than he needs me."

"What do you mean?"

"Before he moved in here, I felt so alone." She shrugs. "I'm not exactly young, Caleb. I'm in my thirties. I spent so many years focusing on school I never got serious with a guy, and with my younger sister getting engaged I realized maybe having my own kids won't be possible. Adopting Marco means creating my own family. Even if I meet someone one day—taking the time to get to know him, getting married, and him wanting kids, it could be years. What if I'm too old by then and can't have my own kids?"

I think about everything she just said and a gut-wrenching feeling of jealousy consumes me. The thought of her meeting another man and getting married makes my hands tighten on her hips. I want to be that man. I want to be part of that family she just described. I don't, however, want to scare her with too much too soon. Hell, these thoughts are scaring me.

"You are amazing, and Marco is lucky to have you. I love that a family to you isn't just biology and that you already consider Marco your child, but don't give up on having your own kids. Plus...you aren't *that* old." I give her a wink and she glares at me crinkling her nose at the word old.

"I'm not *that* old huh? How old are you?"

"Still in my twenties," I say nonchalantly. I'm only a few years younger than Hayley, but it's fun to mess with her. She slaps my chest laughing and I pull her in for a kiss. Her stomach growls causing us both to laugh, so we head out to get breakfast before she goes to work.

On our way out, I notice the car Hayley was talking about parked a few houses down but don't mention it to her. I don't want to scare her. It's the same car from the day I saw Marco talking to Hector and Santos. The third guy that was there got out of that car. He was the one dressed nicer, looking out of place.

We get to the restaurant, a little hole-in-the-wall place Hayley loves, and the waiter comes over to take our order.

"Hey, Hayley, How are you?"

"I'm good. You?"

I can see the look in his eyes. He wants her. It's obvious they know each other.

"I'm good. I haven't seen you in here recently."

"Things have been crazy busy. Can I get a coffee and the breakfast special?"

"Sure thing," he says, giving her a wink. Is this guy serious? Does he not see me sitting right here with her?

"I'm going to use the restroom to wash my hands." Hayley stands from her seat and heads toward the restrooms. Instead of taking my order, the fucker watches her ass as she walks away.

I clear my throat loudly, causing him to turn to face me. Lifting one brow, I glare at him. "You ready to take my order or would you like to continue to stare at my woman's ass?" Holy fuck. Did I just call her my woman? Yes, I did, because she's mine, and she sure as fuck isn't his.

His eyes go wide, realizing I caught him and he at least has the decency to look a little embarrassed.

"I want a coffee and a water, and I'll have the breakfast special as well."

He nods then scurries off to put in our orders.

When Hayley returns, instead of sitting across from her, I move into the booth next to her.

"What are you doing?"

"I just want to sit next to you."

She giggles and it makes my heart soar. I love that fucking giggle.

The waiter sets our drinks down and lets us know our food will be out shortly.

"The waiter has the hot's for you."

"Oh, stop it!" Hayley says, backhanding my chest playfully. "I've been eating here for years. He just knows me."

"He was watching your ass while you walked away." Hayley's head flies back against the back of the booth and she full-on belly laughs. It reminds me of the day at the gym when I saw Stephen make her laugh like that. I love that I'm the one making her laugh now—even if what I'm saying it true and not meant to be funny.

"Well, I can't stop people from watching my ass," she says, sobering up.

"No, but I can. It's my ass."

"What did you say? That you are an ass?" She laughs again.

"Very funny. I said...It's. My. Ass. I don't want anybody looking at it but me."

"How very alpha of you." Hayley laughs softly and then leans in and gives me a peck on my lips, but I want more. My tongue darts out and finds hers. She tastes sweet as fuck, and I can already tell she's going to become my addiction. As we kiss, my hand lands on her thigh and I squeeze it tightly. I've never wanted a woman as much as I want her.

A clanking sound causes us both to jump, and when I glance up, the waiter is loudly setting down our food. My fist tightens on Hayley's thigh and I can feel her silently shaking with laughter.

Taking her face into my hands, I look her in the eyes. "Mine." Her laughter stops but her smile remains as she nods her head. Damn right, this woman is mine.

After we finish breakfast, Hayley heads to work and I decide to have a chat with Jarred about the car. He lets me know that unless there is any type of physical contact there isn't much he can do. Even if it is Hector and Santos, unless they are breaking a law there is nothing we can do. He also tells me he already has a restraining order out on the men who are out on bail, requiring them to stay a thousand yards from Marco and me until the court hearing. Apparently they're looking into Hector and Santos and the man they work for. His name is Antonio and he's been under surveillance for a while now, but they don't have enough evidence against him to make an arrest. At this point all we can do is keep our eyes peeled and if something more happens let him know.

While I'm there, we go over all the specifics, the questions I'll be asked and how I should answer. Because they're trying all of them separately their attorneys have requested extensions. Luckily I will only have to give my recollection of the events once during my deposition. I won't actually have to take the stand four different times unless their attorney calls me in for cross-examination.

When I leave the courthouse, I see a text from Hayley letting me know her family's coming for brunch this coming Sunday. This will be my first time meeting somebody's parents, which makes me think about the fact that I don't even really know where Hayley and I stand. That's definitely a conversation we should have soon. I realize it's almost three o'clock and head home to meet Marco at the bus stop since Hayley is working late.

"Hey bud! How was your day?"

"Really good! I wrote an essay in Language Arts and the teacher said I am a natural writer. Want to read it?"

"Sure."

He pulls the essay out of his backpack and hands it to me suddenly looking nervous. I begin reading it. The topic is asking him who he looks up to. The entire essay is about me, and how he wants to be just like me. But what tugs at my heart is the fact that there is barely anything even mentioned about me as a fighter. Every example Marco gave was regarding me as a person. He writes about how much I care and how patient I am when teaching him to fight. He writes about how protective I am, referring to me saving him and Hayley the day in the parking lot. Then he writes about when I gave him twenty dollars to play video games and let him order anything he wanted from the kid's menu. He even says it was one of the best days of his life. Damn, this kid is just so unbelievable. To most kids, twenty bucks at an arcade is a normal occurrence, but to Marco he writes about it like he was taken to Disney Land.

I can't help but get choked up, and when I look over at him to tell him how much his essay means to me, he looks unsure of himself. "Marco, this is the best essay I have ever read. The things you wrote about me..." I have to swallow the lump in my throat so I can continue. "Can I keep this, please?"

His face lights up. "You want to keep my essay? You like it that much?"

"It's the nicest thing anybody has ever written about me." I lean over and hug him hard, not wanting to let go.

"How about we go surprise Hayley at work and steal her away so we can go do something fun?"

"Really?"

"Yeah."

We get to the gym and I look for the guys to say hi to, while Marco runs over to a couple kids who are about to begin a class. I find Cooper, Bentley, and Kaden bullshitting near the locker rooms with Alex and Stephen and a couple other younger guys who train here as well. They're all laughing and making digs at Kaden.

"What's up?" I ask, fist bumping everyone.

"We're all going out tonight and Kaden is acting like a little pussy not wanting to go out," Stephen says with a laugh,

"Yeah," Alex chimes in. "I get those two not wanting to go out," he nods toward Bentley and Cooper. "They're pussy whipped with kids, but supposedly Kaden isn't even getting any from Ashley because they're just friends, yet he'd rather go sit on her couch and hang out then try to catch some tail. What happened to the playboy you used to be?"

Kaden laughs it off. Only a few people know Kaden's story and why he acts the way he does. "First of all, keep Ashley's name out of your mouth and second, I'm getting plenty of pussy, you dick. Worry about your damn self."

Just as he says this, he looks over my shoulder like a deer caught in the headlights as Tristan comes running past us toward the class, and trailing behind him is Ashley. She clearly heard his last comment.

She looks hurt but quickly smiles and laughs, playing it off. "Yeah, don't worry. Kaden hanging out with me is only slightly putting a damper on his little black book. Feel free to go out tonight. I have to work anyway."

She walks away without saying a word and Kaden runs after her not giving a shit that they're about to argue in front of half the gym.

"What do you mean you're working tonight? I thought you only worked two days a week."

"Things changed. I have...bills to pay."

"Do you need me to watch Tristan? What's going on?"

"Nothing is going on. And no, I have a babysitter watching him but thank you." She smiles softly at him and then stands on her tippy toes, giving him a kiss on his cheek before walking away from him. Kaden doesn't go after her this time. He just stands there with his jaw clenched. I'm not sure if he's mad at himself for the comment he stupidly made or mad at her for blowing him off and acting like she didn't care. But either way, it's the most emotion I've seen from him since I've known him.

I say bye to the guys and call Marco over to join me. We find Hayley in her office where she's typing away on the computer not realizing we're watching her. I clear my throat and she jumps.

"Jeez, boys! You scared me."

"We're here to steal you," Marco says.

Hayley laughs at the excitement in his voice.

"And where are you going to take me?"

"Caleb said to do something fun, but he didn't say what."

"Well, okay then. I'm all yours." She shuts down her computer and we take off. While I'm driving I hand her the essay Marco wrote. When she's done reading it, her face is wearing a matching expression to how I feel—complete love. Words don't need to be exchanged to know how much we both love that little boy.

We pull up to *GameWorks* and its clear Marco and Hayley have never been here. It's a huge state of the art arcade that also has a five star restaurant and a bowling alley. When we enter through the doors I buy the biggest package possible that includes dinner, a ridiculous amount of credits for the video games, and a game of bowling for the three of us.

Once I hand Marco and Hayley their cards with the credits on them, we walk inside. Marco stops and looks around taking it all in, and Hayley looks at me, grinning wide, knowing what I'm up to. Marco thought the tiny arcade was so amazing—well, this place blows it away. They aren't even in the same league of arcades.

"We can play any game we want?" Marco asks in shock, never having seen anything like this before.

"Anything you want, and you earn tickets that will let you pick out prizes at the end. Now lead the way, kid."

His first stop is air hockey. He and Hayley team up against me. Within minutes I'm kicking their asses but they're both cracking up laughing. Hayley tries to put her arm across the goal to block the puck.

"Really? You're going to resort to cheating?" I taunt her.

"I don't know what you're talking about," she says, leaning over the goal and giving me a tiny peek at her ample cleavage.

"Okay, but when the puck bruises your arm I don't want to hear it." I grab the striker and line up the puck, pretending like I'm going to hit it across the table. Hayley's eyes narrow and her head tilts slightly, daring me to try it.

I hit the puck to the left, knowing Marco will hit it, and sure enough he does. He knocks the puck into my goal and they both jump up and down giving each other a high five. They lost miserably, but it doesn't stop them from cheering about Marco's goal. Hayley walks over to me and gives me a peck on my cheek.

"I knew you wouldn't hurt me."

Taking her by her waist, I say softly so only she can hear, "The only thing I ever want to do is bring you happiness, baby."

Her lips curl up into a gorgeous grin that makes my heart melt.

"C'mon, guys!" Marco yells over the noise of the arcade.

We work our way through the various arcade games. We race each other in Mario Cart, challenge each other shooting hoops in Super Shots Basketball, play the classic Skee-ball game where I know Marco distracts me so Hayley can run up and put her ball into the highest slot, and after we're done playing probably every game imaginable, we take our cards and Marco picks out several dozen crappy prizes that he believes are the best prizes ever. We take a gaming break for dinner and afterward, we take Marco bowling for the first time.

When there is nothing left to play or win, we head home and Marco thanks us no less than a dozen times before he passes out in bed.

Hayley and I cuddle on the couch and partake in a hot make out session while watching *The Bachelor*.

"Thank you, Hayles."

"For what? *GameWorks* was all because of you."

"Yeah, but this life...my newfound happiness...it's all because of you."

Nineteen

HAYLEY

IT'S FRIDAY EVENING AND EVERYBODY'S DECIDED TO MEET at a club on the strip for drinks. While I'm at work I can't help but think about where Caleb and I stand. We haven't had sex yet, but it feels like everything we've done has been even more intimate. The late night talks that lead to the late night kisses and cuddling. If he's able to make my body feel that alive without bringing me to an orgasm, I can't even imagine what will happen when we finally do have sex. My pent up sexual needs are at an all-time high for sure. But I'm letting Caleb run this show even if I die from sexual frustration in the process.

Since I knew I had a late meeting with one of the fighters, I brought a change of clothes with me, and Caleb is dropping Marco off at Bentley's parents' house. Kayla and Ashley are both dropping their kids off there as well. Liz and Cooper are coming out, but his mom is watching their two little ones, wanting some grandma time. As I'm unlocking my car door, I text Caleb to let him know I'll meet him at the club. I'm getting ready to drive off when I notice a piece of paper on my windshield. Ugh! It's probably one of those advertisements to lose weight or for a free dental cleaning. I swing the door open and hop out to grab it from underneath the windshield wiper and shove it into my purse.

I get to the club and valet park. The guy hands me a ticket and I thank him. I spot Caleb waiting for me near the front door and walk up to him. He pulls me into his embrace, giving me a kiss that ends far too soon. We go straight to the bouncer and Caleb must know him because they shake hands and we go right in without having to wait in line.

When we get inside, I see everybody is already here. Kaden and Ashley are sitting together laughing, Bentley has Kayla on his lap, and Liz and Cooper are slow dancing next to the booth. I also notice Alex is there with a couple other guys from the gym. I invited my sister and her fiancé, Gavin, and they're both there talking to Kayla and Bentley. Kayla and Liz both know my sister from her visits over the years. I met Liz and Kayla while working at a bistro with them years ago when I was in medical school.

Caleb and I walk up and everybody's eyes turn to us. I look down nervously, wondering if maybe I have my dress on backward or inside out, but it seems fine. Then I notice Caleb's hand is still in mine, and everybody is staring at our hands. I go to pull my hand away from his, but he grabs ahold of it tighter, giving me an *I don't think so* look. Nobody is sure what to say, so they choose to ignore what is happening and greet us.

Hannah gets up to hug me, but it's a one armed hug since Caleb still won't let go of my hand.

We walk over to Gavin and make introductions. After everybody knows everybody, we find an empty seat and order drinks from the waitress. I go with my favorite, a Lemon Drop martini, and Caleb orders a beer.

"C'mon girls, let's dance!" Kayla yells over the music. She grabs my hand and Liz's with Ashley and Hannah following behind us. We get to the center of the dance floor and the song is one I love. *Somebody* by Natalie La Rose is pumping through the speakers making me want to dance that much more. I get into the song with Ashley. While I can definitely hold my own, this woman has got some serious moves. We're grinding up against each other playfully when a couple of guys come over and ask us to join in. We look at each other, laugh and politely decline, continuing to dance with each other.

After a few minutes I see some of the guys have joined. Kaden steals Ashley away, and since I don't really want to dance with a stranger, I turn to go back to the booth when I run right into Caleb smirking at me. He pulls me close, and even though the song is one people are gyrating to, he slow dances with me.

"The way your body moves is fucking sexy, Hayles," he whispers into my ear. "I want you...tonight." His words send a shudder down my spine. I back up a little to look at him and see the lust in his eyes. I nod and put my head against his chest, continuing to slow dance in the middle of the fast song, not caring about anything other than how much I want this man. His hands go to my ass and he grabs ahold of me pulling me closer into him. I can feel his hard-on rubbing against me making me want to grind on him. When his leg hits my center I can feel how turned on I am as sparks fly straight to my core. I don't just want this man. I need him, like now. He chuckles softly into my ear as if he knows exactly what I'm thinking.

When the song ends and the emcee announces some drink specials before playing the next song, we head back to the booth to get another drink. We all hang out for a few hours, but I don't drink anymore. I want to be fully sober tonight. I want to remember everything. Then I get nervous...We haven't discussed what we are to each other, but hopefully tonight won't be a one-time thing. How should I act? Do I just lie there and let him do everything? I'm probably overthinking this, but I don't want to screw it up.

"What's got you frowning?" Kayla asks nudging me. I confide in her since she knows about Caleb's past.

"You know what you have to do, right?"

"Umm...no...what?"

Her face lights up with mischief. "We need to leave early and handcuff you to the bed!"

I'm unfortunately taking a sip of my drink as she says this so my water sprays all over the place.

"Excuse me?" I whisper, looking around to make sure nobody else heard her.

"Handcuffs...If you're handcuffed, you're giving him one hundred percent control, and then you don't have to worry about what you should be doing. He'll be doing it all."

I hate to admit it but she has a point. "Where would I get handcuffs this late?"

"Oh, I have them in my glove box," Kayla says like it's perfectly normal to have handcuffs in one's glove box. I raise my eyebrows up in question, but she just tells me it's a long story.

She whispers something to Bentley causing him to laugh then she announces our departure, saying she needs me to give her a ride somewhere before I head home. She grabs my phone and texts Caleb to meet me at home in a half hour before dragging me along behind her.

We get to my house and it's pitch black. Caleb must have forgotten to leave the outside light on. I walk inside, flip the light on, and step back outside to make sure it's working when I see that same car parked down the street. I need to remember to let Caleb know. Something is definitely off, and he mentioned getting a threatening note when we got back from Boulder. What if it's the same people? Before I can think any more about it, Kayla dangles the handcuffs in front of my face making me nervous.

"C'mon! Strip down into nothing but your bra and underwear."

"WHAT??" I squeal out.

"If you're handcuffed he won't be able to take your clothes off," she says like *duh!*

I quickly rinse off in the shower and then after taking several calming breaths put on my sexiest bra and panty set and get onto the bed to be handcuffed.

Kayla takes the handcuffs and puts them around the bedpost and then locks them around my wrists loosely. I look at them and see they're made of pink feather-like material so they won't rub my wrists raw.

"I don't even want to know why you have pink feathered handcuffs."

Kayla laughs. "Looking at you all sexy on this bed, if I swung that way I would totally be having my way with you right now."

I crack up laughing. "Get out! I'm going to lose my courage."

"Sorry, girly, but it's a little too late for that. I'll leave the key on the nightstand though."

"Oh God! I can't believe I'm doing this."

Kayla laughs again, shaking her head. "Since Caleb has a key, I'll lock the door on my way out. Good luck!"

"Wait! How are you getting home? We took my car."

"Bentley is outside waiting for me." She winks and then turns off all lights, leaving only the glow of the nightlight from the bathroom. A few seconds later, I hear the door close, leaving me here by myself to do nothing but second-guess myself.

Twenty

CALEB

WHEN KAYLA SAID SHE NEEDED HAYLEY TO TAKE HER somewhere I thought maybe Hayley was trying to get out of being with me. I made it clear to her that I want her tonight, but instead of going home, she's running errands with Kayla? After they ran out, I felt my phone buzz in my pocket.

Hayley: Meet me at home in thirty minutes ;)

Okay, I'm not sure what is going on, but I will definitely be meeting her at home in thirty minutes. Bentley says he needs to get going, but not before slapping me on my back and laughing. "Good luck tonight, bro."

I hang out with everyone else for a few more minutes and then excuse myself for the night. The drive home feels like it takes forever wondering what the hell Hayley is up to.

I get home and walk into the dark, quiet house. "Hayley?" I call out but don't hear anything. I turn on the living room light, so it's not pitch black and make my way to her bedroom first. When I open the door it's dark, but there's a small light shining through, and on the bed I see the most exquisite image laid out right in front of me.

Hayley is spread out on the bed in nothing but a tiny black bra and matching panties. They are nothing more than scraps of material barely covering her, and as I get closer the faint light shows me they're see-through. Her nipples are hard and poking through the cups of her bra and her legs are closed tight together. She looks absolutely breathtaking...and nervous.

"This was Kayla's idea. We thought it would give you control, you know, so I can't touch you. You can touch me and do whatever you want to me. But while I've waiting for you, I started to think, what if me lying here isn't giving you control because I'm initiating the sex by lying here in the first place, but you did say you want me tonight, so technically you initiated it..." She's rambling on, afraid I'm going to push her away, and all I have stuck in my head is the part where she said I could do whatever I want to her. My dick twitches at the sight of this woman handcuffed and willing to make herself completely vulnerable and uncomfortable just to make me comfortable.

I step up next to the bed and lean down to kiss her, mostly to stop her from second-guessing herself, but also because I need to taste her. She tastes of toothpaste with a hint of lemon from her drink earlier. She tastes amazing, and then I wonder what her other lips taste like. My dick twitches again at the thought.

When I break the kiss, she opens her mouth to say something else, but before she can speak I put my fingers to her lips to quiet her, shaking my head.

"You are absolutely breathtaking, baby." She looks down and if the lights were on, I would bet her cheeks are shaded with a light pink tint in embarrassment.

"Don't be embarrassed, Hayles. This is the most selfless, thoughtful thing anybody has done for me."

I remove my shirt and walking boot and then my jeans, leaving myself in only my briefs, and crawl over her to sit on top of her legs.

A flashback begins to hit me...A time from my past when I was in this same position with another woman, but I shake it off immediately. I refuse to let my past ruin this moment. I take in a deep breath and focus on the beautiful woman in front of me.

"Baby, I can't wait to make you scream my name." I reach forward and tweak one of her nipples through her bra. She wiggles and I know she's turned on. I don't really know where to start. Every time I had sex somebody was telling me what to do, what she wanted, what she needed. I never had to think about how to please a woman. I just did what I was told.

Looking at Hayley, all I want is to please her. I want to explore her body and find out for myself what turns her on. I want to see what makes her scream and squirm and orgasm. I want to know every inch of this woman. I lift myself off her and spread her legs so I'm now between them. I lean over her and start with kissing her. If I could spend the rest of my life simply kissing this woman I would be a satisfied man.

While still kissing her, I take one hand and pull her bra cup down, exposing her pert nipple. I break the kiss and move my mouth to her nipple, licking around the tight pink nub. She squirms a little, releasing a soft moan that causes my dick to remind me he's still here. I push the other cup down and lick around her other nipple while pinching the one I'd just licked.

"Oh, Caleb."

Her soft sounds let me know she's enjoying this. I take the bud into my mouth and suck on it. I notice her tits fit perfectly in my hands while I massage them, switching from nipple to nipple, sucking hard on each one and then licking the pain away.

"Caleb, please..." The handcuffs clink against the bedpost as she attempts to move. She wants more. She wants to tell me what she wants, but she stops knowing I need this. I need the control.

I suck on each nipple one more time before I begin to trail kisses down her flat stomach toward her pussy. When I get to it, it's covered with the same fabric as her bra, but it is glistening wet. I touch her middle and feel the wetness covering the material. My girl is dripping for me. I pull her panties down her legs and throw them to the side.

Her pussy is trimmed neatly and all I want to do is put my nose right up to the center to smell her scent...so I do. I inhale deeply and can smell the strawberry scented body wash she uses with a bit of something else that is just her. I spread her lips, so I can lick up her slit and I'm addicted. She moans out my name and her legs try to close. I push them back apart and lick from bottom to top, lapping up her juices.

"Do you like that, Hayles?"

"Yes, please," she says, sounding out of breath.

I push a finger into her and then another. Her ass comes off the bed meeting my thrusts as I fingerfuck her. It's even more fulfilling knowing I'm causing this woman's pleasure by choice and doing as I want to. I take a third finger and push it into her warmth continuing to lick her clit. Moving my fingers inside her in a come-hither motion I feel when I hit her G-spot. She screams out and my fingers are instantly coated with her arousal. I keep moving them inside her while licking and lapping at her clit. Her pussy tightens, so I lick faster and harder until she comes all over my hand and mouth.

"Oh my God! Caleb!" Hayley screams out, but I don't stop my fingers or tongue until she completely rides out her orgasm. Once I know she's satisfied, I grab my shirt from the floor and wipe off her juices. Then I climb up the bed on top of her.

"I want..." she begins to say but stops. That's when it hits me. Everything with this woman is so different. I want to do what she wants. I want to please her. And while I want to be in control, I also want her to be in control. I don't want her to ever not be able to tell me what she wants or needs because of my past. Trying to find my control has caused her to give up her own and that doesn't sit well with me at all. We need to find a balance.

"Tell me, baby. Tell me what you want."

"I want..."

"It's okay. I want to know. Tell me, Hayles."

"I want your dick in my mouth...please."

And if that request doesn't cause my already hard cock to get harder...

I move to release the handcuffs and she stops me. "No, just move up on my chest and put it in my mouth."

Fuck! This woman is just full of surprises. I straddle her upper body and move my cock slowly toward her mouth, not wanting to force it in. She lets out a frustrated huff and a few seconds later her knees hit my ass pushing me closer. Then she lifts her head to take me in her mouth. I move close enough so she can suck me but not too close that I'm choking her. She licks the slit and then swirls her tongue around the head, causing me to almost come on the spot. In my defense, it's been over seven years since I've been with a woman, and never one I wanted as badly as I want Hayley.

She takes me in farther and I know if I let her continue I'm going to explode in her mouth.

"Baby, stop." I back away and undo the handcuffs before climbing back on top of her. I need to make love to this woman and I need her hands on me.

Her hands are freed, but she lies still, unsure of what to do.

"Thank you for tonight. For giving me the control. But I was wrong, Hayles. I want you to be in control, too. I want you to touch me. Please, baby."

I see tears glossing over her eyes and then one falls down the side of her cheek. I bring my lips to her cheek to kiss the fallen tear, as I slowly push into her.

"Wrap your arms around my neck, baby." And she does. Her arms come up around my neck tightly as her legs wrap around my back, pushing my cock into her, and for the first time in my life I make love to a woman willingly.

Twenty-One

HAYLEY

I CAN FEEL THE SUN HITTING MY FACE SO IT MUST BE morning. I stretch my body and can feel the soreness between my legs. After Caleb made love to me, we showered together and once back in bed made love again before falling asleep wrapped in each other's arms. Sometime early this morning my phone went off waking us up. It was Ashley letting me know she's picking up the kids and will pick up Marco as well so we can sleep in. I was so exhausted I immediately fell back asleep.

Now I'm awake and when I look over I see the bed is empty next to me. Caleb must have already woken up. I jump in the shower quickly and while I'm washing myself it hits me we didn't use protection nor am I on birth control. I highly doubt I'll get pregnant from one night of unprotected sex, but isn't that what everyone says before they find out they're having an *Oops! Baby?*

I make a mental note to pick up condoms until I can get on birth control. I inhale deeply and smell the coffee beckoning me. I throw a shirt on and grab a pair of underwear from my drawer before following the aroma of caffeine. I also remind myself I need to let Caleb know we didn't use protection. When I get to the kitchen, he's sitting at the table with a piece of paper in front of him, looking pissed off.

"What's up?" I ask, ignoring the coffee calling my name and forgetting the birth control talk we needed to have.

"Why didn't you tell me about this?" he growls, causing me to stop in my tracks.

I look at the paper that looks like the one I grabbed off my windshield last night and read what it says. I was wrong. It's not an advertisement...it's a handwritten threat.

Snitches get stitches. Tell your boyfriend to back off or you'll both regret it.

I drop the note on the table and feel myself shaking. "Caleb, I didn't know it said this. I thought it was an ad, like for weight loss or something. It was on my windshield when I got into my car last night. I threw it into my purse without looking at it. Is that where you got it? My purse?"

His anger morphs into worry and he pulls me onto his lap. "I'm sorry, Hayles. I thought you saw this and kept it from me. Yes, I got it from your purse. I was moving it from the counter to the desk to make coffee and it fell over. The note fell out. We have to report this to the police. This is a threat. Just like the one I found at the airport. My guess is, this is Hector and Santos trying to scare us so I won't testify against the guys who tried to kill me. Get dressed and we'll go by the station before we pick up Marco."

After bringing the note to the station and reporting the threat, where they said they can run fingerprints but can't really do much because it could be from anyone, we go to Ashley's to pick up Marco. When she answers the door, her eyes look red and puffy like she's been crying, so I ask Caleb to go check on the boys to give us a minute alone.

"What's going on?"

She slumps in defeat and the tears start again.

"Kaden and I almost had sex last night, but he totally pulled the brakes on it when things got hot and heavy. I just don't get it. He's with women all the time, but he won't sleep with me. It just doesn't make sense. I'm so stupid. I know we aren't anything more than friends. I never should have let things get that far. Hopefully he'll act like it never happened. He has become one of my best friends.

Then we got into a fight this morning when I told him I wouldn't take money from him when he saw a couple of my bills on the counter. I can't let him pay for my mistakes. We aren't even together. I'm just so exhausted from working two jobs. I'm tired of having to have my parents and the babysitter watch Tristan so often, but it's what I need to do."

Ashley seems to purposely leave out what bills she needs to pay, so I don't press her. I wrap her up in a hug and tell her it'll be okay not really sure if that's true but not sure of what else to say. We hear the loud footsteps approaching and when we look up Caleb is standing in the doorway.

"What's wrong?" Caleb asks, clearly worried for Ashley.

"Umm..." I'm not sure what she wants him to know, so I give her a look telling her to tell him what she wants.

"Why won't Kaden sleep with me?" she blurts out.

Caleb's eyes go wide with shock and maybe even a bit of nervousness before he quickly composes himself. "Ashley, I can assure you Kaden really does care about you, however, I can't answer that question for you. That's Kaden's story to tell."

Ashley and I exchange confused glances, but Caleb walks away calling out to Marco it's time to go, making it clear he's not going to say anything else on the topic.

"That's interesting...So Kaden has a story to tell?" I whisper to Ashley.

"I have no idea," she says clearly as puzzled as I am.

"Ready to go?" Caleb asks with Marco by his side. Tristan plops onto the couch and begins to flip through the channels.

"Hey, sweetie!" I give Marco a kiss on his cheek and hug him tightly. I missed him last night. He has become a part of us and when he isn't around, it feels like a piece is missing.

I hug Ashley once more goodbye.

"Call me if you need anything," I whisper to her.

"Thank you."

After leaving Ashley's house, we decide to stop at a local restaurant for lunch and to figure out what to do the rest of the day. Grabbing a newspaper, Caleb looks at what is going on locally. While flipping through the pages the real estate section falls out causing me to ask the question I don't really want to ask but know I need to.

"Have you looked at any apartments?"

Before Caleb can answer, Marco grabs the paper. "What do you mean? Who's moving?"

Caleb takes the paper from Marco. "Nobody, buddy. We aren't moving anywhere."

"Oh, good. I like where we live. Plus you guys just painted my room. You would have to paint it again. And if we move, I would have to switch schools and I like my school."

"We aren't moving anywhere and you definitely don't have to switch schools, but Caleb..." Before I can finish my sentence, Caleb cuts me off.

"Nobody is moving anywhere." Caleb glares at me and balls the paper up. "Now let's figure out what to do today." He's shut down the conversation of moving just like he shut down the conversation regarding Kaden. While Kaden isn't my business, he must know our living situation is and it's something we need to discuss. Maybe he just wants to wait to discuss it until we are alone.

"There's indoor miniature golf, Hershey's Chocolate World, The Children's park, or the Aquarium."

Marco gives it some thought. "Can we go to the aquarium? But can we invite Bella? She loves dolphins and I know she would love it."

"Sure," Caleb says. "Let me call Liz and Cooper and see what they're up to today."

He gives them a call and since they have no plans they join us.

And that's how we spend our day, at the aquarium as a family. I wonder in this moment if life can possibly get any better.

Twenty-Two

CALEB

AFTER I PUT A STOP TO THE APARTMENT HUNTING TALK, we enjoyed the rest of our day at the aquarium. Sure it's probably not a good idea to ignore the obvious, like the fact that I'm capable of living on my own and shouldn't be shacking up with a woman I may or may not be in a relationship with, but can you blame me? When everyone you want and need is under the same roof, who in his right mind would want to move out from under said roof? Sure as hell not me.

I'm not ignorant to believe by ignoring the facts they'll go away, but I'm hoping maybe I can come up with a plan to keep myself under the same roof as the two most important people in my life, especially with the recent threat to Hayley. It's even more important I continue to live with them...for their safety, of course.

Being at the aquarium with Marco is like experiencing everything again for the first time. He has got to be one of the most grateful, innocent kids I've ever met. He's truly thankful for everything he is given. It just sucks he's come to be this way because of the shitty life he was raised in. I would rather him be a spoiled brat than him having witnessed his druggie mom being raped and then committing suicide.

Every single time Hayley or I bought him something he would light up like he was being given the most incredible gift. It made me want to just keep buying him stuff to see his face light up. We walked around the aquarium all day with Cooper and his family and as I compared us to them I realized to the naked eye we look just like them—a family. And that is exactly what I want—a family with Hayley. Biological or not, I don't care, as long as it's with her, and Marco is a part of it.

We get home and Marco showers and passes out from exhaustion. We both fall onto the couch equally exhausted and laugh. I could listen to her laugh forever.

"Your family will be here in like twelve hours for brunch. We should probably get some sleep." But even hearing myself say these words, I don't believe them.

"Mmm...I know, but I just want to cuddle with you." And if by cuddle she means rubbing her palm on top of my dick making it jump, then cuddling is definitely what we're about to do.

"Can you be quiet?" I whisper into her ear. A slow mischievous smile creeps across her face and she nods. I stand and, taking her hand in mine, guide her to the room and close the door behind us.

We aren't even all the way in the room before she's pulling her clothes off her body while I'm doing the same to mine. She finishes quicker and before I can push my boxers down she grabs hold of them and pushes them down for me, her body going to the floor with them. Out of instinct, I almost push her off me but catch myself at the last second. My head hits the back of the door with a thump and I close my eyes for a second to calm myself down. A flashback hits of a woman giving me head and I have to open my eyes to remind myself it's Hayley and not another woman in this moment with me.

I look down at Hayley on her knees before me as she takes my cock in her hand and, after kissing the tip and swirling her tongue around the head, deep throats me like she doesn't have a gag reflex.

My hips thrust forward as the pleasure of her mouth assaults me causing me to almost come on the spot. Not wanting to come in her mouth in two seconds, I reach down and force her mouth off my dick, picking her up and tossing her onto the bed on her stomach, ass in the air. I land a playful smack to her ass cheek when another flashback assaults me of the last time I had sex in Boulder, but I shake it off willing my brain to remain in the here and now with Hayley. She deserves my full attention.

She looks back at me with a smirk and then wiggles her ass without saying a word. Lying down on the bed, I lift her pussy up into the air a little more and then attack her clit with my tongue from behind. I lick and suck and then move the juices with my tongue to her ass, sticking one finger into her tight hole. I feel her tighten up and know she hasn't been taken there. It's probably a horrible thought to have but knowing she's never been claimed in the ass makes me want to try to replace my old memories with new ones that are with Hayley.

I go back to licking her pussy and sucking on her clit until she's coming all over my mouth.

"Baby, I'm going to claim your ass." She doesn't give me anything but a moan, letting me know she is down. Knowing her juices won't be enough, I grab some KY jelly from the drawer and smear it onto my dick and into her tight hole. I start off by sticking one finger back in her ass, fingering it slowly.

"I need more," she begs, so I give her more. I add another digit and continue fingerfucking her ass. I reach over and have her sit up straight so I can massage her tits. Pinching her nipple, she shivers and begins to ride my fingers with her ass, needing a release.

Once I know she's ready, I remove my fingers from her ass and replace them with my dick, slowly lowering Hayley onto me until she's taken me all the way inside of her. I bring my hands to her breasts and massage them.

She wiggles her ass, needing me to move, but instead of me being in control, I give it to her.

"Ride my dick, Hayles. Move up and down." And she does. She begins to bounce her ass on my cock and fuck if it doesn't feel good in her tight ass. Bringing my hand down from one of her breasts, I fingerfuck her to the same rhythm she's bouncing on my dick. I add another digit and one more and within minutes she's coming all over my fingers. "Oh my God, Caleb. I feel so full." Her orgasm causes her to push down farther onto my dick and within seconds I'm releasing my seed into her.

We both come to a stop, and moving her sweaty hair off her shoulder, I give her a kiss on her neck before she pulls herself off me.

"Shower with me?"

"I wouldn't have it any other way, baby." I give her a kiss and we make our way to the shower where we end up making love against the wall.

Twenty-Three

HAYLEY

AFTER WE HAVE SEX UP AGAINST THE SHOWER WALL, CALEB washes my body from head to toe and then I gladly return the favor. Once the water goes cold, we get out and Caleb runs to his room to grab a change of clothes. While I'm drying off I feel the excess of cum in me. I can't believe we seriously forgot to use protection again. I'm a freaking doctor for God's sake. I know the risks.

When Caleb comes into my room, dressed, he can tell right away something is wrong.

"We didn't use protection," I blurt out.

"I'm clean, Hayles. I was tested after I left Boulder years ago and you're the only person I've been with since then. Wait...have you been with someone else? Alex?"

"Whoa there! Back up. I haven't been with anybody but you. My point is I'm not on birth control and we had unprotected sex several times. I know better than this."

He just shrugs "Oh."

"Oh? What do you mean 'Oh'?"

"You said it yourself, Hayles...you're getting older..."

I'm in the middle of putting on my comfy reading socks when he says this and my head whips around to glare at him. "Excuse me?"

He throws his head back with a laugh. "I'm just kidding, babe." He walks over and sits next to me, turning my head to face him. "I'm just saying if you get pregnant, would it really be that bad? You said you wanted to have a baby..."

"So I shouldn't get on birth control?" I ask, just making sure I'm hearing him correctly.

"No, and if it happens it happens."

"But we aren't even together, Caleb..."

"Yes, we are. You're mine and I'm yours, Hayles. I have already told you that before. I'm not going anywhere, ever."

"Okay," I say, trying to remain calm and not run through the streets shouting that Caleb just said he's mine. Instead, I give him a chaste kiss on his lips and say, "I like the sound of that." Then we climb into my bed and he holds me close. We lie in silence for a few minutes and I think he might be asleep when he says, "You know how you mentioned talking to your sister for me? If she agrees to help me, I'm going to have to tell her my story."

I roll over to face him and, taking his chin in my fingers, give him a soft kiss. "She isn't going to judge you."

"I know. I just don't know how I'll feel if I have to start telling everybody especially in the open, like in court."

"What's really going on, Caleb?"

"What if everybody finds out and thinks I'm a pussy? I spent years fucking women. Most guys would high five each other over it, not cry rape."

My blood boils at the way he thinks people would view what happened to him. "Anybody who would want to high five someone for being blackmailed and forced to have sex at fifteen years old needs some serious help. Nobody that matters will think any less of you, and I'll be there every step of the way."

Caleb nods and gives me one more kiss before rolling me back over to spoon me from behind. Within minutes I can hear the evenness of his breathing and know he's asleep. I vow to myself, if I ever get the chance, I will destroy Gloria for what she's done to Caleb.

I wake up to an empty bed and hear cartoons on the television out in the living room. Caleb must have let me sleep in and gotten up with Marco. After showering and getting dressed, I make my way out to join my guys.

"Morning sleepyhead," I say to Marco, fluffing his hair as I walk by him cuddled up in his blankets, barely awake, watching cartoons. I head to the kitchen to grab a pen and paper to make a list of items we need for brunch. Before I make it to the kitchen, Caleb grabs me by my waist and pulls me toward him. I bend over and give him a kiss without thinking about it.

"Are you two boyfriend and girlfriend?" Marco asks, obviously seeing the kiss.

Caleb looks at me then to Marco. "Would it be okay with you if we were?"

Marco rolls his eyes. "I told you a long time ago you wanted to give her cooties."

I'm not sure what he's talking about but I can't help but laugh.

"Yeah, yeah. Marco told me months ago I liked you."

"Smart kid." I give Caleb a wink and make my list.

Marco and I head to the store while Caleb picks up the house and waits for everyone to arrive. After walking up and down the aisles and me agreeing to get all the junk food Marco suggests, we head to the register to check out. After bagging up the groceries, Marco pushes our cart to the car. My phone dings with a text, so I check it.

Hannah: On our way! See you soon.

Me: Sounds good!

I'm hoping Hannah will be able to help Caleb get the clubs from his stepmom, so he'll be rid of her for good, but that would mean he would have to tell her everything. I'm not sure he'll be comfortable doing that.

I look up from my text and run right into the back of Marco. When I begin to ask why he's stopped, I glance around him and see words written across the side of my vehicle.

LAST WARNING BITCH!

Instinctively, my hands grab Marco's shoulders. While scanning the area for any sign of threat, I practically drag him and the cart back to the store. Once we're inside, I call Caleb.

"Hello?" he answers on the first ring.

"I need you," I say, trying to hold back my tears. I need to be strong for Marco. I don't want to scare him.

"What's wrong?" he practically shouts, hearing the fear in my voice.

"We're at the store and someone wrote on my car. I need you to come and get us. I don't know what to do."

"I will be right there. Stay in the store, in plain sight. Okay? I'm going to three-way the police, so we don't have to get off the phone." Caleb calls the police and tells them to meet him at the store.

Once Caleb and the police arrive, they take pictures and ask questions. They say they're going to ask the store about cameras to see if they can see who did it.

"Why are they threatening me?" I ask the officers on scene. I'm not even the one testifying against them. I wasn't there. Only Caleb is testifying. Marco is underage, so he gave his statement, but we agreed it's best for him not to testify.

"My guess is they're hoping the threats will force Caleb to drop the charges out of fear for you."

"Which I won't do," Caleb says, putting his arm around me and pulling Marco into his side.

"The court date has been moved up because the prosecutor found significant evidence of drug trafficking and is ready to nail several of the guys," the officer says. "I think this is their way of trying to get Caleb to back down. With his testimony to the attempted murder charges, these guys will be going away for a long time."

Caleb offers to take my car through a car wash on his way home and insists I take his truck home with Marco.

We get home just as my parents are pulling in. I don't want to worry them, so I don't bring up why we're running late. They help me bring in the groceries and then I make introductions.

"Marco, this is my mom and dad, Lori and Bill. Mom, Dad, this is Marco."

My mom grabs Marco in a hug and tears spring to her eyes. Even though she hasn't met him yet she's listened to me talk about him the last couple months and has seen all the photos I've posted and sent her. She already views him as her grandson.

"Nonsense! You call me Nana and him Pop." She continues to wrap Marco in a hug until I insist she let him go so he can breathe.

"I don't really mind," Marco says with tears shining in his eyes. The thought of a child crying because of receiving love and affection makes me want to pull his mother out of the grave and beat her, but I stop the thoughts because the truth is she was sick. She had a lot of problems and wasn't given the chance or opportunity to fix them. I can't waste my energy being mad at her. I just want to feel blessed I get to have Marco in my life.

Caleb walks in and sees all of us practically in tears and looks horrified.

"What the hell happened?"

"Nothing," I say, laughing through my tears. "My mom was just very excited to finally meet Marco. Mom, Dad, this is Caleb. Caleb, this is my mom and dad."

"Nice to finally meet you, Bill and Lori." He gives my dad a handshake and then gives my mom a kiss on her cheek.

There's a knock at the door and in walks Hannah and Gavin with presents in their hands. Hannah has met Marco several times and insisted he call her Aunt Hannah once she found out I'm adopting him.

"Hey, kiddo!" Hannah hands him the gifts and gives him a hug.

"Are these for me? But it's not my Birthday." Marco looks confused.

"I don't need a reason to buy my favorite nephew gifts. Now go open them!"

My mom says she's going to the kitchen to start brunch and insists we all hang out while she cooks. Since Marco is busy with the new stuff Hannah and Gavin brought him, I mention to Hannah about Caleb needing an attorney.

"So, it's not really my story to tell but Caleb was left some clubs his dad owned, and his stepmom is fighting him for them. Do you think it would be possible to help him?"

"I can pay you of course," Caleb says. Hannah waves him off. Money is the last thing she needs. Gavin comes from old money and between the two of them being attorneys they're not struggling to make ends meet.

"Caleb, why don't you come and see me this week?" She hands him her card. "We can sit down and discuss your options." She looks at her phone and then says, "Actually I have a cancellation for tomorrow morning. Would that work for you?" He looks over the card and then to me. "Yes, we'll be there," I tell her.

"Thank you," Caleb adds.

"Hayley! Look what Aunt Hannah got me!" Marco waves a pad

of paper and colored pencils in the air. He had mentioned he loved coloring to us one day at lunch and of course she remembered.

"Thank you so much!" He runs over and gives her a hug.

"You're very welcome, kiddo."

Hannah and I join mom in the kitchen to help her finish up brunch while the guys set the table and pour drinks. Once the food is set out and we're about to dig in, Hannah says they have an announcement to make.

"So, we were hoping to do the whole engagement, marriage, then baby thing in order but..."

"Oh my God!" Mom yells, springing from her seat to give Hannah and Gavin a hug.

"Yep! We're expecting. I'm only three months along, but we have decided to move the wedding up so we're married before the baby comes."

"Congratulations!" I say, getting up to give each of them a hug. My dad and Caleb both congratulate them as well. We all start eating, when Marco says, "So that's what it takes to have a baby? You just have to be together?"

I drop my fork on my plate and look to Caleb for help. But of course he has a shit-eating grin on his face. He's such a damn guy. I guess I'll be handling this one myself.

"It's more than that. Two people have to love each other and when they're ready, they choose to share a bed and they create a baby."

He nods and goes back to eating. I hold my breath, hoping he's done. I definitely plan to have the sex talk with him, but I'm hoping this will pacify him while we're all eating and we can discuss this in private.

"Okay, so does that mean you and Caleb are going to have a baby since you guys shared a bed and you're boyfriend and girlfriend?"

Oh my word! He just had to go there. He is lucky I love his cute little behind.

Caleb cracks up laughing until I give him a death glare. He attempts to control his smile, but I can still see it peeking through.

"You and Caleb are together?"

"When did this happen?"

"How did I not know?"

Between my mom, dad, and Hannah, I'm being bombarded with questions that I have no idea how to answer. What I would like to do is take a biscuit and chuck it at Caleb's head. I grab ahold of the biscuit in one hand and just as I'm about to take aim and fire, he takes my hand in his and smiles warmly.

First, he answers Marco's question. "Marco, there's a little bit more to creating a baby, and after Nana and Pop and everyone leave, we'll sit down and discuss it, okay? As for right now, no we're not having a baby."

Then he says, "And yes, Hayles and I are dating, and yes, we slept in the same bed last night. I care a lot about her."

Everybody seems to accept his answer and thankfully goes back to eating. I look over at him and he leans in and whispers, "And I fully plan to practice those baby making skills...Every. Single. Night."

His words cause my cheeks to heat and I quickly look around

grateful nobody heard him. I squirm a little in my seat and he chuckles next to me, then reaches over and takes a bite out of the biscuit I had envisioned hitting him on the side of the head with.

Twenty-Four

CALEB

IT'S MONDAY MORNING. AFTER PUTTING MARCO ON THE bus, Hayley and I head downtown to her sister's office to speak with her. On our way I stop at the bank to get the recording my dad left for me in the safety deposit box. I figure if Hannah is going to hopefully represent me she should be aware of all the evidence I can bring to the table in hope of Gloria dropping her lawsuit for the two clubs. And I'm hoping we can get her to drop them sooner rather than later. There are employees that need to work to make a living and if we don't figure this out soon I'm going to eventually have to dish out more money to keep them employed.

After I run in to get the recording, which was exactly where my dad said he left it, we go to Hannah's office. Once inside, she ushers us straight back to her office and closes the door.

"Okay, what do you have for me?"

How do I even begin to explain all this? Thankfully Hayley is here and takes over.

"Caleb received two clubs from his father when he passed away. Technically his stepmom ran them, but his dad owned them outright and left them to Caleb. Now his stepmom, Gloria, is fighting for them."

"Okay...what am I missing?" She's a lawyer—of course she senses there is more to the story. And she isn't asking Hayley—she's asking me.

I clear my throat and then proceed to tell her everything—starting with my stepmom forcing me to have sex with her at fifteen to her pimping me out to other women.

"And you said your dad left you a recording of her confessing?"

"Yeah." I pull the flash drive out of my pocket and hand it to her. "I haven't heard it yet. I just grabbed it out of the safety deposit box on my way over."

"Do you mind?"

"No, go ahead."

She plugs it into the side of her computer and, after clicking on the file, presses play. I hear my dad's voice come over the speakers. It's crystal clear like he knew he would be recording.

"Gloria, I want a divorce."

"I don't really think that's what you want, Adam. I would hate to have to turn you in for insider trading."

"I don't care what you do anymore. I can't be with you knowing you forced my son to have sex with you and then forced him to have sex with other women. It's disgusting. I should have divorced you sooner."

"Don't be mad because he was better in bed than you! And give me a break. I'm less than ten years older than him. You're almost twenty years older

than me, Adam."

"That's true, but you had sex with him when he was fifteen years old, Gloria! You were of legal age when we got together. And then when I caught you guys, you made it sound like it was entirely his fault. None of this was his fault. I lost my son because of you."

"No, Adam. You lost your son because you are self-centered and chose to save yourself over him."

Hannah hits stop on the computer. "Well, I would say we have enough to definitely scare the shit out of her, and if she still wants to go to court, between the letter from your dad, the will, and the recording, we have a very strong case. What you need to understand, though, is if this goes to court it will become public knowledge about you being raped and used as a male escort. Are you okay with that?"

I know what she's saying. In today's society a man being raped isn't the same as a woman being raped. As a UFC fighter, the attention this will get will be ridiculous, even if I'm not extremely popular. This is exactly what I said to Hayley, but when Hayley told me she would be by my side I knew my decision. I'm not letting Gloria get away with this.

"I understand and I'm willing to deal with the shit storm that will follow. I can't let her win. Let's hope she walks away without fighting."

"Okay, I'll file a response with the court requesting mediation and hopefully when she sees the evidence laid out against her she'll be smart enough to cut her losses and walk away."

"What should I do about paying the employees? I've had to pay them all for several weeks now. It was only supposed to be one week then it turned to two. Now I've been paying them for weeks."

"I'll also put in that if she chooses to take it to trial she'll need to pay half of the employees' incomes while the clubs assets are frozen. I'll give you a call once I know anything."

Damn, she's good.

"Thank you so much. If you need anything from me please let me know. Who do I see to pay your retainer fee?"

"Don't be silly, Caleb. We're practically family. Family doesn't charge family."

"Thanks, Hannah."

Hannah comes around her desk and gives Hayley a hug and then we head out.

After we leave the office, Hayley says she's going to pick up Marco from the bus and then she needs to go to the gym to meet with a couple fighters.

"I think I'll join you guys. Kayla mentioned I'm allowed to do light workouts again."

"Okay, sounds good. Let's go home first, so you can change and grab your gym gear. "

Once we get home, I run into my room to grab some workout clothes. I'm walking through the house half-dressed checking my phone when Hayley stops me.

"You can't walk around the house like that Caleb. It's not fair. You're such a tease."

"How long do we have until we need to get Marco?"

She glances at her watch. "Not long...like half an hour."

"I know a lot we can do with that time." I pick her up over my good shoulder and, giving her ass a smack, bring her into the room, where I spend the next thirty minutes proving to her I'm not a tease.

Once we get to the gym, Hayley takes off to her office to get some work done, Marco heads to the ring to check out the guys fighting, and I head to the treadmill to warm up.

"Well, look who it is." Kaden jumps on the treadmill next to me. "You ready to get back to training, yet?"

"I'm getting there. Doc said I could do a light workout, but no fighting yet. I need to strengthen my leg and shoulder first, plus my chest still hurts like a bitch."

"Well I'm ready when you are," Kaden says, staring down at his phone. Whatever he's reading must piss him off because he shoves it back into his pocket and turns up the speed so fast one would think he's trying to literally run from whatever is bothering him.

"You good?" I ask, trying not to sound like a gossiping little girl.

"Yeah, just dealing with a stubborn ass woman."

I laugh at that. "Ashley?"

"Yeah, she's working as a cocktail waitress at a shitty strip club to make extra money instead of letting me help her out with her bills. Like I said...Stubborn."

"She was crying the other day when we went to get Marco from her house. Some shit about you two almost fucking, but you stopped it..." I just let that hang there.

Kaden winces slightly at my words then lets out a strangled breath. "Fuck, man...She's my best friend. I'm not about to treat her like all the other no-named women I've hooked up with over the years. She deserves better than a drunken fuck."

"Better like more...like you want to be with her?" Yeah, we totally sound like chicks right now.

"No, like I don't do the whole wife and kids shit. She's my friend and that's the way it needs to stay. If I fuck her, it'll ruin everything and that's not going to happen."

It's common knowledge Kaden was married at some point years ago. So he definitely did the wife shit, but this was all before I met him. Whatever went down must have been bad because he doesn't discuss it and he always makes it clear he will never settle down again.

A few minutes later Bentley and Kayla walk over. She's holding Chloe, and Bentley is holding Faith. Kaden and I both stop running to say hi.

"We have some great news!" Kayla says.

"Oh yeah? What's that?" Kaden asks. We both wipe the sweat off our hands and face before grabbing the babies from their parents. I can easily imagine Hayley and I having one of these one day soon. Faith coos and giggles at me as I hold her above my head and blow raspberries on her belly.

"DCF approved for us to adopt Chloe! We go before the judge next week to make it official."

"That's amazing!" Hayley says, coming over and giving Kayla and Bentley each a hug.

Marco joins us and takes his sister from Kaden, giving her kisses on her cheeks. She smiles and coos at Marco.

"I'll still be able to see her, right?" he asks Kayla.

Her eyebrows furrow and she steps closer to Marco. "If I didn't know how much Hayley and Caleb love you and how much you love living with them, Bentley and I would be adopting you and your sister together. You are welcome to visit her any time you want, Marco, and she will *always* know you are her brother and how much you love her. I will always be grateful to you. You brought her into our life. You cared for her when your mom wasn't able to."

Her answer seems to make him happy, but it upsets Hayley. "Marco, do you want Kayla to adopt you? Do you want to be with your sister? I would never want you to be away from her if you want to be with her. I know you originally said you wanted to live with me, but I will understand if you want to live with her now." Hayley's eyes fill with tears but she wills them not to spill over, trying to stay strong for Marco.

She looks at me and my heart breaks for her. She loves him so much she would do anything to make him happy, even if that means giving him up before she even adopts him.

"Marco, sweetie. If you want to live with Kayla, I promise I won't be mad."

I walk over to Hayley and put my arm around her.

"Please don't cry," Marco says, giving her a hug.

"Hey, bud, listen. She isn't crying because she's mad. She loves you and wants you to be happy."

"It makes me happy living with you guys. I don't want to leave. I just wanted to make sure I could still see Chloe all the time like I do now." He hugs Hayley again.

She sniffles. "I'm so glad you want to live with us and you will always be able to see Chloe any time you want."

"Well, on that note, I think we should all go out to dinner and celebrate," Bentley says, breaking up the emotional tension.

"I agree!"

"But after my MMA class," Marco chimes in. We all laugh and head over to the kids' ring to watch their class. Since I got hurt, Cooper has been running most of the classes and when we get over there we see him and Bella warming up with a few other kids.

"Hey Marco!" Bella calls out, waving him over. Marco runs over to her and warms up with her.

Kaden spots Ashley dropping off Tristan and goes to speak to her. I'm not sure what is being said, but they almost look like a couple arguing. She shakes her head and then storms out of the gym.

Kaden comes back over and rubs his palms over his face clearly agitated. I can't help but laugh. The guy almost never loses his composure. Then again he's usually the one in control. Hopefully he'll realize soon how bad he has it for Ashley.

While we're watching the kids' MMA class my phone goes off with a text from Hannah.

Hannah: Mediation set for Friday at 9 a.m.

Me: That was quick.

Hannah: When I petitioned for Gloria to pay half the employees' wages her attorney agreed to speed things up. Friday was the soonest I could get. If all

goes well you should have the clubs in your possession by Friday afternoon.

Me: Thanks!

Hannah: No problem!

"What has you smiling?" Hayley asks.

"Your sister got mediation set up for Friday. It might all be over by Friday afternoon."

"That's great, Caleb." She gives me a small kiss. Before she can pull away, I grab ahold of her and deepen it. I don't care where we are. I can't control myself when I'm around this woman.

The guys all call out insults and tell us to get a room.

"Leave him alone." Kayla laughs. "He has years of celibacy to make up for."

Everybody laughs and I ignore them all, grabbing my woman for another kiss. I definitely have a lot of time to make up for.

We all decide to go to a local bar and grill to celebrate the adoption of Chloe. After we're all done eating the girls decide to take the kids home and have a late night play date and gossip session. The guys end up hanging out here at the bar to watch some basketball. Since we knew we would be drinking we agreed to have the ladies take the vehicles home and we would grab a taxi once we are done.

After Kaden slams his phone down on the bar for the millionth time, Bentley says, "Man, I don't know what's going on with you and Ashley, but maybe you need to find a way to release some of that pent up tension. It's not like you to be wound so tight."

Kaden glares at him. "I didn't see you sleeping all over town when you and Kayla were having issues. Plus, Ashley and I are just friends."

Bentley puts his hands up. "Whoa, there. Nobody said anything about having sex. I was thinking you need to go a few rounds at the gym...but if sex is on your mind, I see a pretty little thing looking in our direction and out of the four of us you're the only single one."

We all look over to see who Bentley is talking about and that's when I see her...Gloria, and she's looking our way. As soon as she makes eye contact, she saunters over. I've had too many drinks to deal with this woman, but it looks like I don't have a choice. "Cooper, call a cab, now."

"Well, hello there, stranger." Gloria steps into my personal space. She grabs my bicep and squeezes. Because I'm damn near drunk, it takes me a second to get caught up, but once I see her hands on me, I push her away.

"Don't touch me. We were just leaving." I throw down enough bills to cover our drinks and get up from the stool about to walk around her, but she steps in front of me. The alcohol is definitely slowing me down.

"I just want to talk. Maybe we can work something out regarding the clubs." She trails a finger down my arm. To an outsider it looks like a pretty woman flirting with a man. To me, it's my rapist threatening me once again, and although I'm drunk, it sobers me up enough to stop this.

I move her fingers off me and grab her by her arms roughly, setting her on the bar stool I was just sitting on. The guys are all staring at the scene in front of them not saying a word. "Are you fucking serious right now? Wasn't forcing me to fuck you and then pimping me out for money enough for you? Do you have any idea the shit storm you have created in my fucked up head? I'm going to take you to court and let every fucking person know about your pedophile cunt ass."

For a second she looks shocked, but the bitch quickly composes herself. "Nobody would believe you. I'm a woman and you are a man, a man who beats people up for a living. What proof do you have?"

I almost blurt out I have a recording of her confession safely locked away but decide to keep that information to myself. I can't wait to see the look in her eyes on Friday. Looking at this nasty cunt all I want to do is get home to Hayley and Marco.

"I'll see you in court," I say and then turn and walk out of the bar with the guys following after me. Luckily the cab driver is waiting for us in front of the bar, so we're able to get right in and give him the address to Bentley's place, where all the women are.

The entire ride is silent. They obviously all heard the conversation. I'm not sure if I should bring it up or pretend it didn't happen. I thought maybe Kayla would have told Bentley after I told her. I wouldn't ask her to keep a secret from her husband, but she insisted it would stay between us. I guess she meant what she said and didn't tell him.

Cooper pays the cab driver, and as we're all walking up to Bentley's house, the three of them stop and wait for me to say something.

"I don't know what you guys want me to say."

"The truth," Kaden says.

"My dad fucked up, did some illegal insider trading, my stepmom found out and blackmailed me into having sex with her and other women for a few years. He died and left me everything. She's fighting with me over a couple of clubs."

"Damn, man. I honestly thought all those years you were gay," Bentley says with a laugh.

Cooper hits him in the stomach. "Look, what she did was shitty. I hate that you felt you had to hide it from us. We would have been there for you."

"You were. All three of you were. You barely knew me, but you took me away from that place. The day you offered me a way out was the last time I had to have sex against my will. You three saved me. You just didn't realize it. I will always be grateful to you guys."

Each one of them gives me a hug. Nothing else ever has to be said. We have each other's backs and always will.

AFTER EVERYBODY HEADS OUT AND WE SAY GOODNIGHT to Marco, I jump in the shower to rinse off. The thought of Gloria's hands on me earlier at the bar makes me want to scrub my body until it's raw. Once I'm clean enough, I switch the water off, grab a towel, and step out of the shower.

When I look up from drying my bottom half off, Hayley is leaning against the bathroom sink wearing only a white lacy bra and matching panties, looking fucking gorgeous. I can see her dark pink nipples poking out through the thin material and I want nothing more than to put my mouth on them...So I do. Dropping my towel, I stalk over to her, pick her up and place her on top of the counter, then take one of her pert nipples into my mouth. I suck on it for a few seconds and then give the other one the same attention. Hayley moans loudly, squeezing her legs together around me.

"Baby, you have to be quiet. Marco just fell asleep." She nods in understanding.

Taking both breasts out of the cups of her bra I bring them together and put both her nipples into my mouth at the same time sucking hard. Her hands fist into my hair as she pulls my face even closer to her chest moaning softly.

"Oh my God, Caleb. That feels so good." She tries to whisper, but she sucks at staying quiet.

Keeping my hands on her perfect breasts, I massage them softly, my fingers tweaking her nipples while my mouth moves to her neck. She moves her head to the side granting me access and I waste no time trailing kisses down her neck to her collarbone. She squirms in pleasure tightening her legs once more. I back up a little bit and, moving her panties to the side, insert a finger and then two into her tight pussy.

"Damn, Hayley. You are wet as fuck." While my fingers thrust in and out of her, my thumb rubs her clit. She grabs the back of my head and brings my face to hers, kissing me like her life depends on it. The deeper my fingers go, the harder she kisses, and within minutes, her pussy is clenching around my hand as she orgasms. Her body shakes and she tries to close her legs to stop me, but I don't stop until I know she's completely ridden her orgasm out.

"Mmm...that was so good," she says.

Before I can do or say anything in response, she's pushing me backward and hopping off the counter. A second later she's on her knees in front of me, guiding my shaft right into her warm, wet mouth.

"Fuuuck, Hayley."

She looks up at me and laughs. "Baby, you have to be quiet," she says, repeating my words back to me. This woman is going to be the death of me.

With one hand, she brings my dick back to her mouth while the other cups my balls massaging them gently. I stare down at her while she fucks my dick with her mouth. She stops for a second, swirls her tongue over the head and then slowly glides her mouth upward as she takes me fully inside her mouth until I can feel my head hit the back of her throat causing her to slightly gag. The action causes a flashback and before I can think too hard about it, I'm grabbing Hayley by her arms, lifting her up into a standing position, and bending her over the sink.

I rip her panties off her body, tossing them to the side. Then cupping her mound, I pull her ass toward me, pushing my dick into her pussy a little too roughly. Luckily she's soaking wet so my dick slides in easily, but that doesn't stop her body from hitting the edge of the countertop from the force of me entering her. She grabs ahold of the edge while I continue to pound into her almost violently, my hands tightly holding onto her hips while my fingers dig into her skin. My eyes meet hers in the mirror and I then remember I'm not fucking one of the women from my past—I'm fucking Hayley...no, I'm making love to Hayley. Because it doesn't matter whether it's hard or soft, every time I touch her, it's out of love.

With my eyes never leaving Hayley's, my thrusts slow down and we quickly find our rhythm—Hayley meeting me thrust for thrust. I know when my cock hits her sweet spot because she moans loudly. I keep hitting the spot over and over again until we're both finding our release at almost the same time.

Twenty-Five

HAYLEY

IT'S BEEN ABOUT A MONTH SINCE WE CELEBRATED BENTLEY and Kayla's adoption news, and it feels like our life hasn't stopped moving in full speed ever since. In the past month the threats have become more frequent and instead of them saying things like "Last chance Bitch," they now say things like "Watch your back." The police can't prove who's sending them so their hands are tied. Thank God the court date is coming up and soon we will be able to put it all behind us.

On a more positive note, Hannah convinced Gloria it would be in her best interest to walk away from the clubs without going to court. I must admit getting to see my little sister in action was awe-inspiring. She said I was her assistant to get me in, but I had to promise not to reach across the table and strangle Gloria. My sister is such a badass!

"Good morning. My name is Lyrica Goldstein. I'll be mediating today. Who would like to begin?"

Before Gloria's attorney could even speak, Hannah was all over that shit.

"Good morning, we're here for mediation in hope of not having to go to trial so we don't have to waste more time and money. My name is Hannah Roberts and I'm Caleb's attorney. I'll be presenting the evidence that will be shown to the judge should Gloria Michaels feel it is necessary to go to trial."

"Okay, Ms. Roberts. Please show your evidence and then we'll go from there."

Hannah walked around the table with her laptop and sat it right in front of Gloria. On the screen was a digital copy of the letter Adam wrote to his son. Leaning over Gloria's shoulder, Hannah read the letter out loud. When she was done everybody knew in the room what Gloria had done.

"It's his word versus mine. And he's not even alive!"

Gloria's attorney told her to close her mouth.

"I understand that completely," Hannah went on. "That's why the next piece of evidence is absolutely crucial."

She pressed play on the recording and the room filled with Gloria's voice as she confessed everything to Caleb's father, not realizing she was being recorded. I could see the look of horror streak across her face.

The entire room went quiet.

"Would you like a few minutes to speak to your client?" Hannah asked Gloria's attorney.

"No, there's no need," Gloria whispered. She said something to her attorney and then walked out the door.

"My client has decided to drop the lawsuit against your client for the clubs. She waves all rights to anything club related."

"She never had any rights," Hannah pointed out with a smug look on her face.

With Gloria's bullshit behind us, Caleb insisted on immediately flying to Boulder to get the club handled so he could come back home and handle the one closer to us, and this time when he took Marco snowboarding he was able to join him. We all flew out together and spent spring break relaxing and having a good time.

Caleb was able to weed out the people loyal to Gloria, hire new help, and even hire Jacob, a bouncer who's been there for years and has his business degree as the on-site manager.

Once we returned back home my sister and Gavin got married. They found out they're having a little girl and are so excited. They found a house right down the street from my place and their offer was accepted last week. They're having some renovations done to the house first so they won't be moving in for a couple months but I'm so excited to have my sister as a neighbor.

Now Caleb and I are sitting in the adoption agency at the DCF office. Karen called me in to let me know she has some good news.

"I'm happy to say your adoption request has been approved. You and Marco are scheduled to go before the judge next week to swear you in as his legal guardian."

"Thank you so much!" I look over to Caleb and see the sad smile he has on his face.

"I know the adoption system frowns upon two people adopting a child when they aren't together, but do you think there's any way they could make an exception?"

"Unfortunately the DCF doesn't do exceptions. If you two were married, you could file the application together, but that would mean starting the entire process over again. The other option is you adopting Marco now and once you two are married Caleb can legally adopt Marco. Since you'll be his legal guardian you won't have to go through DCF at that point."

I hate that I'll be adopting Marco and Caleb isn't but she's right. The second option would be the easiest way to go. I don't want to start the adoption process over and who knows if or when Caleb and I will be getting married.

"Thank you," Caleb says and then stands shaking the attorney's hand.

Our entire ride home is silent. I know that it's breaking Caleb's heart not being able to legally adopt Marco right now. He said it was okay before, but now it seems like he has changed his mind. Does he want to be the one to adopt Marco? But if he does and then decides to move out, that would mean he would take Marco with him. I love Marco too much to let him go.

I go to work for the rest of the day and once I get home, Caleb and Marco go to the gym while I make dinner. I take out the pork roast I put to season yesterday, but when the scent hits my nostrils my stomach roils, forcing me to run to the bathroom. I make it to the toilet just in time to throw up everything in my stomach. I seriously hope I'm not getting sick on top of everything else.

After I am done throwing up, I make dinner and then clean up the house a little bit. I can't get this whole situation off my mind and if I stop moving I know I am going to drive myself nuts.

About an hour later dinner is ready, just as Caleb and Marco walk inside. We eat dinner, take showers, and watch a movie until it's time for Marco to go to bed. And this is how our routine continues for the next several days: Work, gym, dinner, family time, and bed. Caleb and I share a bed, and every night we make love, but we don't discuss anything. I'm getting so frustrated and confused and I know it's only a matter of time until I lose it.

Twenty-Six

CALEB

EVER SINCE WE LEFT THE DCF OFFICE MY THOUGHTS HAVE been running crazy. I know I told Hayley I was okay with her adopting Marco, and I am, but at the same time I hate the fact that they will legally be a family and I won't be a part of it. What if she decides one day she doesn't want me in her life? I have no legal claim to see Marco. I would have to walk away without having a say in anything. I hate the feeling of not being in control.

It's Saturday night and Marco's just gone to bed when Hayley finally snaps. We're sitting on the couch with her feet in my lap, watching a TV show.

"Talk to me, Caleb, please." Hayley's eyes are filled with tears and I would do anything to stop her from being upset.

"I don't know what to say, Hayles. I know you adopting Marco alone is the best choice. I just feel left out." I edge closer to Hayley and, bringing my hand to her thigh, rub up and down her legs hoping to relax her. I hate seeing her so upset and I hate that it's my insecurities causing it. She jumps slightly at my touch, but then relaxes not saying anything else. I massage the tops of her legs and she moans in appreciation. Sometimes it makes me sick, knowing my expertise of what a woman wants comes from years of being with women unwillingly, but it makes me feel better knowing I can apply those skills to a woman I actually want to be with.

I'm expecting her to argue with me, to want to talk some more, so I'm shocked when she moans out, "Caleb, rub harder." Something in my brain goes fuzzy, taking me back to an older memory from my past...and this time I can't seem to shake it off.

"Caleb, I had the hardest workout at the gym today. My muscles are so tight. Rub my body, now." Gloria lies on her stomach on my bed and I want nothing more than to choke the shit out of her so she'll disappear from my life, but we both know I'm not really capable of murder. So instead I do as she says. I sit on top of her ass and begin rubbing her shoulders like she has taught me to do.

I move my hands down her back and massage circles into the muscles and then move lower, scooting down to sit on her legs, massaging her ass. Once I get to her thighs, I think she might be asleep until she says, "Caleb, rub harder." I do as she says and rub harder into her muscles.

She flips over and gives me a devious smirk. "Come back up here. I want a full body massage. Massage my breasts, Caleb." I do as she demands because what choice do I have? I could tell her no, but then my dad would end up in prison. I continue to massage her body and of course my dick betrays me and gets stiff in my pants. Gloria thinks it gets hard because I want her. I think she has to tell herself that to justify how fucking wrong this is.

Of course she wins and we end up fucking, as I pray to God that I somehow find a way out of this shitty situation.

"Caleb...are you okay?"

My mind snaps back to the present and I realize that while my girlfriend is sitting on the couch next to me wanting me to touch her, I was having a flashback of massaging my stepmom and then fucking her. I look down and see my dick is hard. Bile rises in my throat and I just make it to the bathroom before I throw everything I've recently eaten up.

I hear her come up behind me and then her hands touch my shoulders. I know it's only out of care for me, but I can't have her touching me with the memories of my stepmom in my head.

"Don't touch me," I bark. She removes her hands from me but doesn't leave the bathroom.

"What's the matter? Did I do something wrong?" Her voice is so soft and insecure and I know it's my fault. How do I explain to her that my body is a fucking traitor and gets turned on by the thought of touching my stepmom when it should be soft by the thought of it? I shouldn't have snapped at her, but I can't stand the idea of her innocent, perfect hands touching me while I'm having sick thoughts. I don't want her tainted by my shit.

"Caleb, please, talk to me." I can't even look at her. I feel gross for even having the flashback. I feel even more disgusting for having the flashback while touching Hayley.

"I'm just not feeling well. I'm going to bed." I get up from the floor of the bathroom, flush the toilet, and walk by her without making eye contact. Instead of going to the room I've been sharing with her, go to mine and shut the door. How could I have ever thought I could live a normal life with a woman? How could I have thought it would be a good idea for me to adopt Marco? My life is tainted. Hayley deserves so much more than this. Marco deserves better than me. Hayley adopting Marco on her own is the way it should be.

And for the first time in weeks I sleep alone in my bedroom without Hayley curled up next to me.

Twenty-Seven

HAYLEY

I SAW THE SAME LOOK ON CALEB'S FACE LAST NIGHT THAT I saw the first night we made out like teenagers as well as the several nights since then we've made love. I don't know what exactly was going through his head, but I would bet my life it wasn't something as simple as him not feeling well. It doesn't go unnoticed the pained look he gives me too often when we're intimate. He doesn't realize I notice, but I do. I would bet it has something to do with his past. When he told me not to touch him, I wanted to grab him and pull him closer. I wanted to beg him not to push me away, but what right do I have?

I have to remember that even though Caleb has come a long way these past couple months, and while I know what he's been through because of the little he's told me, I'll never fully understand what goes through his head. The fact that it was bad enough to make him throw up tells me I need to give him space. He doesn't need me nagging him when he's got enough of his own shit to deal with. I hated going to bed without him. I hated that once again we didn't have the necessary conversation we need to have regarding Marco's adoption.

I drag myself out of bed knowing I'm going to have to face whatever is going on with Caleb head on. After showering, I get dressed and then make my way out to the living room. Marco is watching Sunday morning cartoons as usual and Caleb is on his laptop.

"Morning," I say, grabbing a cup of coffee.

"Morning," they both say in unison. I look over Caleb's shoulder and see the rental ads pulled up. My heart sinks. He's decided to move out. I guess I know where we stand after all.

"Hey Marco, want to head to the park to go skateboarding?" I need to get out of here and get some fresh air.

"Yes!" he yells, running to his room to get his skateboard.

"Make sure you brush your teeth after you get dressed!" I yell down the hallway. I sip on my coffee and think about how to approach this conversation. I don't want to fight with Caleb. We've never fought before. I want him to open up and talk to me.

"Do you want to come with?" I ask Caleb after a few minutes of silence.

"I can't. I have some apartments I need to look at." He says it quietly, so Marco can't hear, but do you know any kids who don't have supersonic hearing?

"Why are you going to look at apartments?" Marco asks, coming around the corner dressed and with his skateboard in his hand.

"Marco, I think we should talk," Caleb says solemnly. "When I moved in here with Hayley and you it was never to be forever. I was hurt and couldn't walk up the stairs. But I'm better now so I have to find my own place."

Huh. That's ironic considering he told me he was mine and wasn't going anywhere, ever. I guess *ever* was a lot shorter than I thought.

Marco looks absolutely crushed and for the first time I understand what parents mean when they say they want to shelter their children from all possibilities of being hurt. "You don't want to live with us?"

I should probably jump in and help Caleb, but I feel the same way as Marco.

"It's not that...this isn't my home. This is your home and Hayley's home."

"But you said you were together...Plus," Marco adds without waiting for an answer, "Hayley has been really scared about the people leaving the threats. You can't leave us. Please."

Oh damn...how will Caleb react to that? I keep my mouth shut. Caleb looks at me, begging for help and I just raise my brows in defiance. He's choosing this, not me. I'm certainly not going to help him push us away and run.

He sighs. "How about I look at a couple apartments, but I'll wait to move until I know you're both safe? I'll wait to move until after the trials are over."

Marco doesn't seem satisfied by the answer but nods anyway. Caleb gives him a hug goodbye and leaves without saying a word to me. Something in me snaps and I send him a text without thinking too hard about it.

Me: If you want to be a coward and leave...fine! But you are choosing this. I don't even know what I did wrong...I deserve better than this.

A few minutes later I get a text back.

Caleb: You do deserve better. I'm sorry.

He's sorry? Seriously? That's all he has to say...well fuck him then! I'm not going to get run all over because of his past while he doesn't even give me a chance to be there for him.

Twenty-Eight

CALEB

I LOOK AT THREE DIFFERENT APARTMENTS AND EVERY single one I compare to Hayley's home. None of them feel right. Sure, they're nice as hell—the money my dad left me means I can pretty much rent or buy anywhere I want. The apartments I looked at have enough square footage to fit Hayley's house inside the kitchen alone. They have state-of-the art appliances, and one of them even comes furnished. No, the problem isn't the apartments themselves. The problem is none of them include Hayley and Marco. There's not a single item money could buy that would compare to what it feels like being with Hayley and Marco. If only it were that easy.

Now I'm at the bar drinking away my sorrows that I've created myself.

"Another one?" the bartender asks with a wink, letting me know if I wanted to I could take her into a bathroom and fuck her right there on the sink. The thought makes me feel sick. The only woman I want touching me is Hayley.

"No, thank you. Just a water please."

"Sure thing," she says with another flirtatious wink.

I don't even know how long I sit at the bar thinking, but my mind goes to the last couple months and how happy Hayley has made me. I realize for the last seven years I've been doing nothing more than simply surviving. But the day Hayley brought me to her house I finally started living. And what do I do when shit gets rough? I push her away, when the truth is, I should've pulled her closer. I should have explained to her how I've been feeling. I'm so hell bent on trust being so important, yet I didn't even give Hayley a chance to prove I could trust her. I tell her I would love to have a baby with her, yet I haven't even told her how much I love her, how much she means to me. I want to adopt Marco and instead of asking her to marry me so we can do it together, I get upset and run away.

I look around the bar and wonder what the hell I'm doing here when every single solution to my problems lies within two people and both of them are at home.

When I arrive at the house, I notice Hayley's car isn't in the driveway. I look at my cellphone and see it's after two in the morning. Where the hell could she be at this time of the night...well, morning...

I unlock the door and walk through the entire house. Nobody is here. The lights are all off and the beds are still made from this morning. I pull out my cell phone again and pull up the tracking app I set up for Hayley months ago. It shows about an hour ago she was in Marco's old neighborhood. I hit update, but it says her phone is offline. I try again, but it doesn't update. Why the hell is she in that shitty neighborhood?

I dial her number, my hands shaking. I have the worst feeling in my gut, but I'm refusing to think it out loud. Her phone goes to voicemail and I start to freak out.

I pull back up the app and click Marco's name. It shows he's here in the house. I run to his room and see his phone sitting on the desk in his room. Fuck!

I try Hayley's number once more, but it goes to voicemail. I send a group text to all the guys, asking any of them if they've seen or heard from Hayley. I know she went to the park with Marco today, but she should have been home by now. I call the number on the card to speak to the detective in charge of my case.

"Detective Bradley, this is Caleb. Hayley and Marco are both missing. I don't think it's a coincidence she received several threats and now I can't find them. Hayley's phone last showed her in Marco's old neighborhood before it was turned off."

"Okay, Caleb. We'll head over there now to check things out."

"Thank you, sir."

I should wait for the police to see what they can find, but I can't just sit and do nothing. I grab the gun from the lock box I purchased a while back when the guys and I used to frequent the shooting range for fun. After I got approved for my concealed weapons permit, I purchased a *Smith & Wesson .40*. I keep it locked up and out of Marco's reach with the ammunition separate, but it makes me feel better knowing I'm prepared in case anything happens, especially with Hayley feeling like she's being watched and all the threats we've received. I put the gun into the front of my pants and grab my keys, jump into my truck and head to Marco's old neighborhood. If the app is correct she was somewhere around the industrial building near where I saw Marco meet Hector and Santos to exchange money that day I was following him.

I don't even want to think about the possibilities of what Marco and Hayley could be going through right now. I'm praying this is all a misunderstanding and they're safely at one of our friend's houses, but I would rather expect the worst and hope for the best. While I'm driving I get several texts from our friends and her family saying they haven't seen or heard from her. Hannah texts saying Hayley posted a picture of Marco skateboarding earlier at the skate park. I forward it to the detective remembering I didn't mention the park during our conversation. Then I text Cooper, Bentley, and Kaden telling them I think Hayley and Marco were taken.

I get to the neighborhood and drive around looking for anything suspicious. I don't see Hayley's car anywhere. I drive by Marco's old house and it's vacant. I get out and walk around the house, but it's empty. I feel my phone buzz and see a text from the detective.

Detective Bradley: Officer found her car abandoned at the skate park earlier and reported it.

Fuck! There's no way she would have just left her car there.

Me: Hector and Santos had to have taken her!

Detective Bradley: Meet me at your house. Don't do anything stupid.

I want to keep searching for Hayley, but I know driving around isn't going to get me anywhere. I need to be smart about this. If it was Hector and Santos who took Marco and her it's because they want something. I head back home and when I get there the detective is there along with his partner. I think his name is David.

We walk into the house, and as I sit down on the couch to get down to business, David is bent over in the doorway. "Did you see this?"

I get up from the couch and grab what he's holding. It's a photo of Hayley and Marco both tied up and looking scared. Hayley looks to have a large bruise on her face. I flip it over and on the back is a note.

I warned you over and over again, but you didn't listen. Maybe now you will listen. One million in cash dropped off to the park under the bench where the car is parked by 10 a.m. or they will be killed.

"What the fuck! How did I not see this shit before when I came home?" It was dark, that's why I didn't see it, and I wasn't looking on the ground for fucking clues.

"Fuck! Since I didn't drop the charges, they want money…and I am what? Supposed to sit here for eight fucking hours and wait to drop off the money and hope they're okay?"

"No, you aren't," Bradley says. He's making calls and trying to get intel on the guys. I feel so fucking useless. I don't even know where to start looking. This is entirely my fault! If I hadn't left Hayley to go look at apartments I would've been with them at the park and this never would've happened. It doesn't go over my head every time she received a threat she was alone. I should have taken the threats more seriously. I should have insisted the police do something more. I kept thinking the trial would come around and these guys would be locked up with the other two that didn't get out on bail. I shouldn't have let my guard down. Now Hayley and Marco are God knows where scared and possibly hurt.

"What do we do?"

"We're having a couple officers go to Hector's and Santos's houses to check things out. We're also having the tech department pull up the cameras at the park from earlier today. Unfortunately other than a few anonymous threats since the graffiti on her car, there hasn't been much to go off of.

"I can't just sit here. The tracker showed her near the industrial building. I need to go there and check it out."

The front door swings open and I pray it's Hayley and Marco, but it's not. It's Bentley, Cooper, and Kaden.

"What the fuck is going on?" Bentley asks.

"They were taken?" Cooper asks.

"Yeah." I show them the picture.

"So what the hell are we doing here? We need to go find them," Kaden growls.

This is why these guys are my best friends. They would do anything for me and the people I love.

"We're having forensics take the picture. We're hoping they can pinpoint a location the photo was printed at or taken from," the detective states, taking the photo from me and handing it to someone on his team.

"A million? We can give the guys that, and they must know if they hurt them, they won't get their money," Bentley says.

"Yeah, well, I'm not sitting and waiting seven more hours to find out." I grab my keys and head out to my truck.

"Wait, you aren't going without us," Kaden says.

"Do you have your guns on you?" I ask.

"Yeah, when you said you thought Hayley and Marco were taken, we grabbed them," Bentley says as we all jump into my truck.

Detective Bradley: I can't stop you, but if you find them please call for backup. Don't go in on your own.

I don't bother texting back. I don't want to have to lie to a cop, and there's no way I'm going to find my girl and kid and sit around and wait for him to get there.

We're driving around the neighborhood for about thirty minutes and I'm getting frustrated as fuck having no clue where Hayley can be when I see the same expensive vehicle I've spotted several times now.

"That's the car," I point out. "Hayley and I have seen this car parked near us several times."

I park my truck and quickly text the detective, sending him a live location of where we are.

I take my gun out and take the safety off—the guys do the same thing.

We all walk up along the side of the building. It's the same warehouse Marco met the guys at but around back. The only way to get to the door is a small alleyway. If it weren't for the car being parked here I would have completely overlooked it. We stop at the vehicle and look inside. Nobody is in there, but on the floor of the car I can see Hayley's phone. She has to be close by. When I feel the hood, it's cold telling me it's been parked here for a while.

I hear soft footsteps coming up behind us and I turn and point my gun ready to shoot anybody that's a threat. It's the detective and several other officers. The detective puts his fingers to his lips and I nod. We walk toward the door of the building, when I hear a woman scream so loud it send chills down my spine. I know I should wait for the detective to give some kind of orders, but I don't. I try to open the door, but it won't open, so I step back and shoot the lock out.

When the door flies open the scene in front of me is one I'll never forget for as long as I live.

Twenty-Nine

HAYLEY

Nine Hours Earlier

"OH MY GOODNESS! MARCO! YOU'RE LIKE A SKATEBOARDING god! Who taught you to skateboard like this?" I'm watching Marco do ridiculously cool tricks using his skateboard and I'm absolutely amazed. The kid is so talented.

"I used to skateboard here all the time before Cooper started the MMA classes, and usually after the classes I would come here to practice, plus my friends and I practice at school during gym."

I pull out my phone and switch it to live mode to record him doing his tricks and then post it to Facebook. It's a beautiful day here and getting out helped take my mind off Caleb and the fact that while I'm here with Marco, he's off looking at apartments.

A little while later Marco comes over to me and sits down.

"Umm...so I have a question," he says nervously.

"What's up?"

"Your parents said I can call them Nana and Pop—those are

nicknames for grandparents, right?"

"Yes," I say, pretty sure where this is going but scared if it's not going in the direction I think it is, I'll be heartbroken.

"And if they're my grandparents, it's like you're my mom. Right?"

"Well, I would definitely be honored to be your mom if that's what you're asking. I know you already have a mom, so I think that would be up to you."

"My mom wasn't a good mom. I'm old enough to know that."

"She wasn't perfect, but she loved you the best she could." I seriously hope I'm not botching this entire conversation. I probably should have looked up the right things to say. I'm already messing up this whole parenting thing and it's not even official yet.

"What if I wanted to call you mom?"

My heart tightens in my chest at his words. "Then you would make me the happiest woman in the entire world, but only on one condition."

"What's that?" he asks, nervous again.

"I can call you my son."

"That would be awesome. Do you think Caleb would let me call him Dad?"

The heart constricts at the idea of Caleb and I being parents to Marco. He's been close to Marco for so long, I could never keep that title from him, even if he doesn't want to marry me and formally adopt Marco.

"That is something you would have to ask Caleb, but I'm pretty sure he would be honored. He loves you *almost* as much as I do," I say with a playful wink.

Marco laughs.

"Speaking of new names. I have some good news. The adoption went through and on Friday we'll be going before the judge to make it official. You're legally mine, kid."

I reach over and give him a hug and he hugs me back. "I love you, Mom."

I choke up, but compose myself quickly. "I love you too, Son."

Marco runs back to the ramps to skateboard some more. I want to text Caleb to tell him about this conversation but don't want to bother him while he's apartment hunting. He needs his space. If he needed or wanted me he would be here with us. I can't make someone try.

I look at the time and see it's almost dinnertime, and since it's a school night we need to get home to eat and get ready for tomorrow.

"C'mon, Marco, let's go."

"Coming, Mom!" he yells. He has no idea what the significance of those three little letters mean to me. All I can do is make sure I do everything in my power to earn the title that precious little boy has given me.

I hit the button to pop open my trunk. Marco takes his pads off his elbows and knees and then takes his helmet off, throwing it all into the trunk, slamming it closed when he's done. I hit the key fob to unlock the doors, and just as we are about to get in hands come around me, one hand covering my mouth. I try to scream, but it's muffled. I'm then blindfolded and handcuffed with my hands behind by back and then thrown into the back of a vehicle where I can hear Marco screaming.

"*Cállate*," I hear a man bark out. Marco immediately stops screaming. I shift my body, so I'm touching Marco's body with mine, letting him know I'm here with him.

The guys talk minimally in Spanish and a few minutes later the car comes to a stop. Since I'm blindfolded I have no idea where I am. Then I remember I have my cell phone in my back pocket. Without being able to see, I try to unlock it and dial whatever number comes up first. But before I can even get it unlocked, the phone is smacked out of my hand and I hear it crack like it's being stomped on.

"*Puta cuidadosa o morirás!*" a man spits out before grabbing me and dragging me out of the car. I hear Marco crying and saying something in Spanish. The man smacks me across the face hard and then throws me onto the ground. I curl up into a fetal position while I'm kicked several times in the back and a few times to my ribs. Eventually it's too much and I throw up. They finally stop and I'm picked up and brought somewhere where I'm thrown onto cold hard cement. I try to stay calm, but my body is aching. I can taste the blood coming from my mouth, but I don't want Marco to know anything is wrong.

I only know Marco is with me because I can hear him breathing loudly. The place goes quiet a few minutes later, and I take the chance and speak.

"Marco, sweetie, are you okay?"

"Yeah, Mom, I'm okay. Are you?"

"Yes, I'm okay. Do you know what the man said to me in Spanish?"

"He said to be careful or you will die. I tried to tell him to stop."

"It's going to be okay, Marco."

He doesn't say anything back.

A little while later the door opens and our blindfolds are removed. I've read enough books to know this isn't a good thing. If the kidnappers are okay with letting you see them they don't plan to let you live. Once my eyes adjust, I see we're in an empty room in a warehouse and sure enough it's Hector and Santos along with the two guys who got out on bail. There's another guy there as well, dressed nicer than the other guys, and I wonder if he's the owner of the expensive vehicle that has been parked down my street.

"You know why I took off your blindfolds? So you can see who is in charge of your life. Let's hope you and the boy are worth a million dollars," one of the men says in his heavy Spanish accent. He takes his cell phone out and snaps a picture of Marco and me.

"And then you will let us go?" I ask.

"We'll see."

"Please just let Marco go. You can keep me. He's just a child."

"Just a child? He's the reason for this shit! Him and his druggie mother!"

"He's a child!" I yell back! The man backhands me so hard tears spring from my eyes and blood coats the inside of my mouth.

"Mom!" Marco yells. He looks so scared. All I want to do is hold him and make him feel safe even if neither of us are.

"Shut up! Both of you!" They put the blindfold back on Marco and then on me.

The door slams shut, leaving us once again in the dark.

"I love you, Marco." It's all I can say. I don't know at this point if we will live or die, but I need him to know I love him. "You are the best treasure ever brought into my life. No matter what happens I need you to know I love you, Son."

"I love you too, Mom. Thank you for saving me."

There's so much more I want to say, but I can't speak without crying, and I don't want Marco to hear me crying. My body is in so much pain and it's hard to breathe. I take a slow deep breath and pray to God somebody finds us soon.

After telling Marco over and over again I will protect him he finally falls asleep with his head in my lap. It seems like hours before the men return. I'm exhausted and it's got to be well into the night or early morning, but I'm too scared to sleep. I need to protect my son.

I hear the men getting closer. They're yelling back and forth in Spanish and while I have no idea what they're saying, it doesn't sound like they're very happy. Every few words I hear one I can translate like police and money. Damn it, I wish I had paid better attention in Spanish class back in college.

The voices keep getting closer and before I know it I hear the door swing open. Before I can react, Marco is no longer sleeping on my lap and my shorts are being ripped off me. Marco is screaming out my name and I'm just so thankful he won't have to actually see me being raped. I'm pushed onto my back and because my hands are still handcuffed, I can't stop myself from falling backward, my head hitting the concrete hard. I feel dizzy but try hard not to blackout.

"Your boyfriend made a grave mistake, you little bitch. He involved the police. His mistake is your punishment." He grabs my breasts hard and then spreads my legs so wide I scream out loudly in pain. I can't just let him rape me. I need to fight, but how can I fight without my hands or sight. I attempt to kick him hard and must make contact, because when my foot hits him, he grunts out what sounds like curse words in Spanish. I take the opportunity to begin screaming again trying to get away.

I expect him to come back at me to take my underwear off, so I bring my legs up ready to kick him again, but instead I hear a loud gunshot ring through the air, what sounds like a door swinging open, and then loud voices yelling, "Police. Put your weapons down." Suddenly several gunshots go off.

I bring my shoulder up to my face as I try to move the blindfold the best I can, but it's not working. A few seconds later, hands are on me and I jump, screaming out loud. "Shh...it's okay, Hayles. I got you." The sound of Caleb's voice allows me to relax. He removes my blindfold, and that's when I see Kaden, Cooper, and Bentley, as well as several armed police officers all pointing their guns at the five men who are on the ground bleeding, having been shot. It looks like at least two of them might be dead and the others are definitely injured.

I search for Marco and see him curled up in the corner. I get up the best I can and hobble over to him. I can't hold him, but I attempt to soothe him with my words.

"It's okay, sweetie. Caleb and the police are here. They saved us." I sit close to Marco, blocking him in case anything goes bad, hoping my body will protect his.

The officers handcuff the three guys who are alive but injured and another officer calls for more ambulances saying there are several injured. One of the officers comes over to Marco and me, and using a key, unlocks our cuffs. I immediately grab Marco, taking his blindfold off, and hold him tight, vowing to never let go of him. First date? Hope he enjoys a third wheel. College? He better be prepared for me to join him. I might even have to homeschool him.

While I'm holding him and refusing to let go, I feel hands encompass us, and when I look up I see Caleb with tears in his eyes, holding both of us.

"I thought I was going to lose you both," he says through his tears. "I'm so sorry, baby. I'm so sorry for leaving you guys."

I'm not sure why Caleb is apologizing. He didn't do this. He can't control what those men did. Then it hits me. He blames himself because he left us to go find an apartment, and I know I should be grateful we're all okay and I should tell him it's not his fault or at least say it's okay, but the fear that has consumed me for so long turns into anger. As I get up to grab my shorts, I feel a sharp pain in my side hit me and I double over before blacking out.

Thirty

CALEB

I FUCKED UP. I KNOW I FUCKED UP, AND NOW I'M GOING TO have to fix this. I walked out on Hayley and Marco to find an apartment in an attempt to push her away. All she's done this entire time is fight for me, and instead of pulling her closer and leaning on her, I pushed her away. I should have just told her about the flashbacks. I should have explained what was going on in my head, but instead I walked away like a scared little bitch.

I should have been at the park with her and Marco. If I were there with them, they never would have been taken. She never would have been so close to being raped.

I grab ahold of both Marco and Hayley apologizing over and over again. I can see when her fear turns to anger and then she gets up to walk away. What I'm not prepared for is when she doubles over in pain and a loud scream rings out in the warehouse, and I realize something is very wrong.

Luckily when the police came they also dispatched ambulances.

The EMTs come running in and cut her shirt open. That's when I see all the bruises. She had to have been beaten. There are bruises all over her stomach and legs. Her face has several bruises and her lip is split completely open.

"We're going to bring her to the nearest hospital. They'll be able to assess her and check for internal injuries," the EMT says, carefully placing Hayley on the gurney. As they're rolling her out, Hayley comes to and starts calling for Marco. She's hurt and her only concern is to make sure Marco is okay.

I run over to her side and tell her Marco is with me and we'll follow her to the hospital.

Marco starts crying and I grab ahold of him, holding him close. "It's okay. She's going to be okay."

"They hurt her!" he cries.

"Did they do anything to you?" I ask. "Are you hurt?" I look over his body, making sure he's okay.

"No, they didn't do anything to me. Can we please go to the hospital? I want to make sure Mom's okay."

Hearing him call Hayley Mom warms my heart. I wonder if she knows he's calling her Mom.

Cooper comes over. "Why don't we head to the hospital with you guys and stay in the waiting room with Marco until they say it's okay for him to go back and see Hayley?"

"Okay."

On our way to the hospital I give Hayley's sister a call to let her know what's happened. She lets me know they're on their way and she'll call their parents to let them know.

When we arrive, the nurse won't tell me anything. I try to play the fiancé card Hayley played to get in to see me, but this nurse isn't having it. Thankfully Hannah comes running through the door demanding answers and since they're sisters and she's on her emergency contact list, the nurse will speak to her.

"Ms. Roberts is okay. She has a couple bruised ribs and is currently receiving stitches for her lip. They're running tests because she hit her head pretty hard, and they'll keep her overnight in case of a concussion. Once the doctor gives the okay, I'll let two at a time go back and see her."

Knowing Hayley is alone back there and in pain makes me feel sick, but at this point, we're lucky she's okay. I sit with Marco and hold him like Hayley would have done until he falls asleep.

A little while later Hayley's parents arrive, then Ashley, Kayla, and Liz all come in.

"You guys didn't have to come here. She's okay."

"Are you crazy? Of course we're here. Once I can see her for myself I'll bring Marco home with me," Kayla says.

Marco tenses up, telling me he's awake and listening. "I don't want to leave my mom. Please don't make me leave her." He starts crying and shaking his head, clearly scared of losing another mom.

"Hey, it's all right. You don't have to go anywhere. As soon as they say it's okay, I'll bring you back to see her."

We all sit and wait for another couple hours and then finally the nurse comes out and calls Hayley's name. We all stand. "Hayley is ready for visitors, but she requests that Caleb Michaels not be allowed in—I'm sorry."

Everybody's eyes fly to me and I don't know even know what to say. I should have seen this coming. You can only push someone so far before they give up fighting for you.

Thirty-One

HAYLEY

ONCE I'M BROUGHT TO THE HOSPITAL AND ADMITTED, THEY draw blood to run tests, perform scans to check out my head and ribs, and hook me up to an IV. Luckily I'm just sore with bruised ribs, but nothing major that will require surgery or a cast. The worst part is them having to sew up my bottom lip with a few stitches. I think I'm finally done being checked out when another doctor comes in and shocks the ever-loving shit out of me.

"Good morning, Hayley, my name is Dr. Jones. I've been looking over your chart and it appears you're pregnant. Were you aware?"

Immediately, my hands go to my stomach, to the flashbacks of those horrible men kicking me. I had no idea I was pregnant. "I didn't know, but I can't imagine after the beating I had I'm still pregnant," I say, feeling numb.

"You would be surprised how well the womb protects the fetus, but instead of assuming one way or another, why don't we do an ultrasound." He rolls the ultrasound cart over.

"It says you're a doctor as well. What's your specialty?" I know he's only making conversation to calm me, but I'll take it.

"I specialize in sport's medicine. I work with UFC fighters at a local gym."

"Very nice. Since I don't know how far along you are, I'm going to do a vaginal ultrasound," he says, rolling a condom over the wand and then inserting it slowly into me.

The monitor is on, but I can't look at it. I wish Caleb were here with me to hold my hand. But then I remember why I'm here. He ran, instead of fighting for us, he walked away and wasn't there when Marco and I were taken. I hate feeling so consumed with anger, but I can't help it.

Caleb doesn't deserve to be here. He didn't want me. He wanted an apartment and to be away from me. He chose to let whatever was wrong, probably his past, win out over me, over us.

"...And there's the heartbeat." I completely forgot about the ultrasound. I bring my face up to look at the screen and sure enough there's a lima bean-size baby and a heartbeat. Tears spring to my eyes and spill over.

"It's a strong heartbeat, Hayley. I don't see any tears in the uterine walls. The amniotic fluid looks good. Your body did its job. It protected your little one. You look to be close to six weeks. It's still very early and while I don't want to scare you, I'm going to recommend once you're released you take it easy your first trimester. Your body needs time to heal. I'm not putting you on bed rest, but don't overdo it."

"Thank you, Dr. Jones."

The doctor prints out a couple pictures of the cute little lima bean and then says he'll let the nurse know I can receive visitors.

"Umm, wait. Can you please let her know I don't want Caleb Michaels visiting?"

He nods once and then leaves.

A few minutes later my sister walks in with Marco. He bursts into tears and I welcome him in my bed so I can hold him. He lies next to me and within minutes passes out.

"Everything is okay, right?" Hannah asks.

It won't be long until my parents and friends are fighting to all come back so I need to tell her now. "I need to tell you something, but you can't tell anyone, not yet."

"Does this have anything to do with why you wouldn't let Caleb back? He's completely torn up. A tornado couldn't rip him from that waiting room."

"He left, Hannah!" I yell, but take a calming breath before I continue. I don't want to wake Marco or do anything to put the baby at risk. As a doctor, I know it would take more than yelling to do anything to my baby, but as a mom-to-be I'm not going to take any chances by working myself up.

"What do you mean he left?"

"He was giving me a massage and I think he had a flashback of some sort. I don't know for sure, but I have seen them happen a few times, except this time, instead of fighting through it, he left. Then he said he was moving out. Marco and I were at the park alone while Caleb was looking for an apartment to rent."

"Hayley, that's not fair," Hannah says. "I know you're upset right now, but think long and hard before you place that blame on Caleb. People get upset all the time. People leave and many women take their kids to the park alone. Most just don't have psycho drug dealers stalking them, waiting to kidnap them. Caleb leaving isn't why you're upset. He came back a few hours later. He's the reason you were even found. You know this. So, what's going on?"

I sigh loudly. I know she's right and that's why I didn't want Caleb coming in here. I'm a mix of emotions and I imagine being pregnant isn't helping.

"I'm pregnant."

"Oh my goodness!" Hannah squeals. Then she sobers. "Is the baby okay?"

"Yes, the doctor did an ultrasound and I'm roughly six weeks along. He wants me to take it easy for the first trimester to be on the safe side, give my body time to heal."

"So you aren't going to tell Caleb? Was this planned?"

"That's the thing. We knew we were having unprotected sex and we knew this could happen, but I had it in my head it would be harder to get pregnant than it actually was, and while I'm so excited about this baby, I'm afraid Caleb will regret it."

"I think you need to give him a chance, Hayley. I don't know all that happened, but the guy out in the waiting room doesn't look like a guy who would ever regret having a baby with you. On the plus side, we'll have our babies months apart." We both squeal, and it wakes Marco up.

"What happened?" Marco asks.

"Nothing, sweetie. We're okay. Go back to sleep," I say, threading my fingers through his soft hair.

Hannah and I chat for a few minutes and then she goes back to get our parents. They give me hugs and kisses, thanking God I'm oaky. As much as I want to tell them about my being pregnant, I think it's best to keep it to myself for now. Anything can happen and every person I tell will be another person I have to tell if I lose the baby.

Once they leave, my friends take turns coming in and out. Finally Bentley and Kayla are last.

"He's a mess, Hayley. I know you're upset, but he's a freaking mess out there. Please don't punish him for too long. Even if you're ending it with him, just let him know," Bentley says.

After spending the evening with Marco by my side, the nurse lets Marco know he can't spend the night. He's not happy at all, but when Kayla tells him he can have a sleepover with Chloe, he reluctantly gives in.

The next morning I'm released. Since Kayla had taken Marco home with her, she picks me up and brings us home. Marco and I both take showers. When I tell him I'd like for him to stay home one more day to get some rest, he asks if he can sleep with me. I can't even imagine how traumatized he is from all of the recent events. He obviously doesn't want to be alone and the truth is I don't really want to be alone either. I thought maybe Caleb would try to come home, but I guess not. Marco cuddles into bed with me and I put on a kid movie hoping he won't have nightmares. The kid has been through way too much.

I LOOK AT THE CLOCK AND SEE IT'S TWO IN THE AFTERNOON. I go to grab my phone and remember it was smashed the day we were taken.

Marco stirs awake, and I decide I'm not going to let what happened bring us down. It will definitely be discussed at his weekly therapy session, but I'm not going to dwell on it. We're both okay. My baby is okay, and the men who are alive will be locked away for a long ass time.

"Hey sweetie, did you have a good nap?"

He nods and cuddles up next to me.

"I need to go to the mall to get a new phone. Why don't you get dressed and we'll stop on the way and get lunch?"

"Okay."

After we're both dressed, we walk out to my car to head to the mall. I stop short, seeing Caleb's truck parked in the front of my house. "What's he doing out there?" Marco asks.

"I'm not sure. Why don't you get in the car and I'll go speak to him?"

I get to the truck and see Caleb is texting on his phone. I knock lightly on the window, and when he sees it's me, he rolls it down.

"What are you doing out here?"

"I couldn't leave you guys alone. I just figured it would be better to sit out here since you didn't want me to be around you."

God, I'm such a bitch. I refused to see the man who saved us and he sat in his truck because I didn't want him near me.

"Thank you."

"There's no need to thank me. This was entirely my fault. I saw his threats but didn't take them serious enough. And then I walked out, and while I was looking at apartments, you both were kidnapped. Do you think maybe we can talk?"

"I would like that, but Marco and I are heading out to the mall. The guys who took us smashed my phone so I need a new one. I also need to get him lunch."

"Would it be okay if I went with you guys?"

I want to say no because being around him hurts, but at the same time being around him completes me. It also doesn't help that I feel guilty for hiding this pregnancy from him. This whole situation sucks.

"Sure."

He gets out of his truck and runs in the house to change quickly and is back a few minutes later. On our way to the mall he asks Marco how he's feeling and Marco says he's okay. He also says he wants to eat at the food court, so we head straight to the mall. After we park, we go straight to the wireless store. I let them know my phone was destroyed and decide to upgrade to a new phone.

Marco and Caleb are looking at the latest technology when a salesman walks over and starts talking to Marco. "You should ask your dad to buy this for you."

I hold my breath, praying Caleb doesn't deny it. It would hurt Marco's feelings. Instead, he pats Marco on the back and says, "He just got a new iPad. We can't spoil him too much. We'll have to see how his report card is this semester."

Marco laughs and points out his grades are really good.

After the gentleman sets up my new phone, we head to the courtyard to get something to eat. Marco is so hungry he wolfs down all of his food and asks for more.

"Hey, Mom, can I go grab another chicken sandwich?"

"Sure, sweetie." I hand him money and watch him walk the ten feet over to the counter to order a sandwich.

"I don't know how I'm supposed to let him go to school. I don't want him leaving my sight."

I look at Caleb and realize I said that out loud. He's staring at me weird...like with adoration maybe...I'm not sure.

"What?"

"He called you Mom again. He did it when you were brought to the hospital."

"Oh, yeah." A big smile graces my face. "He asked me if he could call me Mom at the park. I also told him I was approved to adopt him." Tears spring forward and blur my vision.

"Why are you crying?" Caleb leans over to wipe the tears falling down.

"When we were being held hostage, I thought that moment in the park would be the only time in my life somebody would call me Mom, and I was just so glad it was Marco. And then I found out..." I stutter, realizing I almost announced my pregnancy to him right here in the food court, so I try to play it off. "Umm...when I got out of the hospital and we were lying in bed watching a movie, I realized how short life is. I really want to be a good mom." I laugh, knowing my hormones are going crazy. I seriously need to stop talking. I'm barely making any sense.

"Hayles, you deserve it all. More than anybody I know. I'm glad Marco is calling you mom. You are his mom. You're amazing with him, and you will be just as amazing with any kids you have in the future." And insert guilt because I haven't told Caleb he is going to be a father.

I look over to see Marco heading back and think back to him saying he wants to call Caleb Dad. "He asked if he could call you Dad but didn't get a chance to ask you."

Caleb doesn't have a chance to respond, but his face says it all. He would like nothing more than to be a father to Marco. I know regardless of what happens between us, he'll be an amazing father to this baby as well.

The rest of the day goes by quickly. We walk around the mall and shop a little. Marco picks out a new game for his PlayStation and asks if we can go home so he can play. My body begins to feel achy and Caleb notices, insisting we go home. When we get home, Caleb heads back to his truck, but I stop him.

"Come inside, please. I know we have stuff to work out, but until you find a place you're welcome to stay here."

He says okay and then follows me inside. I can tell he wants to say more, but this isn't the time to talk.

We sit on the couch and watch Marco play his game. Caleb joins in for a little bit but excuses himself to make a few phone calls. While he is on the phone I let Marco know it's time for bed.

"Can I go to school tomorrow?"

"Are you sure you're okay to go to school? You have your therapy session in two days...Maybe you can wait to meet with her."

"I'm okay going back. I know what happened sucks, but I like going to school and I don't want to get behind. Please."

How can I possibly say no to my kid begging me to go to school. He's so much stronger than me and I won't let my parental fears scare him.

"Okay, fine. But why don't I pick you up from school and you can practice MMA while I work in the afternoon?"

"Sounds good. Can you ask Caleb to come in as soon as he gets off the phone? I want to talk to him."

"Sure thing." I give him a kiss on his forehead and say goodnight.

When I get back out to the living room Caleb is sitting on the couch with his head sagging down.

"You okay?"

He looks up and shrugs. "They have enough evidence to put the guys who survived away. They need yours and Marco's statements but they won't need us to be at the trial. They'll be held without bail. It's over."

"So why are you sad then? That's a good thing."

"I walked away. I know I messed up, Hayles. I should have been there at the park with you guys and none of this would have happened. Please tell me you'll be able to forgive me."

I can see he's beating himself up over this and I know I need to forgive him and tell him about the baby. We need to figure this all out together, but I can't find the words.

"Marco wants to talk to you. He asked for you to go say goodnight."

"Okay, thanks."

Thirty-Two

CALEB

I PRACTICALLY BEG HAYLEY FOR FORGIVENESS AND SHE can barely look me in the eye. How can I expect Hayley to be on the same page as me when the last thing I said to her was not to touch me and then told her I was looking for apartments to move into? She's hurt and justifiably so. I need to speak with her, but first I need to go talk to Marco.

"Hey buddy." I walk into his room to sit on the edge of his bed. "Hayl—I mean, your mom said you wanted to talk to me."

Marco's face lights up at the word mom. He might have had another mom for the first twelve years of his life, but she wasn't one percent of the mom Hayley is to him.

"Yeah...umm...before we got taken, we were talking and she said I could call her Mom...and I was wondering...I know you can't adopt me, but well, I've never had a dad before. I was wondering if maybe you would be my dad. I know I'm older than a baby, but..."

"Marco, stop. I don't care if you are two, twelve, or twenty-two. I would love to be your father. You are never too old to have a dad and I don't care what the courts say. I love you, and since the moment you walked into that gym, I have thought of you as my son."

Marco sits up and gives me a hug and I swear in that moment it feels like all is right in the world.

"Get some sleep, bud. I love you."

"Love you too, Dad."

I walk back to the living room feeling like I'm floating in the clouds and see Hayley wiping her tears.

"You were totally listening, weren't you?" I say jokingly.

She laughs. "Yes! I had to hear for myself. Is he not the sweetest kid, ever?"

"When he asked me to be his dad, I wanted to go out and buy him a car."

Hayley cracks up laughing and shakes her head. God, I love to hear that woman laugh.

"I know we need to talk, but I'm fucking exhausted, Hayles. Would it be okay if we talk tomorrow? I just want to lie in bed and hold you, please."

She nods, and after we both change into clothes to sleep in, we climb into her bed. She lies facing away from me and I pull her close so I'm spooning her from behind. I wrap my arms around her body and nuzzle my face into her hair, inhaling her scent. I'm pretty sure today was one of the best days of my life. Hayley and Marco are both safe, I'm lying in bed with the woman I love, and Marco wants me to be his dad. The only thing left to fix is Hayley and me.

I wake up to an empty bed and when I look at the clock I see it's nine in the morning. Hayley must have snuck out without waking me up. I have some serious groveling to do. I walk through the house and see both she and Marco are gone. I grab my laptop and cell phone and begin working on a plan.

Thirty-Three

HAYLEY

AFTER GETTING MARCO OFF TO SCHOOL I GO TO THE GYM to check on my fighters. If it wasn't for me working for Cooper I imagine I would have been fired a long time ago. I need to let him know about the pregnancy so he knows I'm planning to go part-time, and once the baby comes, I would like to stay home. I don't know what things will be like for Caleb and me, but I have money put away and I'll use it if I have to. Thinking about it, it's probably best if I let Caleb know first.

I see a couple fighters and then receive a text from my sister asking if she can please take Marco this weekend for the entire weekend. He's never been away from me for that long. so I let her know I'll speak to him and get back to her. Marco and I go to court Friday to sign the papers. I plan to surprise him by having him play hooky and spend the day with him.

I consider texting Caleb so many times throughout the day, but I don't know what to say. I don't know how to deal with him walking out. I know he's sorry, but it doesn't change the fact that he wanted to move out.

When the afternoon rolls around and it's time to go get Marco I run into Ashley who's visiting Kaden.

"Hey girly," she says, giving me a hug. "How are you feeling?"

"I'm okay. What are you up to tonight?"

"Nothing much. I'm off tonight."

"Marco and I can come over and we can do dinner." I'm totally avoiding Caleb, but I also want to spend time with Ashley. She's seemed all over the place lately and nothing works better to ignore your own problems than to focus on someone else's.

"Sounds good!"

I grab Marco from the bus stop and don't stop at home. Within a few minutes, there's a text from Caleb.

Caleb: Are you coming home?

Me: Having dinner with Ashley. Don't wait up.

Caleb: If you're staying away because of me, I can leave.

That is definitely what I'm doing, but I'm not about to tell him that.

Me: That's not what I am doing...

Caleb: Okay

As Marco and I walk up to Ashley's house, I bring up the subject of Hannah wanting to spend some time with him. "Hey Marco, Hannah asked if she can take you for the weekend. What do you think?"

"Are you okay with me going?" I love that he's worried about me, but his job isn't to worry. His job is to be a kid. My job is to worry about him and me.

"Hey, I'm fine, and I'll be okay with you at Hannah's. Your job is to have fun. Got it? No worrying."

"Okay, then I would like to go. Aunt Hannah is cool."

We knock on Ashley's door and I text Hannah to let her know this weekend is a go. Ashley answers the door and lets us in.

The boys run to Tristan's room to play video games and I follow her into the kitchen where she grabs a bottle of wine. I notice a few notices on her counter. Some say first notice, one says third notice, and one says final notice. I look away, not wanting to be nosy, but Ashley sees what I was looking at and, with an embarrassed look on her face, grabs the papers and shoves them into a drawer.

She brings the wine to the couch and I follow with two glasses, setting them down on the table so she can pour.

"Kaden brought this over the other night," she says by way of explanation.

"Who's judging?"

"I know you saw the notices, Hayley. I just don't want you to think I'm behind on my bills, yet I'm buying bottles of wine."

"Trust me, I'm the last person to judge anyone. But if you want to talk, I'm here."

Ashley lets out a heavy sigh and shakes her head. "I just don't even know where to begin. Talking about it won't change anything." She begins to cry and I cross over to the side of the couch she's sitting on and just let her cry it out while holding her.

After a few minutes, she composes herself. "Jeez, I am a horrible host."

"Hey now, I pretty much invited myself over." We both laugh.

"The truth is I'm kind of hiding from Caleb. Before Marco and I were taken, we got into a fight. Well, not really a fight...I don't even know what happened. Anyway, it ended with him saying he was moving out. At some point, we're going to have to talk, but I'm just not ready yet."

"Well, you're welcome to hide out here as long as you need to."

We decide to order pizza for dinner and after we all eat and the boys play some more video games for a couple hours, Marco and I finally takeoff so he can take a shower before bed since it's a school night.

We get home and Caleb's truck is in the driveway, but he isn't in the living room. I notice his bedroom door is shut. Marco takes a shower, and after I say goodnight, I take a quick shower as well and go to sleep.

Sometime in the middle of the night, I feel Caleb's hands on me. It feels like he's spooning me and at one point it even feels like his hand is running across my stomach, but when I wake up and the bed is empty, I chalk it up to a dream.

I get ready for work and head out just like yesterday, except today I invited Marco and myself over to Kayla's place using the excuse he would love to see Chloe. After dinner and dessert we head home and once again Caleb is in his room. I say goodnight to Marco and go to sleep, having the same dream as the previous night.

IT'S FRIDAY MORNING AND CALEB'S DOOR IS OPEN AND empty. He must have already left for the day. Marco is up early and excited for two reasons: I sign the adoption papers this morning and later tonight he'll be going to Hannah's for the weekend. She's told me she'll be by right after work to get him. I offered to bring him to her, but she was adamant I meet her at my house. So much for avoiding Caleb tonight...

"You ready to do this, kid?"

"Yeah, I am."

We get to the courthouse and have a seat in front of the room number Karen let me know the judge will be in. I'm so excited to finally get to formally adopt Marco, but it breaks my heart Caleb isn't here with us. I know he wouldn't be able to adopt Marco, but I still wish he were here to share this moment with us.

Karen arrives with the paperwork and shortly after the judge calls us in.

He reads off the required legalities asking me to confirm who I am and then asks me to repeat after him promising to care for and provide for Marco. When we're done, I sign on the dotted lines and then handed copies of the adoption paperwork. I have tears in my eyes and am seconds away from crying. I can't believe this is real. I am a mother and to the most amazing, genuine, and selfless child. I feel so completely blessed. I turn around to smile at Marco, and that's when I see Caleb sitting on the bench next to him. He has his phone out like he was taking pictures, and I lose it. The tears stream down my face and I walk over to give them both a hug.

"I love you, Son."

"I love you too, Mom."

Caleb takes pictures of Marco and me and then Karen offers to take a couple pictures of the three of us. Once we're done, we head out to the parking lot. I don't want to be rude to Caleb, but I had planned to spend the day with Marco, just the two of us.

"Umm...So..."

Before I can say anything, he saves me. "I have to get going. I have a couple errands to run. I'll see you both later. Okay?" He gives Marco a hug. "Congratulations, buddy. You have the best mom there is."

"That's because I got the best kid," I add.

We say goodbye and Marco and I head to his surprise.

After we stop at the store to pick up lunch to go, we arrive at Hollywood skate park. It is known to be one of the best skate parks. We get out of the car and I walk around to my trunk to grab Marco's skateboard.

"Are you serious?" Marco fist pumps into the air and runs around to grab his skateboard from me. He gives me a huge hug. "Thank you so much. This is so awesome."

He runs over and joins the teens that are all skateboarding. We spend the rest of the day at the park. I take picture after picture of him. When he gets hungry, he takes a break and we eat lunch together. He tries to show me how to ride on the board, but I suck at it. By the end of the day, he's exhausted and ready to go home. This time I know our day won't end with either of us being taken.

This is our second chance. Our fresh start.

"Thank you for today," Marco says.

"You're welcome, sweetie."

I give him a kiss on his forehead and then we head home.

We aren't even home thirty minutes when Hannah shows up to get Marco. I give her Marco's backpack with clothes for the next two nights and kiss him goodbye. I'm not sure what I'm going to do this weekend, but I know staying home and sulking isn't it. Just as they're leaving, Caleb pulls up and blocks my car in.

"I'm leaving. Can you move your truck for me, please?"

"No, I can't. I gave you a few days, but now we're going to talk. But first we're going out. Go get changed, please. "

I don't bother arguing. The look on his face tells me he isn't playing around. I guess tonight we'll be talking.

Thirty-Four

CALEB

WATCHING HAYLEY LEGALLY ADOPT MARCO WAS ONE OF the most beautiful moments I have witnessed. I wasn't sure how she would feel about me being there, but I couldn't imagine not being there with them. Hopefully one day it will be my turn to sign those papers, but first I need to fix Hayley and me.

I have everything planned. I purchased the engagement ring, made the reservations, wrote down the show times, and have written out an itinerary for the weekend, so I don't forget anything. I spoke to Hannah and she was more than willing to take Marco for the weekend.

Now, I just need to pack for Hayley and me. I would tell her to pack, but that would give away the surprise of where I'm taking her and what we're doing, so I'm doing it myself. I grab a luggage from the hallway closet and pack for myself first and then make my way to Hayley's room to pack for her.

After grabbing a bunch of outfits I've seen her wear, I head to her bathroom to grab her toiletries. When I open the cabinet, I see a prescription that wasn't there before. Prenatal vitamins. Why would Hayley be taking these? Unless...Holy shit! Is it possible? Is she pregnant?

Then it hits me—if she's pregnant, she's keeping it from me. She watched what happened to Kayla and Bentley when Kayla hid her pregnancy from Bentley. She listened to me tell her how hard it is for me to trust a woman. She heard my stories of my sister and mom hiding shit from me. There's no way Hayley could be pregnant and keep something this important from me.

Thinking about it...she's been emotional lately. We've been having sex for months and she hasn't gotten her period at all. Then like a punch to the gut, I remember she was beaten up when she was taken. What if she lost our baby? What if the reason she's avoiding me is because she lost our baby because I left them and they were taken. But wouldn't she be more upset?

I should be mad that Hayley hasn't told me if she is indeed pregnant or if she lost our baby, but I know Hayley and she wouldn't keep something this important from me. She went through a huge ordeal and needs time. I'm going to show her this weekend I love her and want to spend my life with her, and I have to believe if those pills mean she is or was pregnant she'll open up and talk to me. Hayley has done nothing but fight for us and I'm not going to assume she's like every other woman who has proven they can't be trusted. I'm going to trust Hayley until she proves otherwise.

I finish grabbing her stuff from the bathroom and haul the suitcase out to my truck. I drive to the jewelry store and pick up the ring. I was able to grab another ring Hayley wears on the same finger occasionally and have them size it.

When I return home, Hayley is home and Hannah is about to take Marco for the weekend. Hayley asks me to move my truck so she can run away like she's been doing the last two nights, but that shit stops now.

Once she's dressed, we jump into my truck and head to the strip. When we arrive at the Bellagio, Hayley gets excited but tries to tone it down, remembering we need to talk. I don't want our weekend to be tainted, so I decide to have us go to the room to talk first, and then hopefully we'll enjoy the weekend.

After I'm done checking us in, we make our way up to our room.

"What are we doing here?" Hayley asks, sitting on the couch.

"I thought it would be a good place to talk." I kneel in front of her and spread her legs a little so I'm face to face with her. "Baby, I cannot even begin to apologize for leaving on Sunday. Saturday night when you were upset and I was giving you a massage you said something and I had a horrible flashback. The truth is, I get them often, but this one lasted longer and it scared the shit out of me."

"A flashback from your time with Gloria and those other women?" she asks softly, putting her hands on both my cheeks.

"Yes, I'm so sorry. It feels like I'm cheating on you when I have them."

"Caleb, don't say that. You can't help where your brain goes. You aren't cheating on me. You went through a lot as a teenager. Something like that doesn't just go away. Would you consider seeing a therapist?"

I think about it for a minute and know it's the right thing to do. Maybe speaking with someone will help me work out what goes through my head.

"Yeah, I will. Will you come with me, Hayles? I need you."

She leans down and gives me a soft kiss, and it has me craving her, but right now it's more important we talk.

"I promise you I will never run again. No matter how rough it gets, I'm in this for the long haul. There's nowhere I would rather be than with you and Marco. I looked at three apartments and in every one all I thought was that none of them are home unless you guys are with me."

"Caleb, I feel the same way. But you seriously hurt me by running. It's not fair and I won't tolerate it. You have to trust me enough to talk to me or we will never make it. I care so much about you. Aside from Marco, you have practically become my entire world. These last couple nights I even dreamed you were holding me at night. I don't want to live without you."

I laugh softly. "Oh, Hayles, I'm so sorry. I have so much to work on and I will. I promise. And baby, those weren't dreams. I was there in your bed, every night after you fell asleep, holding you. I couldn't go that long not holding you in my arms."

Hayley wraps her arms around me and I pick her up in my arms. "I need you, Hayles. Right now I just want to make love to you."

"Caleb, there's something I need to tell you." I can tell by the sound in her voice she's going to tell me about the baby, but I stop her because when I propose, I need her to know it's about us and not because she's pregnant or was pregnant...

"Whatever you need to say can wait, baby. I need you now."

"But—" she attempts to cut in, but I cut her off with a kiss.

Thirty-Five

HAYLEY

CALEB PICKS ME UP AND CARRIES ME TO THE BED. I TRY TO tell him about the baby, but he isn't having it.

"I'm not going anywhere," he whispers into my ear. "Whatever you need to tell me can wait until after I worship your beautiful body."

He lays me down on the bed and kisses me. The kiss start off affectionately. It's slow and sweet and he tastes so good. But after a few minutes, it gets rougher and more intense, causing my sex to clench, wanting and needing more. He sits up on my legs and unbuttons my blouse one button at a time, until my shirt falls to each side, leaving my bra exposed.

"I never imagined ever wanting to willingly be with a woman. I didn't trust women. Now I can't imagine not being with you. I trust you with everything I am, Hayles. But most importantly, I trust you with my heart."

He takes my bra cups and pulls them down, and taking both nipples in between his fingers, pinches and pulls at them just enough to send shivers straight to my core. My legs tighten at his touch, seeking relief.

"I want to spend the rest of my life touching you." He pinches my nipples again. "Kissing you." He leans down and gives each nipple a soft, wet kiss. He moves up, and kisses my lips, then trails kisses down my neck. My breathing goes erratic at his touch.

"I want to spend every day tasting you." He slides down the bed, taking my skirt and panties with him. He throws them to the side and plants a single kiss on top of my mound. Then his tongue hits my clit and he licks it with such expertise I almost come on the spot.

"Oh my God, Caleb!" I yell, grabbing his hair so I have something to hold on to. He doesn't back off, though. He licks my clit until my orgasm hits, causing my ass and pelvis to lift off the bed, as I come all over his tongue. "Fuck, baby, you taste so good."

He climbs back up my body and crashes his mouth against mine. His tongue plunges past my parted lips, and I taste myself on him, and holy hell, if that doesn't turn me on even more.

"I want to spend the rest of my life making love to you," he whispers against my lips as he pushes himself into me, slow and deep.

I wrap my hands around his neck as he makes love to me with his mouth and cock simultaneously. Kissing me passionately, while continuing to thrust in and out of me. I have never felt so loved and cherished before. Within minutes, we both find our release and I know without a doubt I don't want to spend another day without this man. When we both come down from our orgasms, Caleb looks into my eyes and says, " Baby, I want to spend the rest of my life with you," and then kisses me one more time before pulling out. I want to believe him so badly, but I'm scared.

He must sense my fear because he takes my chin between his thumb and forefinger and kisses me softly. "I meant what I said, Hayles. I want to be with you for the rest of my life. I'm not running anywhere. I know it's going to take time for you to believe me, but I will prove it to you. I love you, baby."

Tears spring to my eyes, hearing him tell me for the first time he loves me.

"I love you too." And it's the truth. I love him more than life itself.

We both clean up, and when I think we're going to get into bed to relax, he says, "Oh, no. Tonight has just begun. Get dressed. We have somewhere to be in"—he looks down at his watch—"thirty minutes."

I want to tell him about the baby but figure it can wait until after we go wherever he's so excited to take me. After we're both dressed, we head down the elevator. He stops at the concierge desk for a couple minutes and speaks to the man in charge. He won't let me listen in, which causes me to pout.

"It will ruin the surprise."

Once they're done chatting, he takes my hand in his and walks us back to the elevator and back to our room. When we walk in, I notice the curtains are no longer covering the back doors and at the table is chocolate-covered strawberries. Rose petals are littering the floor and bed.

He walks us out to the balcony and that's when Celine Dion starts singing *My Heart Will Go On*. Not even a second later, the fountains and lights begin to dance beautifully in tune. Caleb reserved a room where we can watch the Bellagio Fountain show right from our room! I watch the entire fountain show in amazement. It's one of the most beautiful shows I've ever seen, the way the music and water dance in synchronization. I'm glad my first time seeing the show is with the man I love. It's simply magical. Caleb stands behind me holding me close while we sway to the music playing. I can't keep the smile off my face. I'm blown away that he not only remembered I've never seen the show but put forth so much effort for us to watch it.

The show ends, and Caleb's body leaves from behind me. I twirl around to tell him thank you, but he's gone. That's when I notice he's down one knee with the most exquisite pink diamond engagement ring in his hand.

"Hayles, the moment I spilled coffee all over your blouse I knew you were the one." I laugh. "I knew you before that day but didn't take the time to see you. When I felt you up on accident and heard you giggle, I was done for. And then when you offered to foster and adopt Marco I saw what a selfless person you truly are and you won my heart over. When I made the mistake of thinking you would be better off without me and went to find my own place...I looked at those places and knew no matter what house or apartment I picked it would never be a home without you and Marco in it. I love you, baby, and I don't want to spend a single day not sleeping in the same bed as you. I know we have a long way to go, but you're the only woman I want to be on this journey with. Hayley Roberts, will you marry me?"

"I'm pregnant, Caleb." I can't believe I just blurted that out. Clearly my conscience is getting the best of me. This man is down on one knee proposing and I'm the worst person in the world for keeping this from him.

Caleb stands and, taking my hand, walks us inside the room to the couch. "You're pregnant, Hayles?"

"Yes, I found out in the hospital. I'm seven weeks along. I should have told you."

I put my face in my hands and start crying. God, these damn hormones are going to be the death of me. Caleb lifts my face and wipes my tears away. "Don't cry, baby. It's okay. You were going through a lot. Is that what you were trying to tell me earlier?"

"Yeah," I sob out.

"Do you want to marry me?"

Oh my God! I forgot to answer him. I felt so guilty for hiding my pregnancy I didn't even give the man an answer to his question.

"Yes, I want to marry you."

He slides the ring onto my finger and kisses me like his life depends on it. He picks me up and moves me to the bed where for the rest of the night my fiancé makes love to me until we both fall asleep in each other's arms.

THE NEXT MORNING, AFTER EATING BREAKFAST IN BED, Caleb takes me down to the casinos to gamble. He said he planned to take me later tonight, but with me being pregnant, he doesn't want me around the cigarette smoke. He also said we would be skipping the strip club portion of the weekend as well because he's not going to bring his pregnant fiancée into a club. I laugh, remembering when he told me he would take me gambling, to a strip club, and to see the fountains in one night. Two out of three are okay with me. We spend half of the day gambling and the other half lounging by the pool at the resort while we spend the night making love to each other.

IT'S SUNDAY MORNING AND WE'RE PACKING UP OUR STUFF to go back home. When we arrive, I see all of our friends cars parked along the road.

"Did you do this?" I ask. Caleb just shrugs. "I told them you said yes."

We spend our day hanging by the pool with our friends and family. The guys grill burgers and when we all sit down to eat we tell them our other news.

"So, it's still early but we wanted you guys to know. I'm seven weeks pregnant. We are having a baby." Everybody cheers and gives us their congratulations. Marco comes over and gives me a big hug.

"I hope it's a boy! We can't let all these girls outnumber us!" Then he jumps back into the pool to splash Bella.

My mom comes over and wraps me up in one of her motherly embraces. "I am so happy for you, Hayley. I can't believe both my daughters will be giving me two more grandchildren in the next year."

I love that she uses the word more. I love that everybody accepts that Marco is just as much mine as this baby I'm carrying. I look around and am so thankful for everybody in my life. Last year I felt so alone and now my life is so full of love.

Caleb comes over to sit next to me. "You okay?"

"Yeah, I just feel so blessed."

"Baby, I have told you this so many times. You deserve this life and so much more. I'll never be able to thank you for fighting for me when I wasn't ready to even fight for myself. I'm sorry it took me so long."

"No, Caleb. It just wasn't our time yet. I believe everything happens for a reason, you moving here, meeting Marco, bringing him into our lives. It was all meant to happen just how it did. Marco has brought us so many blessings. He brought us together. He even brought Chloe into Kayla and Bentley's lives. We owe him more than he will ever know."

He wraps me up in his arms, rubbing his hands on my belly, as we watch everyone around us laugh and smile happily. I'm not naïve to believe life will always be this perfect, but for right now it definitely feels pretty damn perfect.

Epilogue

CALEB

Three Months Later

"WOULD YOU LIKE TO KNOW THE GENDER?" THE ULTRASOUND technician asks.

"Yes!" Marco says, before Hayley and I can even answer.

"I guess so." Hayley laughs.

The technician moves the device over Hayley's belly and then hits a button to freeze the screen.

"Congratulations! You're having a baby girl!"

"Noooo!" Marco sighs in defeat.

"Hey! You're going to be an amazing big brother to this little girl. Just like you are to Chloe," Hayley says.

"I know, but do you think after you have this baby, you can try one more time to give me a brother? There needs to be more boys than girls. Girls are too powerful."

I can't help but laugh at this kid's logic. "Why don't we get through this pregnancy first and then we'll discuss trying for a boy in a couple years."

"Okay."

After the technician prints out pictures, we head out to our vehicles.

"I need to run by the club for a last minute interview and then I'll meet you guys at home," I tell Hayley, giving her a kiss.

"Okay, babe. I have a couple errands to run as well." She gives me a knowing wink. Marco has no idea what is happening tomorrow.

I head to the club thinking about everything I need to get done so I can spend the weekend with my family. I wasn't sure how Hayley would feel about me working so closely to strippers all day, but she's actually really cool about it. She was more concerned with how I would feel working with women all day. It probably helps that I've hired Liz to manage all the books so she splits her time between the gym and *Assets*. I'm working on hiring a manager for the club soon since I was given the go ahead by the doctor to fight again.

Hayley's going to work until her eighth month and then she'll be quitting to stay home fulltime with Marco and the baby. When she told me it was her dream to be a stay-at-home mom I was absolutely thrilled.

I pull up to the rear of club and walk in through the back door.

After I took it over, I learned that Gloria actually did a good job running it—once you remove the illegal shit from the equation. It's now an upscale strip club with a no-touching policy. I renovated it completely and it now has a high-class restaurant where people can watch the dancers while dining or go to the second floor where there is a bar and tables to just watch the dancing going on. There are VIP booths that line the walls and have their own mini dance floor and pole, and in the back, there are several smaller rooms for private parties. Even those have a strict no-touching policy. I added more bouncers and have them making sure to enforce my rules. I was lucky to have found an amazing chef as well. Several people have told me they come here for the food just as much as they do the entertainment.

Once I get situated I text Liz to let me know when the girl coming in to interview arrives. Helping me definitely isn't in Liz's job description, but she is doing me a huge favor by screening through the resumes and weeding out the ones who wouldn't be a good fit here.

"Hey Caleb...Someone is here to see you." Liz pokes her head in my door, looking extremely uncomfortable. "For an interview?" I ask. I glance at my watch and see she's early.

"No. How about I just send her in."

"Okay."

A few minutes later, there's a knock on my door.

"Come in."

I look up to see Ashley standing in the doorway. I stand to greet her and ask her to have a seat.

"Is everything okay?"

She closes her eyes and swallows slowly before opening them back up again. I've never seen Ashley look so nervous.

"I need your help, Caleb. Please. I'm begging you."

I'M TRYING TO CONCENTRATE ON WHATEVER BENTLEY IS saying, but I've been watching Hayley all day and the sight of my beautiful, pregnant wife has me losing my ability to think. Walking around in her bikini with some see-through thing that ties around her waist has my cock constantly hard. Her swollen breasts are perfect, her swollen belly even more perfect. Even seeing her mingling with people, smiling and laughing and touching her belly is turning me on.

I can't take it anymore, so while she's saying goodbye to the last of Marco's school friends and parents, I excuse myself from Bentley and join her. I angle myself against her side, sliding my arm around her back and shoulder. Then I pull her close, so she feels my hard-on pressing against her. She gives me a mischievous smile as she returns my embrace and we wave goodbye to the departing guest. As we lose sight of them, I turn her into me and whisper five simple words to sum up the thoughts of how irresistible she has been today. "You look so fucking hot." I want to say more. Shit, I want to do more, but I have to remind myself this is an important day for Marco on so many levels, so my dick is just going to have to wait until later.

Now that all of Marco's friends from school have left and it's just our close friends and family, Hayley and I go inside to grab the last but definitely not the least of his birthday presents. I swear I'm just as excited if not more excited than Marco is about today. We gather everyone around the outdoor table by the pool. Kayla already knows what this last present is, so she has her camera ready. We watch in anticipation and excitement as Marco rips open the wrapping paper and briefly reads his new-framed official birth certificate and reads aloud "Marco Alejandro Michaels." His reaction of surprise and happiness has us all crying. I pull him and Hayley into a three-way hug and declare, "We are now officially the Michaels family!" and my heart swells.

While Hayley was able to adopt Marco a few months ago, I had to wait until we were married. The day our marriage certificate came in we went down to the courthouse to file the adoption and name-change paperwork. I thought being a husband and father would be scary, but it's honestly the best decision I've ever made. I can't wait to add our little princess to the mix. All in all today has been the best half-year birthday-Fourth of July-official adoption ever.

After the full day we've had I can tell Hayley is getting tired, so I tell her to go inside and relax while Marco and I clean up. He talks my ear off about the most exciting parts of his first birthday party and all the presents he received. I don't think I've ever seen a kid so grateful. After we're done cleaning, I tell him to grab a shower and then he can play one of his new videogames for thirty minutes before bed.

While he's content in his world, I head to take a shower myself. I stop as I enter the room. Hayley is napping on the bed and I contemplate backing out of the room and taking a shower down the hall so I don't disturb her. She looks so gorgeous lying there, her face slightly pink from the sun and the hint of a smile on her lips. I wonder if she's dreaming. Before I can decide whether or not to wake her up, she stirs awake on her own.

"Hey," she says sleepily.

"Hey yourself. You feel rested?"

"Yes, thank you."

"The house is clean and Marco is showered and playing a video game...I was going to take a shower. Do you want to join me?"

"You know it."

I help her up and then lead the way into the bathroom, stripping my board shorts as I go. She playfully slaps my ass in the process and picks up my shorts to throw them in the hamper. I turn on the shower to let the water heat up, while she undresses. When I turn back around, my cock grazes her protruding stomach. Framing her face, kiss her softly. Her mouth is sweet and warm, just like her pussy.

We step into the shower, and my eyes stay trained on her the entire time she soaps up her body—caressing her breasts and rubbing her hand over her mound. I don't know if she's purposely doing it, but she is so damn sexy. I ignore my desire for her and fill her in on what Marco told me about his party.

As soon as we're done drying off, I throw on my boxers and sweats, and then peek into Marco's room. "Hey bud, it's time for bed. Mom and I will be in to say goodnight in a minute."

Hayley is smiling at me as I come back into our room to get her.

"What?" I ask playfully.

"Nothing, it's just that I'm so happy."

"Ditto," I reply as we both head back out to say goodnight to our son. I don't think I will ever get tired of saying those words. *Our son.*

After we say goodnight, we both head back to the bedroom to relax. I'm just going to be real, everyone expects you to love every minute of pregnancy but honestly Hayley's first trimester kind of sucked. She constantly had morning sickness, thought she looked fat and not pregnant despite me telling her every day how beautiful she is, and she didn't want to be touched much less have sex most days.

But if the first trimester sucked, the second has been amazing. She's no longer sick, her belly has become more pronounced, so she feels better about herself, and to top it off, she is horny twenty-four seven. If the rest of her pregnancy stays like this, I can see myself knocking her up at least a couple more times.

I look over at my wife reading on her iPad and hope whatever scene she's reading will help make tonight interesting.

HAYLEY

"ANY GOOD SCENES IN THAT BOOK?"

I look over at my husband, shake my head, and laugh. I swear his brain is hardwired to think about sex at all times of the day. "Yes but not what you're thinking. The couple in the book just said their vows and everyone is clapping for them as they kiss."

"Do you regret not having a wedding like that?"

I don't even need to think about my answer before responding. "No, all I wanted was to be married to you. I didn't need or want any of the glitz or glamour. I just needed and wanted you."

After everybody left our house after celebrating our engagement we cleaned up, put Marco to bed, and then sprawled across the couch to watch some television. The movie What Happens in Vegas *was on and Caleb made a joke about it then laughed.*

"Huh?" To be honest I wasn't really paying attention to the movie or to him. I was staring at my beautiful engagement ring and on cloud nine.

"We live in Vegas. We wouldn't even have to elope. We should go to the courthouse tomorrow and just get married."

I sat up straight and assessed whether or not he was serious. I couldn't tell.

"Are you being serious or fucking with me?"

"I don't know...if I was serious would that be something you would consider? I mean, do you want the big wedding? I want you to have whatever you want."

"Let's do it."

Caleb sat up mimicking my position.

"Hayley, are you being serious or fucking with me?"

"Are we playing copy-cat?"

"What the fuck is copy-cat?" He looked confused.

"Never mind. Yes, I'm serious. Let's get married tomorrow, just you, Marco, and me. Let's go to the courthouse and get married, and then file for you to adopt Marco."

"Hayley, are you sure? I know most women want a big wedding..."

"No, I don't. I just want you."

And that's exactly what we did.

"Earth to Hayley. You there?"

I put my iPad on the nightstand and then roll over to straddle my husband. "I'm sorry. I was remembering the night we decided to elope. Do you have any regrets?"

Caleb puts his hands on my belly and gently massages my front.

"Baby, my only regret is not making you mine even sooner."

He takes me by my hips and carefully lifts me off of him, laying me on my back so he's hovering over me. Then he drags his body down mine until his face is level with my protruding belly. Lifting up my shirt until it reaches just below my breasts, he gives my belly a kiss and then looks up at me. "Have I told you today how beautiful you look knocked up with my baby?"

I shake my head, laughing at his choice of words.

"Well, that's a damn shame, because you do. You look fucking gorgeous with my baby in you. I think I might have to keep you pregnant for the next several years."

He gives my belly one more kiss then moves downward toward my pussy. He pushes my pajamas bottoms and panties down my legs and throws them on the ground. Spreading my thighs, and then spreading my folds, he softly blows onto my clit, eliciting chills straight up my spine, causing my nipples to harden.

"Baby, grab your nipples for me." I do as he says and remove my shirt, adding it to the pile of clothes on the floor. With my eyes locked on Caleb's, I take both of my nipples between my thumbs and forefingers and twist them to the point it just not hurts. I can't help but let out a moan.

Caleb gives me a sexy smirk and then his face disappears between my legs. He blows one more time on me, and then his mouth is on my clit, biting and sucking on it. My hips buck, needing more. He inserts two fingers into my soaking wet pussy and I damn near come on the spot.

He continues to lick my swollen clit while fingering me. I'm wound so tight, I need to release. I can feel my orgasm right there on the edge, and I just want to fall. I twist my sensitive nipples one last time and that's all it takes to push me off the ledge, my orgasm spilling over. My eyes close from the intensity and I swear I feel light headed.

When I open my eyes, my beautiful husband is staring at me with a huge grin on his face.

"Get up here," I demand playfully. He crawls back up my body and without saying a word enters me. His hands are on either side of my face and I can feel his abs rubbing up against my belly. He leans his face down and gives me a kiss. I taste myself on him and it's such a turn on. He lifts his upper body off me, and grabbing one of my legs, hooks it on his forearm, angling himself to go deeper. With his other hand, he begins to rub my clit. I'm already sensitive from my last orgasm and within minutes I'm coming again. Once he knows I've come, he picks up his speed and seconds later is spilling his hot seed into me.

He gets up to clean himself and grabs a washcloth for me. After we're both clean, he throws the washcloth into the hamper and lies down in bed, spooning me from behind and wrapping his arms around me with his hands splayed out across my belly. Ever since he found out I was pregnant this has become his go-to position. Some nights I would seriously like to push him away and tell him I need my space, but when he told me he read the baby can feel his warmth, I knew I better get used to sleeping in this position.

"Did your interview go good today?" I ask, remembering he's in need of a new dancer since one of the girls had to quit suddenly.

His body tenses but quickly relaxes. "I filled the position."

"That's good. You know if you ever need a fill-in once I'm no longer pregnant I can totally be your girl. I bet I could bust out some serious moves on a pole."

He nuzzles his face into my hair and chuckles quietly.

"The only place I want to see you busting out any moves is in this bedroom, baby. You are mine. Mine to touch. Mine to kiss. Mine to love."

"And you are mine."

"Damn right, baby. I am yours."

The end!

About the Author

Reading is like breathing in, writing is like breathing out.— Pam Allyn

Nikki Ash resides in South Florida where she is an English teacher by day and a writer by night. When she's not writing, you can find her with a book in her hand. From the Boxcar Children, to Wuthering Heights, to the latest single parent romance, she has lived and breathed every type of book. While reading and writing are her passions, her two children are her entire world. You can probably find them at a Disney park before you would find them at home on the weekends!